BRIAN

REVERSE TH.

BRIAN FLYNN was born in 1885 in Leyton, Essex. He won a scholarship to the City Of London School, and from there went into the civil service. In World War I he served as Special Constable on the Home Front, also teaching "Accountancy, Languages, Maths and Elocution to men, women, boys and girls" in the evenings, and acting in his spare time.

It was a seaside family holiday that inspired Brian Flynn to turn his hand to writing in the mid-twenties. Finding most mystery novels of the time "mediocre in the extreme", he decided to compose his own. Edith, the author's wife, encouraged its completion, and after a protracted period finding a publisher, it was eventually released in 1927 by John Hamilton in the UK and Macrae Smith in the U.S. as *The Billiard-Room Mystery*.

The author died in 1958. In all, he wrote and published 57 mysteries, the vast majority featuring the super-sleuth Antony Bathurst.

BRIAN FLYNN

REVERSE THE CHARGES

With an introduction by
Steve Barge

DEAN STREET PRESS

INTRODUCTION

"I believe that the primary function of the mystery story is to entertain; to stimulate the imagination and even, at times, to supply humour. But it pleases the connoisseur most when it presents – and reveals – genuine mystery. To reach its full height, it has to offer an intellectual problem for the reader to consider, measure and solve."

Brian Flynn, *Crime Book* magazine, 1948

BRIAN Flynn began his writing career with *The Billiard Room Mystery* in 1927, primarily at the prompting of his wife Edith who had grown tired of hearing him say how he could write a better mystery novel than the ones he had been reading. Four more books followed under his original publisher, John Hamilton, before he moved to John Long, who would go on to publish the remaining forty-eight of his Anthony Bathurst mysteries, along with his three Sebastian Stole titles, released under the pseudonym Charles Wogan. Some of the early books were released in the US, and there were also a small number of translations of his mysteries into Swedish and German. In the article from which the above quote is taken from, Brian also claims that there were also French and Danish translations but to date, I have not found a single piece of evidence for their existence. The only translations that I have been able to find evidence of are *War Es Der Zahnarzt?* and *Bathurst Greift Ein* in German – *The Mystery of the Peacock's Eye*, retitled to the less dramatic "Was It The Dentist?", and *The Horn* becoming "Bathurst Takes Action" – and, in Swedish, *De 22 Svarta*, a more direct translation of *The Case of the Black Twenty-Two*. There may well be more work to be done finding these, but tracking down all of his books written in the original English has been challenging enough!

Reprints of Brian's books were rare. Four titles were released as paperbacks as part of John Long's Four Square Thriller range in the late 1930s, four more re-appeared during the war from Cherry Tree Books and Mellifont Press, albeit abridged by at least a third, and two others that I am aware of, *Such Bright Disguises* (1941) and *Reverse the Charges* (1943), received a paperback release as part of John Long's Pocket Edition range in the early 1950s – these were also possibly abridged, but only by about 10%. They were the exceptions, rather than the rule, however, and it was not until 2019, when Dean Street Press released his first ten titles, that his work was generally available again.

The question still persists as to why his work disappeared from the awareness of all but the most ardent collectors. As you may expect, when a title was only released once, back in the early 1930s, finding copies of the original text is not a straightforward matter – not even Brian's estate has a copy of every title. We are particularly grateful to one particular collector for providing *The Edge of Terror*, Brian's first serial killer tale, and another for *The Ebony Stag* and *The Grim Maiden*. With these, the reader can breathe a sigh of relief as a copy of every one of Brian's books has now been located – it only took about five years . . .

One of Brian's strengths was the variety of stories that he was willing to tell. Despite, under his own name at least, never straying from involving Anthony Bathurst in his novels – technically he doesn't appear in the non-series *Tragedy at Trinket*, although he gets a name-check from the sleuth of that tale who happens to be his nephew – it is fair to say that it was rare that two consecutive books ever followed the same structure. Some stories are narrated by a Watson-esque character, although never the same person twice, and others are written by Bathurst's "chronicler". The books sometimes focus on just Bathurst and his investigation but sometimes we get to see the events occurring to the whole cast of characters. On occasion, Bathurst himself will "write" the final chapter, just to make sure his chronicler has got the details correct. The murderer may be an opportunist or they may have a convoluted (and, on occasion, a somewhat over-the-top) plan. They may be working for personal gain or as part of a criminal enterprise or society. Compare for example, *The League of Matthias* and *The Horn* – consecutive releases but were it not for Bathurst's involvement, and a similar sense of humour underlying Brian's writing, you could easily believe that they were from the pen of different writers.

Brian seems to have been determined to keep stretching himself with his writing as he continued Bathurst's adventures, and the ten books starting with *Cold Evil* show him still trying new things. Two of the books are inverted mysteries – where we know who the killer is, and we follow their attempts to commit the crime and/or escape justice and also, in some cases, the detective's attempt to bring them to justice. That description doesn't do justice to either *Black Edged* or *Such Bright Disguises*, as there is more revealed in the finale than the reader might expect . . . There is one particular innovation in *The Grim Maiden*, namely the introduction of a female officer at Scotland Yard.

Helen Repton, an officer from "the woman's side of the Yard" is recruited in that book, as Bathurst's plan require an undercover officer in a cinema. This is her first appearance, despite the text implying that Bathurst has met her before, but it is notable as the narrative spends a little time apart from Bathurst. It follows Helen Repton's investigations based on superb initiative, which generates some leads in the case. At this point in crime fiction, there have been few, if any, serious depictions of a female police detective – the primary example would be Mrs Pym from the pen of Nigel Morland, but she (not just the only female detective at the Yard, but the Assistant Deputy Commissioner no less) would seem to be something of a caricature. Helen would go on to become a semi-regular character in the series, and there are certainly hints of a romantic connection between her and Bathurst.

It is often interesting to see how crime writers tackled the Second World War in their writing. Some brought the ongoing conflict into their writing – John Rhode (and his pseudonym Miles Burton) wrote several titles set in England during the conflict, as did others such as E.C.R. Lorac, Christopher Bush, Gladys Mitchell and many others. Other writers chose not to include the War in their tales – Agatha Christie had ten books published in the war years, yet only *N or M?* uses it as a subject.

Brian only uses the war as a backdrop in one title, *Glittering Prizes*, the story of a possible plan to undermine the Empire. It illustrates the problem of writing when the outcome of the conflict was unknown – it was written presumably in 1941 – where there seems little sign of life in England of the war going on, one character states that he has fought in the conflict, but messages are sent from Nazi conspirators, ending *"Heil Hitler!"*. Brian had good reason for not wanting to write about the conflict in detail, though, as he had immediate family involved in the fighting and it is quite understandable to see writing as a distraction from that.

While Brian had until recently been all but forgotten, there are some mentions for Brian's work in some studies of the genre – Sutherland Scott in *Blood in their Ink* praises *The Mystery of the Peacock's Eye* as containing "one of the ablest pieces of misdirection" before promptly spoiling that misdirection a few pages later, and John Dickson Carr similarly spoils the ending of *The Billiard Room Mystery* in his famous essay "The Grandest Game In The World". One should also include in this list Barzun and Taylor's entry in their *Catalog of Crime* where they attempted to cover Brian by looking at a single title – the somewhat odd *Conspiracy at Angel* (1947) – and summarising it as "Straight tripe and savorless. It is doubtful, on the evidence, if any of his others would be different." Judging an author based on a single title seems desperately unfair – how many people have given up on Agatha Christie after only reading *Postern Of Fate*, for example – but at least that misjudgement is being rectified now.

Contemporary reviews of Brian's work were much more favourable, although as John Long were publishing his work for a library market, not all of his titles garnered attention. At this point in his writing career – 1938 to 1944 – a number of his books won reviews in the national press, most of which were positive. Maurice Richardson in the *Observer* commented that "Brian Flynn balances his ingredients with considerable skill" when reviewing *The Ebony Stag* and praised *Such Bright Disguises* as a "suburban horror melodrama" with an "ingenious final solution". "Suspense is well maintained until the end" in *The Case of the Faithful Heart*, and the protagonist's narration in *Black Edged* in "impressively nightmarish".

It is quite possible that Brian's harshest critic, though, was himself. In the *Crime Book* magazine, he wrote about how, when reading the current output of detective fiction "I delight in the dazzling erudition that has come to grace and decorate the craft of the *'roman policier'.*" He then goes on to say "At the same time, however, I feel my own comparative unworthiness for the fire and burden of the competition." Such a feeling may well be the reason why he never made significant inroads into the social side of crime-writing, such as the Detection Club or the Crime Writers Association. Thankfully, he uses this sense of unworthiness as inspiration, concluding "The stars, though, have always been the most desired of all goals, so I allow exultation and determination to take the place of that but temporary dismay."

In Anthony Bathurst, Flynn created a sleuth that shared a number of traits with Holmes but was hardly a carbon-copy. Bathurst is a polymath and gentleman sleuth, a man of contradictions whose background is never made clear to the reader. He clearly has money, as he has his own rooms in London with a pair of servants on call and went to public school (Uppingham) and university (Oxford). He is a follower of all things that fall under the banner of sport, in particular horse racing and cricket, the latter being a sport that he could, allegedly, have represented England at. He is also a bit of a show-off, littering his speech (at times) with classical quotes, the obscurer the better, provided by the copies of the *Oxford Diction-ary of Quotations* and *Brewer's Dictionary of Phrase & Fable* that Flynn kept by his writing desk, although Bathurst generally restrains himself to only doing this with people who would appreciate it or to annoy the local constabulary. He is fond of amateur dramatics (as was Flynn, a well-regarded amateur thespian who appeared in at least one self-penned play, *Blue Murder*), having been a member of OUDS, the Oxford University Dramatic Society. General information about his background is light on the ground. His parents were Irish, but he doesn't have an accent – see *The Spiked Lion* (1933) – and his eyes are grey. Despite the fact that he is an incredibly charming and handsome individual, we learn in *The Orange Axe* that he doesn't pursue romantic relationships due to a bad experience in his first romance. We find out more about that relationship and the woman involved in *The Edge of Terror*, and soon thereafter he falls head over heels in love in *Fear and Trembling*, although we never hear of that young lady again. After that, there are eventual hints of an attraction between Helen Repton, but nothing more. That doesn't stop women falling head over heels for Bathurst – as he departs her company in *The Padded Door*, one character muses "What other man could she ever love . . . after this secret idolatry?"

As we reach the halfway point in Anthony's career, his companions have somewhat stablised, with Chief Inspector Andrew MacMorran now his near-constant junior partner in investigation. The friendship with MacMorran is a highlight (despite MacMorran always calling him "Mr. Bathurst") with the sparring between them always a delight to read. MacMorran's junior officers, notably Superintendent Hemingway and Sergeant Chatterton, are frequently recurring characters. The notion of the local constabulary calling in help from Scotland Yard enables cases to be set around the country while still maintaining the same central cast (along with a local bobby or two).

Cold Evil (1938), the twenty-first Bathurst mystery, finally pins down Bathurst's age, and we find that in *The Billiard Room Mystery* (1927), his first outing, he was a fresh-faced Bright Young Thing of twenty-two. How he can survive with his own rooms, at least two servants, and no noticeable source of income remains a mystery. One can also ask at what point in his life he travelled the world, as he has, at least, been to Bangkok at some point. It is, perhaps, best not to analyse Bathurst's past too carefully . . .

"Judging from the correspondence my books have excited it seems I have managed to achieve some measure of success, for my faithful readers comprise a circle in which high dignitaries of the Church rub shoulders with their brothers and sisters of the common touch."

For someone who wrote to entertain, such correspondence would have delighted Brian, and I wish he were around to see how many people have enjoyed the reprints of his work so far. *The Mystery of the Peacock's Eye* (1928) won Cross Examining Crime's Reprint Of The Year award for 2019, with *Tread Softly* garnering second place the following year. His family are delighted with the reactions that people have passed on, and I hope that this set of books will delight just as much.

Steve Barge

CHAPTER I

I

A MARCH evening was at its wildest and wettest. Wind and rain vied with each other in violence. Most of the roads were empty, dead and dark. Save for an occasional car which made its quickest way homeward, there was no life in road or street. And there were absurdly long intervals of time between these occasional cars. P.C. Percy Wragg hunched his shoulders for the umpteenth time and stared out solemnly from his coign of vantage in a convenient doorway into the wet, dim silence. Then, in an effort of protection, he attempted to bury his chin in the upturned collar of his uniform overcoat.

"Might be Sodom and Gomorrah," he muttered to himself. "Looks like it and, what's more, feels like it."

Wragg's spirits, low as they were, sank still further. Many hours of the evening and of the night to follow, loomed heavily and horribly in front of him. To add to his intense discomfort, the rain was increasing in severity. Whipped by the merciless wind, it now blew into his doorway and beat in his eyes and on his cheeks. Again he criticised the lamentable error of judgment on his part as a result of which he had entered the Police force. The sound of an approaching car made him look up and he glanced with little interest, it must be admitted, across the dark surface of the road which faced him. It glistened almost savagely with the rain that lay on it. The car towards which Constable Wragg looked was travelling fast. Considerably faster than any of the other cars which during the evening had arrested Wragg's attention. As the car passed Wragg, its horn blared twice. Wragg looked across the road. As he did so, a yellow light shone suddenly from a window in a tall house. The car swept on and Wragg turned his head idly and watched it. The watching lasted a matter of five or six seconds. Then the sight of the car was lost in the distance and Constable Wragg slumped again into his harbouring doorway. He shook the gathered drops of rain from the surface of his cape and his dismal spirits fell to their lowest ebb. Wragg shivered. But the shiver died on the instant almost that it had been born. For as the constable shivered, a far-away scream tore in two the wet curtain of the night.

II

Wragg started to run. To run hard. Towards the place from which the scream had come. As he ran, he found himself wondering what distance away his nearest colleague was. Too far for him to be comfortable, he considered. After Wragg had sprinted a hundred yards, he began to lose his breath. His heart began to beat fast, with heavy, disordered thumps. His mouth got dry, but he ran on. More efficiently now, for he ran with long, loping strides. He must have been running, he thought to himself, for several minutes. He had forgotten the wind and the rain. He was cold and he was wet. He knew that! In addition, he was frightened. Because he knew for a certainty, through the operation of a sixth sense, which he hadn't known before that he even possessed, that he was about to encounter something terrible.

Wragg continued to run towards the place from which he judged the scream had come. Suddenly, as he ran, he turned a corner and saw a car standing almost at right angles to the road upon which it stood. Wragg knew at once that this was the car which he had noticed a few moments previously. What had happened to it? There was no obvious sign of collision or accident, but despite this Constable Wragg knew beyond the shadow of a doubt that something was terribly wrong with this car and also with the people who were in it.

Wragg raced up to the car and turned the handle of the door on the near side. As he opened the door, Wragg caught his breath. The body of a man lay slumped over the steering wheel. The constable let the light of his torch play over the man's face. What he saw there made him more fearful than ever. For on the man's face there was a look of convulsed, contorted horror. The features were twisted into a spasm of pain which had creased the lines round the nose and mouth and turned them into an appalling leer.

"Struth!" muttered Wragg. "I'd like to know what got him—that I would."

Then he raised his nostrils to the air above him and sniffed. "Something burning," he muttered, "and in here too. I wonder where the—"

Wragg broke off abruptly and flashed the light of his torch round the interior of the car. But he was unable to trace where the smell was coming from. He came away from the car and looked in both directions, up and down the road. There was no sign of any life whatever.

The road led from the town of Mallett to the adjoining villages of Fell and Forge, but the night was bad and there would be few cars travelling in that direction before the morning came. Wragg scratched his head and, that action failing to produce inspiration, rubbed his chin. He felt that he was in a quandary. He went back to the car and put his hand against the man's heart. He felt convinced that he could feel it beating. Yes . . . the man was still alive. The realisation of this stung Wragg into more definite action. He knew that there was a Police box some little distance on the road to Fell. To get there and to ask for help would be the best course that he could possibly take. Wragg began to run again. Towards the Police box on the road to Fell. He made it in a matter of some three minutes and telephoned to the Police headquarters at Mallett.

"Police-Constable Wragg speaking . . ."

III

The necessary car left the Police-station at Mallett with the least possible delay. It carried two people. Inspector Venables and Dr. Pegram. The latter was in a bad temper. That is to say in a worse temper than usual. He knew, he argued to himself, at least twenty-two better ways of spending an evening than this particular one which had been so recently forced on him. He surveyed the weather from the window of the car with moody disfavour and found words of trenchant criticism.

"Without this poisonous weather, Venables, it would have been bad enough. As it is—"

Dr. Pegram shrugged his shoulders. Inspector Venables brushed his top lip with the back of his hand. But he was a man of few words. He made no comment on the doctor's statement. Pegram continued in his previous vein.

"Which constable did you say it was who 'phoned through?"

"Wragg."

"Good man?"

"Yes. All right—as far as he goes. Nothing particularly brilliant about him."

"Well—he's gone far enough to-night. I'll say that for him."

Venables said nothing to this. He contented himself with nodding. Doctor Pegram, sore and annoyed, came again.

"Reliable man? Or given to being fanciful?"

"Oh—reliable. Certainly not the latter. Minus imagination much more than plus."

Pegram grunted at Venables's assessment. "Where is he exactly did you say?"

"Out towards the western boundary of the town. Out towards Fell. He spoke from the Police box on the Fell road. Take us another ten minutes at least." Venables slumped into his seat.

The doctor looked out of the window again. "What a night," he moaned. "Makes me think of Macbeth's witches and people like King Lear. They'd be having the time of their lives."

The car swept on. Venables glanced at his watch. "Not so long now. We ought to be on the Fell road in a minute or so."

"In the fell clutch," rejoined Pegram disconsolately; "that would be a more apt description."

He thrust his hands deeply into the pockets of his Burberry and pushed his back hard against the upholstery of the car. The next few minutes passed in silence. Suddenly Venables leant forward and spoke to the driver through the speaking tube.

"Just ahead, I fancy. Keep your eyes open, Foster. It's wretchedly dark along here."

The chauffeur gave the sign that he had heard and understood. Dr. Pegram took his hands from his pockets and tried to rub some of the mist and moisture from the glass of the window. As he did so the pace of the car began to diminish.

"Here we are, Doctor," said the Inspector; "you'll be on the job now in a brace of shakes."

"You sound as though you regard it as a pleasant prospect," growled Pegram. "Are you aware, my dear chap, that I *might* have been playing bridge at this blessed moment."

The car stopped and the two men got out. Constable Wragg emerged from the shadows and advanced to meet them.

"Now, Constable Wragg," said the Inspector, "what's all this about?"

Wragg amplified the report that he had already supplied on the telephone. Dr. Pegram had gone to the big black car, the bonnet of which was pointing almost straight to the near side of the road. Still talking, Venables and Wragg went nearer to where the doctor was standing. They could hear him muttering and mumbling to himself as his hands worked on the body of the man by the steering-wheel. Suddenly he jerked his head back and called to the Inspector. There was an unusual note in his voice.

"Venables! Come here, man, will you?"

Venables pushed his head and a portion of his body into the interior of the car. Dr. Pegram half-turned from his task to speak to him.

"This fellow's dead, Inspector. But he hasn't been dead for over long."

Pegram took his hat off, tossed it on to the seat at the back of the car and then scratched his head.

"What's the matter, Doctor?" inquired the Inspector.

"Well—I'm damned if I know quite what's killed him. Frankly, Venables—I'm puzzled."

"Why—what's the trouble exactly?"

Pegram shook his head. "Wish I could tell you. But I can't. It's death from shock of some kind, though what the shock was, I'm still wondering."

Then as Police-Constable Wragg had done before him, he lifted his nose and sniffed. "Can you smell something burning, Inspector? In the car somewhere? I'll swear that I can."

Venables did an exercise in sniffing. "I agree, Doctor. I get it distinctly."

Wragg, who had heard the conversation, coughed discreetly. "I noticed it too, sir. When I first came along. I attempted to trace where it was, but I was unsuccessful."

Dr. Pegram sniffed again. "It may sound ridiculous, but it seems to me—here, give me a hand with this fellow. I'll soon settle the matter. Take him out and we'll lay him on the grass part of the path here. I can run the rule over him better down there than stuck inside as he is now."

The Inspector and Wragg helped the doctor to move the body from the car on to the path. Pegram went on one knee and busied himself with the man's clothing. The others saw him push his hands under the body.

"More light," he said curtly. "Shine your torches right on my hands."

The light flooded the prostrate body. Pegram heaved it over on to its face. By the light of the torches Inspector Venables saw a puzzled look come over the doctor's face.

"Something here, Inspector! Can't make it out. Extraordinary business. Between his clothes and his flesh."

Suddenly a look of understanding showed and he thrust his nose in the direction of the man's back. "What I smelt and what you smelt, Constable Wragg, was burning flesh! Neither more nor less. The clothes are burnt as well. But what the hell it all means—"

Pegram glanced up to the Inspector. "I'm going to take this chap back to Mallett. In my car. It's impossible for me to examine him properly here—especially in this foul weather. Wragg can stay and 'phone for help with the first car. We'll put this fellow on the back seat in our own car. There's quite a lot about this business that I don't like at all. O.K., Venables?"

The Inspector nodded his agreement with the suggestion. Wragg helped them to lift the dead body and place it in the car as Dr. Pegram had indicated. Foster, the chauffeur, who had remained in the driving-seat, started on the journey back to Mallett.

IV

Inspector Venables examined certain entries in Police-Constable Wragg's note-book which he had taken from the latter before they parted company. For some time he sat silent and in deep thought. Dr. Pegram was content to sit by the side of the chauffeur with his head half-inclined towards Venables at the back of the car. Suddenly Venables looked up from Wragg's note-book and spoke to the doctor.

"There's one thing. Dr. Pegram: it's a local car all right. XXX555—it's a Mallett registration mark and number. So we shan't be long in establishing the dead man's identity. That means a saving of time, if nothing else. It's a stroke of luck I hadn't anticipated. I was expecting something infinitely more troublesome."

Pegram grunted. His mind was occupied in turning over, again and again, the circumstances of the death of the man whose body lay in the car. It was true that he hadn't been able to give the body an adequate examination under the conditions in which he had seen it, but even allowing for this defection, he was still puzzled by what he had actually seen. And until he would be in a position to carry out a thorough examination in conditions entirely to his liking, he knew that these emotions which now possessed him would remain with him. When the police car entered the main street of Mallett, Pegram gave an order to Foster, the chauffeur.

"When we get to the station, Foster, I shall want you to help me carry that body into the mortuary chamber. We've gained time by bringing it in the car. To have sent for the ambulance would have meant wasting at least another half-hour. So look slippy directly you pull up the car—will you?"

"Very good, sir."

Foster was quick and precise when the moment came to carry out his instructions. With the body on the mortuary-slab and under adequate lighting conditions, Pegram set to work on his task immediately. First of all he removed the dead man's clothing. The coat, waistcoat, shirt and undervest were all burned in the region of the small of the back. Pegram frowned repeatedly at what he saw. For between the clothing and the flesh were six small glowing cinders. Although by now almost all the heat had gone from them, they were still uncomfortably warm to handle. Dr. Pegram found a pair of tweezers and a pie-dish and carefully picked out the smouldering pieces one by one, laying them carefully in the dish. He left them there temporarily and turned his attention to the dead man. Pegram judged him, from his appearance, to be a man in the late sixties. He was tall, thin and had scanty, grizzled hair. On his chest the form of a small snake had been tattooed. His hands were roughish and the doctor mentally assessed him as a man to whom manual labour had been a habit.

Once or twice, perhaps, Pegram looked at the dead man's features. They seemed moderately familiar to him. As though he had seen the man before somewhere and not so very long ago at that. But after a time he shook his head and decided that he must be yielding to the force of fancy. Turning, he saw Venables standing at his side.

"I want these clothes, Doctor," said the Inspector. "Want to go through 'em. Should be something somewhere to help us."

The doctor jerked his head to the chairs on which he had laid the clothes. "Over there. On those chairs."

The Inspector looked curiously at the body. "What exactly was the cause of death, Doctor?"

"Shock from burning. Heart probably couldn't stand up to the shock the nervous system had."

Venables raised interrogative eyebrows. "From burning?"

"Ah-a. And torturing burning at that, Inspector. Cock your eye in that pie-dish on the table and you'll see what I mean. Pretty foul business—if you ask me."

Venables walked over. "Good God!" he exclaimed as his eyes took in the contents of the pie-dish.

"Nice little companions, Venables, for the small of your back! Held in position by the weight of your clothes. How do you fancy the idea? Some improvement on the Star Chamber?"

Venables changed colour. He started to go through the dead man's clothing. "Seven shillings and three pence in small money. Bunch of large keys, bunch of small keys, nail file, silver pencil, cigarette case, box of matches, silk handkerchief, linen handkerchief, receipt for registered packet addressed to John Brooks, 135 Maylott Street, Sear, and one leather wallet. Contents of wallet, three £1 currency notes, one 10s. currency note, picture postcard of Ludlow (new—that is to say, unused), ninepence in stamps, and two letters. Both addressed to 'W. Norman, Esq., Rapson's Farm, Forge,' and quite commonplace in character."

Venables looked at the doctor. "Deceased would appear to be said 'W. Norman.' I'll check up with the Local Taxation licences people with regard to the car. I'll be with you again before very long."

He went out of the room. Dr. Pegram continued to look at the body. He scratched his chin pensively.

"I've a good mind," he commenced to say to himself, then he looked towards the telephone. With an almost startling abruptness he made up his mind. He went to the telephone and dialled a number.

Patiently he waited for the response, his lips pursed in a soft whistle. "Dr. Pegram speaking. From the Police-station at Mallett. Is that Dr. Chavasse? Yes? If you're not too busy, Martin, I'd like a couple of words with you . . . yes . . . something tremendously interesting. Right down your street, I should say. Tired? So am I. Back from what? A confinement?" Pegram chuckled. "This'll make a nice change for you—believe me. Right away from the humdrum. Well—I'm expecting you within the next few minutes. Don't let me down. You know the way in. Walk straight along and ask for me."

Pegram hung up the receiver. Feeling for his cigarettes, he found a packet and lit one. Smoking hard, he walked round the body twice, cocking his head and regarding it from several angles. Venables came in again.

"All clear *re* identity. No doubt about it. The dead man is William Norman, farmer. Address as given on the letters in the wallet. Rapson's Farm, Forge. The wife's coming up as soon as possible. I've sent another car down for her. Sergeant Coleman's gone along with it."

"Good." Dr. Pegram nodded his approval. Then he added something which sounded to the Inspector like an afterthought. "I've asked Dr. Chavasse to come over. 'Phoned him a moment or so ago. I thought he might be useful. Or his opinion, rather."

Venables grinned good-humouredly. "Losing your grip, Doctor?"

Pegram took the shaft with some degree of seriousness. "No. Not exactly. Just feel that I want another opinion. I'm just willing to admit frankly that I haven't got the hang of things as far as this job is concerned by a long chalk—and—well—two heads are always better than one."

Venables shrugged his shoulders. "Depends on the heads," he replied.

As he spoke, another voice was heard in the corridor of the building and after the shortest of intervals, the door of the room was flung open and there entered the tall, athletic figure of Dr. Martin Chavasse. Pegram advanced to greet him.

"Hallo, Pegram. . . ."

"Glad you decided to come, Chavasse. Stroll over here, will you? Something here that will interest you."

The two doctors walked to the dead body of the man who had been known in life as William Norman.

V

Martin Chavasse was tall, thin and spare. His steel-blue eyes, deep sunken, burnt fiercely in his face. His nose was large and prominent and his jaw held a strong, pertinacious line which proclaimed unmistakably to anybody who contended with its owner that he was facing a resolute and determined adversary. Chavasse had come into the district some years previously and had already established a reputation as a brilliant and dominant personality.

He bent down and looked at the dead man. He frowned at the marks of the seared flesh in the lumbar region. "Curious," he muttered. "Curious and extraordinary. Never seen anything like it before. Flesh looks all the world as though it's been burned."

"Told you you'd find it interesting. Sole reason why I gave you a ring. They're burns all right."

Chavasse's tall figure swayed gently backwards and forwards as he continued to gaze at the corpse. "The shock must have killed him, Pegram. Not a doubt about that. And how on earth did it happen?"

Pegram recounted the details of the matter as he had heard them from Police-Constable Wragg. Chavasse punctuated the story with a succession of quick sharp nods.

"A car—eh? I'm still at sea, though. Don't get anything like the full story. Still—that can wait."

Pegram caught him by the sleeve. "Now look in here." He held out the pie-dish for Chavasse's attention.

Chavasse's brows contracted as he looked into it. Pegram explained. "These smoking remnants were lodged between his vest and the small of his back. Held in position by the impact of the clothes. I had to fish them out. Pretty grim, don't you think?"

Chavasse nodded in agreement. "Ghastly! Murder's murder every time, but to try to turn a man into roast pork—" He turned away in disgust and shuddered.

Pegram proceeded with the story. "We've identified him—or rather Venables has. He was a farmer out at Forge somewhere. William Norman by name. His wife's coming up in a few minutes to clinch the identification. Venables is looking out for her now. Don't fancy being here when she arrives."

Chavasse went back to the body. After a moment's further inspection, he called across the room to Pegram. "Come over here, will you?"

Pegram went to him. "Look at this, Pegram."

Chavasse traced a line with his finger from the nape of the dead man's neck to the small of the back. The marks of the burns were plain to see all the way down. Not bad burns where the burns began, mere seared discolorations and nothing like the terrible places in the lumbar region, but the track of the burning agent could be followed against Chavasse's finger without the slightest difficulty.

"There's the course the red-hot pellets took, Pegram. See it? Plain as a pikestaff. As discernible to us as though they were still there beneath our eyes."

"How on earth were they handled?" demanded Dr. Pegram. "That's where I'm beaten."

Chavasse made no reply. He continued to gaze intently at the dead man. "Extraordinary business," he muttered. "Whoever did it must have hated this fellow's guts—and then some. Can't imagine any motive beyond that. Can you?"

Before Pegram could find words for a reply, Inspector Venables showed at the door again. "I'm bringing Mrs. Norman in here, Doctor. She's just showed up."

"Do you mind if I stay, Inspector?" asked Dr. Chavasse.

"Not at all, sir," returned Inspector Venables.

VI

Caroline Norman was a tall, pale-faced, thin, angular woman who in her appearance at least looked to be considerably past middle age. Her dark eyes held a timid, desperately frightened look. A look almost of piteous entreaty. Pegram, sensing her condition, walked over to the body and covered the dead man's face.

"Sit down for a moment, Mrs. Norman, and pull yourself together," said Inspector Venables. "Take your time and try to compose yourself."

He placed a chair at her disposal. Mrs. Norman sat down and dabbed her dark eyes with the edge of her handkerchief. She said nothing. Chavasse and Pegram talked in low tones. Suddenly Mrs. Norman stood up and addressed herself to the Inspector.

"I'm ready, sir. It's no good putting it off any longer," she faltered.

Venables nodded to Dr. Pegram. The latter moved the covering from the face of the corpse. Mrs. Norman went and stood at its side. She put her hand to her throat and nodded hopelessly and helplessly.

"Yes," she whispered in a voice that was almost inaudible. "It's my husband. What's . . . what's . . . happened to him . . . what . . . what was it killed him?"

Inspector Venables took her by the arm and escorted her back to her chair. "He's had an accident in his car, Mrs. Norman. That's all we shall be able to tell you for the time being. Now . . ." Venables paused. "Do you feel that you're able to answer a few questions, Mrs. Norman, if I ask you them now?"

She nodded weakly. Her wide, dark, staring eyes were turned towards the Inspector in concentrated intensity.

Venables opened his note-book. "Your husband's full name was—"

"William Bateman Norman."

"Address?"

"Rapson's Farm, Mallett Old Road, Forge."

"A farmer?"

"Yes." She nodded. "We farm twenty acres there."

"How long have you lived there?"

"Eleven years come next August. My husband bought the property from Stephen Rapson when he moved into the West Country. It had been in the Rapson family for generations."

Venables wrote steadily in his note-book. "How old was your husband?"

"He would have been fifty-three on the 29th of July next," Mrs. Norman began to cry softly—almost silently.

Venables began to look uncomfortable and started to tap his front teeth with the butt of his fountain pen. "When did you last see your husband alive?"

The sorrowing woman lifted her head to answer. "This morning. About twenty minutes past ten. When he went out after breakfast. My husband left the farm to go to the market in Mallett. To-day was market day. He always went on market days. He had done so for years. Practically ever since we went to live at the farm."

"In the ordinary course of events, what time would you have expected him home?"

"Some time during the evening. He wasn't very late—if that's what you mean. I mean he wasn't very late to-night. He used to stay all through the market and then have his dinner at the 'White Lion' in Mallett High Street. Then he'd drive back to the farm in the car. To-night he didn't come." Mrs. Norman put her face in her hands and began to sob again—great shuddering sobs that shook her.

"Had your husband any enemies that you're aware of?"

Mrs. Norman shook her head. "No. None at all. We've always been people to keep ourselves to ourselves. All through our business life. The farm occupies all our time. As far as I know, my husband was popular with everybody."

"He had no worries?"

"None that I know of."

"In good health?"

"Yes. Nothing much to worry about. His heart wasn't as strong, perhaps, as it might have been—he'd had rheumatic fever as a small boy—but otherwise he was all right as far as I know."

Venables retraced his steps. "There were no financial troubles or difficulties to your knowledge?"

Again Mrs. Norman gave the negative reply. "No." The answer was given simply and directly.

Venables persisted in his line of inquiry. "If there were anything of that kind, would you have known?"

"Oh, yes. I should be sure to have known."

"You mean by that that your husband confided everything to you. Is that so?"

Martin Chavasse, looking at her intently as she faced the Police Inspector's barrage of questions, noticed that she flushed a little. "Not everything, perhaps, but certainly everything that he considered to be of any importance."

"You were on good terms with your husband, Mrs. Norman?"

Again the flush. "Certainly. We seldom had anything like a disagreement. In fact, I can reasonably claim that we were quite a united family. All of us at the farm."

"What is the number of the family, Mrs. Norman?"

"Four. That's all. I have a son and a daughter."

"Please give me their names and ages."

"My son is twenty-six. His name is Christopher. My daughter is twenty-four. Her name is Laura."

"I take it from what you have just said that they both reside at the farm with you."

Mrs. Norman inclined her head in assent. "That is so. Neither of them is married. As yet. Christopher hopes to be very shortly. The marriage actually is fixed for the summer. He and my daughter help us with the farm. But I don't know, of course, what will happen now. To-night may change everything. It's so difficult to say." She gestured in the direction of the body of her husband. "After this."

Venables kept his eyes fixed on his note-book. "Your son didn't accompany you here this evening?"

Mrs. Norman's fingers tightened round the square of her handkerchief. "No. When your call came through to me he wasn't at home."

"Any idea where he was, Mrs. Norman?"

"Yes. I always know where he is. Within a little. I've brought him up in that way. Strange though it may seem in these days, my son has no secrets from his mother."

There was a hard pride sounding in her voice. Something like a challenge had rung out. She continued.

"Christopher had gone to the neighbouring farm. The name of the farm is Walter's. It is kept by Mr. and Mrs. Preston. My son is engaged to marry Joyce Preston, their only daughter. You may guess why he elects to spend most of his evenings there. He'll only be young once. Had he been at the farm with me when your summons came, Christopher would have accompanied me here. You can be quite sure of that."

She was dry-eyed now—dry-eyed, hard and fearless. Lines floated through Martin Chavasse's mind . . . "like mountain-cat that guards her young."

Venables had succeeded in putting her thoroughly on the defensive. The Inspector himself seemed to realise this fact. "Quite so, Mrs. Norman . . . quite so! I understand that perfectly. But you appreciate, of course, that inquiries must be made in an affair of this kind. . . ."

She immediately checked him with a nod. "I understand perfectly, Inspector. And because of that understanding, I answered you as I did."

Venables shot her a quick glance from under his eyebrows and altered his tactics. "It was your husband's habit, you say, to dine on market-days at the 'White Lion' in Mallett."

"Yes. He always had dinner there on market-days. I think I told you that. Very often, the market would keep him until after four o'clock in the afternoon. He would have a snack at midday, carry on until the market finished, and then dine at the 'White Lion' in the early part of the evening. It prevented me being worried to get him a hot meal during the evening. He was always considerate over matters like that. That had been his regular programme for years now. As I told you just now."

"I see. He would have friends, doubtless, who would have dinner with him? People who would share the meal with him fairly frequently? Is that so?"

"Friends?" She questioned the word. "Acquaintances, would I think be a truer term, Inspector. No doubt somebody of that kind would be there."

Venables nodded as he made a note. "Thank you, Mrs. Norman. And I mean that. You have answered my questions very clearly. I don't think I need detain you any longer. I'll make arrangements for getting you back home again."

The Inspector looked across at the two doctors. "Does either of you two gentlemen want to—"

Pegram shook his head. But Martin Chavasse nodded quickly and came forward with a question. "One thing I'd like to ask, Mrs. Norman. If I may. I'm rather interested. Stephen Rapson—did your husband know Rapson before he bought the farm off him?"

Chavasse thought that her sudden glance at him was startled. But the reply came direct enough. "No. Not to my knowledge. It came about in this way. My husband saw an advertisement offering the farm for sale. In one of the agricultural journals. I'm certain he'd never met Mr. Rapson before. But why do you ask? Is it in any way important?"

It was a moment or so before Chavasse brought himself to answer. "I'm not sure," he said. "I was trying to chase a fragment of memory—that was all. But I think I've failed—it's eluded me."

She looked at him wonderingly. Suddenly he half-turned and held out his hand. "Good-night, Mrs. Norman. Try to think it's all for the best."

The woman took the hand offered to her and then, without further words, turned and walked towards the car that was waiting for her outside the Police-station.

CHAPTER II

I

Sir Charles Stuart, Chief Constable of the county, was nearing the end of his second year of office in that capacity. During that period, his reign had been singularly uneventful. Not a single crime of any importance had reared its ugly head to trouble him. To justify himself—and the effort bordered on the frantic—he made a point of telling everybody of note with whom he came into contact that it was a much greater feat to prevent crime than to lay its perpetrators by their slippery heels. But Sir Charles was nobody's fool, and as he stood before his own hearth and addressed himself to his wife this fact was easy of discernment by the acute observer.

"Inspector Venables is coming up," he said rather eagerly, "we may expect him within the hour. Or even sooner than that. Until I hear fully what Venables has to say, I'm not opening my mouth at all. I'm just shutting up, sitting tight and suspending judgment."

His teeth closed with a snap and he rubbed his hands together. Elinor Stuart shrugged nonchalant shoulders at her husband. As she did so, her subtle perfume came to his nostrils and made him even more aware than usually of her beauty. Her intimate personal fragrance invariably had that effect on him. It was one of the reasons why he had asked her to marry him. On this particular evening she was dressed in black. Her hair was blue-black, her eyes dark blue, her skin faultless and her parted lips an almost irresistible invitation. Her long diamond earrings set off the shape of her face and made her alluringly exquisite and superbly *soignée*. People—and this term included her own intimate circle—found it hard to describe accurately what they considered were her feelings towards her husband. Perhaps she herself would have found it equally difficult to describe them. If she had so desired! Which is definitely unlikely.

"Why all the fuss?" she remarked somewhat petulantly. "After all, it seems to me only a very ordinary and extremely sordid murder. The sooner forgotten the better. Why talk about it?"

Sir Charles planted his feet a little further apart and clasped his hands behind his back. With his forefinger he then rubbed the end of his nose.

"Don't know. Don't know that I agree with you, my dear. Sordid perhaps, but I'm sugared if you can reasonably call it ordinary. Far from it, if you ask me."

"You know what I mean. It's just a horrible incident—and nothing more. Wants to be treated as no more than a beastly dream."

Sir Charles's grey brows went up. Furrows appeared on the high, straight forehead and his greying hairs bristled. The blue eyes watching him waited for him to speak.

"I'm afraid, my dear Elinor, that, much as I might like to, it will be impossible and impracticable for me to dismiss the matter as easily and lightly as that." He paused and cleared his throat. "It's murder—that's an ugly word in our language. Whatever it may be in other countries."

She gave a little gesture of disgust. "My dear Charles, I'm quite prepared to agree with you as far as that goes. Concerning its beastliness, its horror and its frightful inconvenience, I merely urge—but why should we talk about it." She turned away and shrugged her shoulders.

Sir Charles stroked his chin which from habit he had thrust forward. "H'm. Quite so! Have it your own way, of course." He grunted, turned away and consulted his watch again. "Venables shouldn't be too long now," he muttered. "He's pretty reliable as a rule. And punctual. I like a man of his class to be punctual."

"In that case, then," said the wife of his bosom, "I'll leave you and the coast clear for him. Then both of you can talk 'murder' to your hearts' content."

She rose slowly to her feet, went over to the door and made her exit from the room. The grace of her carriage was in complete harmony with the rest of her. Sir Charles Stuart watched her go with avid eyes and then resumed his position at the fireplace. The place where he resided, Sandals, was a matter of ten miles from Mallett. Inspector Venables had been in communication with him by telephone that afternoon and Sir Charles had made immediate arrangements for the Inspector to come over to his place as soon as was convenient.

Five minutes after the departure of his wife, the Chief Constable was informed that the Inspector had arrived. He gave orders that Venables was to be shown into him at once. The Inspector took the chair which the Chief Constable offered him. Sir Charles sat back in his own armchair and turned his cold, militant gaze on the Inspector.

"Well, Venables, so somebody's waking us up at long last—eh? Thought we'd been allowed to rust too long. Now—first of all—just amplify what you've already told me over the telephone."

"That was my intention, sir. I'll start with the story of Police-Constable Wragg, who was on duty at Mallett yesterday evening. If I'm not sufficiently clear with regard to anything, please stop me and I'll do my best to explain."

Sir Charles Stuart swallowed hard and in a slightly husky voice replied, "I'll do that, Venables—never fear."

Venables proceeded with his story. Its various points were punctuated by Stuart with grunts, nods and rather aggressive clearings of the throat. When Venables had reached the stage which suggested something like finality to the Chief Constable, Stuart made an elaborate announcement:

"The worst murders, Venables, from our point of view as the Police authorities, are those which appear to be motiveless. Don't you agree?"

The Inspector concurred without demur. "Every time, sir."

"Of course you do. And if I mistake not, this one will prove to be definitely in that category. In addition, there seems ample evidence that it's the work of a madman. Hot cinders down a man's back.

Blast it! The whole thing's fantastic. And absurd. Nobody in his right senses would think of doing such a thing."

Inspector Venables nodded. "I entirely agree, Sir Charles. In fact, I should tell you that I've been in communication with the two mental hospitals in the vicinity, St. Andrew's and Mitford, to find out whether any patient had escaped from either of them. But I drew a blank in each case, Sir Charles. There was no news of that kind from either of the places."

Sir Charles Stuart bristled at the Inspector's words. He looked as though he would like to be indignant at the information Venables had given him.

"H'm," he muttered. "Pity! We might have solved the problem that way, if we'd had any luck. But you say 'No.' Well—there it is. It's no good trying to turn 'no' into 'yes,' just in order to please ourselves. That's no way of doing business."

A silence reigned in the room for a matter of ten seconds. Venables waited to see if Sir Charles were going on. Eventually the Chief Constable did so. He cleared his throat again and said: "There's one thing I don't want, Venables, and I'll tell you what it is. I don't want us to be forced to call the 'Yard' in. I don't want any early confessions of failure. I like to feel, and to think, that we can deal with a crime of this calibre as well as the big noises can at Scotland Yard. And I'd like you to think the same, Venables."

"I do, Sir Charles. Nobody more so. And rest assured that everything that can be done as far as I personally am concerned will be done. At the same time—"

Venables stopped abruptly and shrugged his shoulders.

"At the same time—what?" echoed Sir Charles.

"Well—things don't look any too promising. I must be frank with you. That's what I was on the point of saying, Sir Charles."

The Chief Constable saw fit to administer a reprimand. "Now look here, Inspector. Hold your horses, for Heaven's sake. The case is twenty-four hours old. Not a minute more than that. Have a little patience. Rome wasn't built in a day, remember, Venables."

"I know, sir," replied Venables rather desperately. "I know all about that. Nobody better. But since I've been anything in the Force my experience has always been that if you don't pick up a vital clue in the early stages of these affairs, you rarely pick one up later. It's too much to hope for. The scent's growing cold all the time, you see, sir. That's the main point."

Venables drew a deep breath. Sir Charles, however, scouted the idea. "Stuff and nonsense, Inspector! The main point is to *pick* the clue up, not *when* you pick it up. And it'll come to you in this job, I feel convinced. It's there somewhere and it's your job to find it. Now I want to ask you a few routine questions. You mustn't mind that. Although I can readily see that the case is right away from the ordinary."

Venables prepared to answer them. When they came, none of them occasioned him any uneasiness or surprise. Sir Charles showed neither more nor less imagination than Venables had anticipated. After a time the Inspector found himself dismissed.

"Well," said the Chief Constable, "I think that will be all we can reasonably set ourselves to do to-day. It's not a bit of good wastin' time in merely theorising. I'll come over to Mallett to-morrow morning in the car and have a further discussion with you. You may have some more information for me by then. I hope you will."

Venables rose to take his departure. He felt himself a prey to despondency. He shook hands with the Chief Constable. By a strange coincidence, at that moment, Martin Chavasse 'phoned to Dr. Pegram with regard to certain theories which had come to him concerning the effect on human tissue of any substance like a hot cinder. Dr. Pegram listened attentively and with a tremendous amount of interest. What Chavasse was telling him was distinctly important.

II

Inspector Venables had been quick to visit Rapson's Farm and to make the acquaintance of Christopher and Laura Norman. He intimated to Mrs. Norman that he would like to interview them alone and separately. The son was tall and thin, with rather stooping shoulders and a tangle of unruly, incontinent hair which persisted in straggling over his sensitive forehead. To the Inspector, on first appearance, he looked far more like an unsuccessful artist than the only son of a working farmer. He also looked much younger than the age, twenty-six, which his mother had ascribed to him. Venables explained who he was and put several questions to Christopher Norman. At the same time he pointed out that Christopher Norman was under no obligation to answer if he desired otherwise. Norman nodded his head quickly.

"Don't worry about that, Inspector. I understand the implications of that quite well. What is it you wish to ask me?"

"You were on good terms with your father?"

The young man answered with easy composure. "Perfectly. He was a man easy to get on with. I could hardly have been otherwise."

"You know of no enemies he might have had?"

Christopher furrowed his brows. "*Might* have had?" He emphasised the first word.

Venables was quick to see the point. "I'm sorry," he corrected himself; "had."

The young man shook his head with every indication of emphasis. "I know of none. Absolutely none."

Venables found himself attracted to this young man. "Did your father consult you or confide in you with regard to his business and the working of the farm generally?"

Christopher hesitated. "To a certain extent," he replied eventually. "Perhaps not a lot. I helped him here in many ways and in various directions, so that we had to discuss things sometimes. We were compelled to. But my father was always the boss of the outfit, so to speak, and what he said and thought, went! He invariably formed and dictated policy. I mean by that even if we didn't see eye to eye, he always backed his own judgment—never mine."

He quickened the rate of his speaking as he delivered the last few words. Venables made a note of this. "Let us come to the evening of your father's death," continued the Inspector.

Christopher Norman jerked up his chin. For the moment his face showed signs of agitation. "What about it, Inspector? I'm afraid I can tell you nothing of any importance."

Venables gently reprimanded him. "That will be for me to judge. Let us take our time, please. How did you spend the evening?"

"I walked over to our nearest neighbours at Walters; the farm's about a mile's walk from here."

"What time did you leave here?"

"About half-past six, I should imagine. I can't be absolutely certain. My mother would be able to confirm the time. But that's about my usual time for setting out."

"And you arrived?"

"About ten minutes to seven, I should think."

"You were there the whole evening?"

"As good as. You can call it that. When I reached home again mother was out. Your people had sent for her to go to the Police-station at Mallett. My sister was alone."

Venables made a note of the successive answers. "According to the information that has been given me at the 'White Lion,' the place where your father had dinner, he left there about half-past six. That is to say, just as you were starting away from here to visit your friends at the other farm."

Christopher shook his head disclaimingly. "Very likely, but of course, I know nothing of my father's movements that evening. I can't help you at all with regard to that."

He rose to his feet as though he had been set in motion by a hidden spring somewhere inside him and stood in front of Inspector Venables swaying a little.

"Of course not," returned the latter. Suddenly all trace of anxiety left the young man and he became again complete master of himself and of his emotions. He sat down again.

"Did you stay at Walters all the time during the evening?"

Christopher flushed. "No. For part of the time, say about an hour, I was out walking with Miss Preston. That's the daughter of the house. She happens to be my fiancée. We hope to marry very shortly."

"I see." Venables made more notes with an air of extreme gravity.

Christopher Norman stood up and then sat down. Venables pulled his chair a little nearer to him. He might have been a doctor moving forward a little to question more closely an anxious patient.

"Your father's heart wasn't any too strong, I understand. So your mother has told me."

"It has been a trouble to him for some years. Nothing acute. But he had been ordered by his doctor to go slow and not to take unnecessary risks. He managed all right by obeying doctor's orders. What I mean is—he was nothing like an invalid. Did his work—but took great care in all of it. I want you to be perfectly clear as to the exact position."

Venables nodded again. "I see. Thank you." He sat back a little in his chair. Norman waited for the next question. It came.

"I meant to ask your mother, Mr. Norman, about your father's will. I take it that there is one?"

"Everything is left to my mother. My father's solicitors were Lindley, Tinsley and Mitchell at Mallett."

"Thank you." Venables jotted down the names. "And now if you don't mind, Mr. Norman, I'd like a word with your sister. I take it she's available now." As he spoke, the Inspector looked up expectantly.

"I will tell her," said Christopher.

"Thank you. I should be obliged if you would."

When Laura Norman came in, Venables had a surprise. For the girl was near to being a beauty. Her face was delicate in colouring, she had a mist of fair hair that almost shone in its brilliance and a pair of glorious blue eyes. She stopped short in her stride when she saw Venables, but then drew a step nearer to him before she spoke.

"You want to see me, Inspector?"

He smiled at her. The smile was intended for encouragement. Venables rather prided himself on it.

"Yes, Miss Norman. I've only a few questions to ask you. That's all." He put to her the ordinary questions. "Where were you on the evening of your father's death?"

"Here. At the farm with my mother. All the evening."

"Your brother was not here with you?"

"No. He went over to the next farm. To see Miss Preston."

"What time did your brother return, Miss Norman?"

A slight flush of colour tinged her cheeks. "Late, Inspector. After the police had called to take away my mother. It would have been after ten o'clock." There came a swift change of expression in her eyes as she answered. And then, just as swiftly came tears. They streamed down her face and she made no effort to check them. "Oh, why do you ask me these things. Must you? Is it absolutely necessary?" The words were spoken almost in a whisper.

"The truth can harm no one," declared Venables both pompously and illogically. He waited for her to recover herself. Laura Norman threw up her hands with a gesture of despondency.

"I am sorry, Inspector, if it would appear that I am trying to cut our interview short. But, believe me, I know nothing about this horrible affair. If I know nothing, I am not able to tell you anything—am I? That's sound common sense, isn't it? And I have also told you all I know of my brother's movements."

Venables said nothing in criticism of these statements. But he appeared to come suddenly to a decision. "Very well, Miss Norman. If that's how you feel, I won't trouble you any more at present. But I may find myself compelled to talk to you again later."

The Inspector rose, snapped the elastic band round his official note-book and placed the book carefully in his pocket. On his way back to Mallett, he was forced to admit ruefully that he was making but little progress with the case. So far, none of his investigations had yielded him anything of value. His one remaining hope lay in the further inquiry he was about to make at the 'White Lion,' the hotel at which Norman had dined just before he set out on his last journey. If he drew blank there, Venables knew in his mind, with a strange certainty, that he would be compelled to list the case as a failure.

He had arranged with the landlord of the 'White Lion' to meet the five people who had been present in the dining-saloon on the evening when William Norman had eaten his last dinner, and the appointment was timed to take place immediately upon the Inspector's return to Mallett. He looked at his watch and saw to his satisfaction that he had ample time at his disposal for the journey. When he entered the doors of the 'White Lion,' Denton, the landlord, informed him that the company he desired was all assembled.

"Thank you, Mr. Denton," he replied. "I'm much obliged. I'll see them at once."

III

The five people who had dined at the 'White Lion' on the evening that William Norman of Rapson's Farm met his death were by name, Henry King, Richard Cox, Donald Marnoch, Septimus Waghorn and Horace Marsden Hardwick. King was the principal baker and pastrycook of Mallett and the surrounding district. Cox was a farmer with a small farm near Conniss, a small village which lies on the other side of Mallett to Forge and Fell. Marnoch was a retired Inspector of Police who had come down to this particular part of England a few years previously. Waghorn was the manager of the Western Counties Bank and Hardwick was the Deputy Town Clerk of Mallett.

Venables let Denton, the landlord, do the preliminary talking. Then he suggested that they sat down together, made themselves entirely comfortable, and that he himself would take a convenient seat in the centre of the circle as they had made it. Cigarette cases were passed round, pipes were lighted, and within a very short interval Venables succeeded in obtaining an excellent and most congenial atmosphere. Before asking any questions, he encouraged his companions to conversation, and conversation as he well knew must mean mental exposure. Thoughts were very soon in the process of being dragged from their various hiding places. Suddenly, it became clear to most of the company that the Inspector had begun to ask questions, almost before they had been aware of it. The main point which emerged from the discussion was that Norman, on the evening in question, had dined alone. All five of the company were insistent and positive thereon.

"This," said Septimus Waghorn, "was rather noticeable. If I may use such a word with regard to an ordinary occurrence. And I'll explain why, Inspector."

"Yes," prompted Venables. "I'm listening with all ears. Why was it?"

"Because," replied the bank manager, "it was Norman's habit to dine with another man. I know that without the slightest fear of contradiction. Six times out of every seven, they were to be seen at the same table. On this particular night, however, the man was absent. The result was that Norman dined alone."

Denton nodded. "I know the man by sight—but nothing more than that."

Venables at once asked for details of this man's appearance. The five men looked at each other, as though seeking individual inspiration. Marnoch, the ex-inspector of Police volunteered certain information.

"I know the man to whom Waghorn has referred. He was a tall, heavily-built chap. Say in the early forties. Rather a rough-looking customer, taking him on the whole."

"Was he a local man, do you know?"

Marnoch shook his head. "In my opinion—no. Certainly I'd not seen him anywhere about other than in here with Norman."

"What do you other gentlemen say with regard to that?"

Venables put a pertinent question round the members of the circle. He followed it up with a glance that searched their faces. The four men looked at each other. But they all shook their heads and agreed with ex-inspector Marnoch.

"I've no recollection of seeing him except in here," said Hardwick. "Nor I," said Waghorn.

King and Cox expressed similar opinions. "That seems to be pretty well agreed then," accepted Venables. "Now here's something else I'd like you to tell me." They waited for the question. "Did any of you gentlemen notice Norman leave the table on the evening he was murdered? I mean, when he got up to go home?"

Marnoch and Waghorn shook their heads again. "No," they replied in unison. But from the remaining three, Venables succeeded in getting affirmations.

"I did," said Cox. "I actually called out 'Good-night' to him."

"Did he answer you?"

Cox thought for a moment. "No. Not in actual words. But I remember that he waved his right hand towards me in a sort of salutation. Then he went out through the main door."

"Just a minute. The main door, you say? That door doesn't lead to the street, does it?"

"No. It leads into one of the bars. Have a look for yourself before you go. You'll see how it is."

Hardwick said, "I saw Norman go out on the night he was killed. He passed by my table. Quite close to me."

"Did he make any remark to you as he went by."

Hardwick smiled. "He did. And one that was, I'm afraid, extremely commonplace. He said, 'Lousy night outside.' And I concurred. I hadn't been in from the street much more than twenty minutes or so and was only just finishing the soup course, so I knew all about the weather conditions."

"And he went into the bar just as Mr. Cox stated?"

"Yes. I can confirm that. I should say there's no doubt that he found his way into one of the other bars."

Venables jotted down a note that was to act as a reminder to him to see the barmaid who had happened to be on duty that night in the adjoining bar. Then he turned to King. "Now, what have you to say, Mr. King?"

"I can also confirm what Cox and Hardwick have told you. I was actually sitting with Marnoch. But his back was towards Norman, whereas mine wasn't. I saw Norman pay his bill to Kitty, the waitress. I saw him get up to leave and I also saw him speak to Hardwick here on his way out. He was alone and I sized it up that he was going out to his car and would then drive home to his farm."

"It's on the cards, then," declared Venables with quiet insistence, "that he picked up somebody in the other bar. I shall have to look into that possibility."

Denton nodded at the remark before walking away to attend to something.

"I can help you a little there, Inspector Venables." It was Waghorn who spoke.

"What's your story this time?" demanded the Inspector.

"Well," returned Waghorn, "I happen to know for a fact that Norman *did* speak to somebody in the inner bar. For the best of all reasons. I actually saw him in conversation with this man at the end of the bar. They were standing just by the connecting doors."

"How was that, Mr. Waghorn? I mean, how do you come to know that?"

"Well, Inspector. It's quite a simple matter really. The gentlemen's lavatory is just beyond those doors. I went over there, and as I walked through the bar—you must walk through the bar to get to the lavatory—I saw your man leaning up against the counter talking to another man."

Venables evinced keen interest at Waghorn's statement. "Now this is getting more satisfactory. What was this other man like, Mr. Waghorn? Did you have the luck to notice him particularly?"

Waghorn shook his head doubtfully. "Hardly. I walked by them in a second as you may say. But let me think. I caught an impression, no doubt. Let me see if I can conjure anything up."

Waghorn put his hand to his forehead and thought hard over the Inspector's question. Venables and the others waited patiently for his answer.

After a time, Waghorn nodded.

"Yes. I'm getting a picture of the man. He was a man, I should say, of average height. A little under that, if anything. But with broad, powerful and rather restless shoulders. I have a recollection that he moved his shoulders more than once as I was going by. Darkish hair. Well-brushed and groomed. Wore a dark grey suit. Dark grey flannel, I *think*. His hands moved quickly, too. There was a gold ring on one of the fingers of the left hand, I can remember that well. Black shoes. He was smoking a cigarette and was drinking something out of a round glass. That may sound strange—but I mean by that remark that I don't think he was drinking beer." Waghorn looked up at the company and addressed himself to the Inspector of Police. "I'm afraid I can't recollect anything else about him. Pretty thin effort—what?"

Venables smiled. "Not so bad. You never know. Though you haven't given me a lot to go on, I'm afraid." He leant over and touched the bell. An aproned maid answered the summons. "Ask Mr. Denton to come over here for a few moments, will you, my girl? Tell him Inspector Venables wants him and won't detain him for more than a couple of minutes." The girl nodded her understanding and vanished. Denton was quick to leave his customers and join them. Venables mentioned the story which Septimus Waghorn had just recounted to him.

"Now, Mr. Denton," he said as he concluded, "any idea who this man might have been?"

Denton shook his head.

"Not the slightest. From the description given, I can't recognise him as one of the regulars in the bar over there. I know most of 'em and this chap doesn't strike a familiar chord. But just a minute. I'll ask Jo." Venables lifted his eyebrows.

"Josephine, I mean. My barmaid over there. We usually call her Jo for short."

He walked to the door and called the girl by name. A tall, thin, fair wisp of a girl came into them.

"You wanted me, Mr. Denton?"

"That's right, Jo. Now keep your head and don't get 'jittery.' Nothing to be frightened of. This is Inspector Venables. He's here making a few inquiries concerning the death of Mr. Norman of Rapson's Farm."

Denton turned suddenly towards the Inspector. "Shall I ask her or would you rather do the job yourself?"

Venables nodded good-humoredly. "That's all right. You ask her. She's more used to you than she is to me."

"All right then. Now, Jo—you remember that Mr. Norman was in here on the evening of his death?"

"Yes, Mr. Denton. He dined in the big saloon, I'm told, and after that he walked over into the bar where I was serving."

"Did you serve him yourself?"

"Yes, Mr. Denton."

"Was there anyone with him?"

"A man who was already in the bar called him over. I served them both with drinks. Mr. Norman had a Scotch and soda and the other man had a brandy."

"Did you know this other man—this man who called Norman over to him?"

"No, Mr. Denton."

"Ever seen him before in this house?"

"No, Mr. Denton."

"Anywhere else?"

"No, Mr. Denton. Never seen him anywhere—to the best of my recollection. He was a complete stranger to me."

Denton gestured to the Inspector. "There you are, Inspector. You hear what the girl says. Should be conclusive."

Venables took up the inquiry on his own account. "Tell me what this man was like. Give me as good a description of him as you possibly can."

"He was a gentleman. I mean—according to the way he spoke; That's what I always go by. Fairly short. Dark. Big shoulders. Looked athletic—if you know what I mean. *Broad* shoulders. Not exactly good-looking—but a strong, determined-sort of face. Bit of a he-man."

The girl smiled at the men around her as she added her final fragment of description. "Looked like a man who knew what he wanted and intended getting it—never mind what happened to him afterwards."

Venables jotted down what the girl had said. On broad lines, it tallied satisfactorily with the description that Waghorn, the bank manager, had already supplied. With the barmaid, however, Venables intended to go a step further.

"Now tell me, Miss Jo, how long was Norman with this man?"

"Over five minutes, But well under a quarter of an hour. I only served them with drinks twice. A round, each."

"When Norman left to go, did this man go with him?"

For the first time during her examination, the girl was not able to reply promptly. "I'm not altogether sure," she replied after a short period of hesitation, "but I don't think that he did."

Venables looked straight at her. "You are not altogether sure?" he repeated.

Jo shook her head slowly. "No, sir. That's not an easy question for me to answer. You see, it was like this. There were a lot of customers in the bar just about that time and I was busy attending to them. Here, there and everywhere, as you might say. Just dodging about. A man can leave the bar in a second while your back's turned and your attention's distracted, and you don't see the goings of him."

"I suppose that is so," returned Venables; "but tell me why you don't think this other man went out with Norman when he took his departure. You must have a reason for thinking as you do."

"Well," replied the barmaid slowly, "I'll tell you why I said what I did. I fancy—and it's only fancy, mind you—that I saw the man in the bar *after* Mr. Norman had gone away. If I said any more than that I should be telling a lie." She wiped her hands on her handkerchief rather nervously.

"Thank you, miss," said the Inspector. "I don't think I need bother you any more for the moment, though I may want to see you again later on."

The girl turned and went back to her daily occupation. Inspector Venables had a drink with Denton and the other men, and then, shortly afterwards, followed her example.

IV

Martin Chavasse spent an evening with Dr. Pegram. He liked to do this, and he also liked Pegram. He had dropped in rather unexpectedly, but, despite this, Pegram was pleased to see him and genuinely welcomed him. Each was a man whose range of interests extended considerably beyond the equipment of expert medical knowledge. Pegram had become friendly with Chavasse some years previously when the latter had first come to reside in the district, and the friendship had developed and grown on each side.

When he entered, Chavasse slipped into a chair. "Hallo," said Pegram. "Help yourself."

He nodded towards the tantalus and the siphon. Chavasse faced his host and began to fill his pipe.

"What are you reading?" asked Chavasse with a quick gesture towards the book on the table.

"Poetry," responded Pegram drily. "Oddly enough, I suppose, for a busy man these days, I happen to like it. And I've found a man here who's very nearly another Rupert Brooke."

Chavasse picked up the book and glanced at the title and the author's name. "H'm! Collected poems of Richard Elwes. Why waste your time, my dear Pegram? Why waste your time on flowery froth and nimble nonsense."

His voice was harsh and unsympathetic as he spoke. Pegram smiled. He knew Chavasse's opinions of old. He had heard him in this strain before. Chavasse replaced the book on the table and helped himself to a whisky and soda. Pegram handled the book almost affectionately.

"Poetry to me, my dear Martin, is the literature of elegant escape. That's why I find it so attractive."

"Utter rubbish—that talk," rallied Chavasse almost savagely. "Why can't you be content with Shaw and Gilbert Chesterton. The former especially. He never bores you."

"How do you know?" asked Pegram quietly.

"Well—he never bores me."

"Different matter entirely," replied Pegram. "*De gustibus* and all that."

Chavasse emptied his glass and grinned cordially. His mood had changed. "All right. Game, set, match, I'll take it."

"And now you have done with all that, Martin, what was it you've come to see me about?" His eyes twinkled as he answered.

"'The Hot Cinders Murder,' as the Press call it."

Pegan smiled grimly at the description. "I thought as much. Well—what about the H.C.M. Let me put the boot on the other foot. What information have you brought me?"

Chavasse threw back his head and laughed. "That's a good one, I must say. The boot's on the proper foot if you ask me. Where I put it." He eyed Pegram shrewdly as he made the thrust, and then continued. "And, if you ask me again, it pinches somewhat. Come now—open confession's good for the soul."

Pegram shrugged his shoulders. "If you mean that Venables has made no progress, I'm afraid that I can't contradict you. I was speaking to him about it only yesterday afternoon. Also, the Chief Constable, old Stuart, is on his tail with regard to it. He's a fussy old cove. He's always advertised himself, rather, during a long period of inactivity and now that a real case has come his way, all he can show are completely negative results. Which don't please him and make him fuss about appallingly."

Chavasse laughed. The imps of mischief danced in his eyes. "Why doesn't he pocket his pride and call in the 'Yard'?"

"All," returned Pegram, knocking out his pipe. "As you say—why doesn't he? I expect that's what it will come to before we're finished."

"So you can tell me nothing?" remarked Chavasse. "You have evolved no theories whatever about the crime?"

"Frankly, Martin, I haven't. I don't know that I've worried much about it. I've been infernally busy, and I suppose that must be the excuse. Theories are hardly my pigeon—you know. What are your theories? I'd be interested to hear them."

Chavasse grinned. "You old devil! So you'll make *me* talk, will you, whether I like it or not?"

"That's the idea."

"Well, you're right. I have a theory about the case. And it intrigued me so much that I couldn't rest awhile and went down and had a look at the scene of the crime. There's little doubt, I suppose, in your mind, that the person who murdered Norman was a passenger with him in the car. Agreed?"

"Yes—most certainly. I've never considered any other possibility."

"Well then, it looks to me as though he must have been either a friend or an acquaintance. Do you go that far with me?"

"Yes. All the way."

"Well then, it's passing strange to me that Venables hasn't been able to put his hand on the man or woman who travelled with Norman that night. Had Norman such a tremendous circle of acquaintances?"

Pegram shook his head. "Couldn't say. I should most strongly doubt it. A farmer living as he did and where he did." Pegram nodded. "I should say you were right."

"Look at it for yourself, Pegram. What were his habits? Cut-and-dried routine and entirely stereotyped. According to what Venables tells me, the man made two visits to Mallett a week. Every week. On market-days. The rest of his time he spent on the farm doing his work and minding his own business. Venables says he wrung the wife, the son and the daughter pretty dry with regard to their husband's and father's movements generally, but he didn't extract much that was of value from any one of them. Damn it all, Pegram, where's the motive for anyone to kill a man like this fellow Norman?"

Pegram replied quietly. "Revenge for some grievance, real or imaginary. That's the shot I'd make at the target."

Chavasse darted a quick look at him. "You mean something with its roots and genesis way back in years gone by?"

"Something like that, perhaps. I merely projected it as a possible theory. I have no great faith in it."

"Well then, again taking your theory as a practical proposition, Venables should be able to strike those roots provided he digs deep enough."

"I agree. So that we come, more or less, to a matter of time."

Chavasse nodded. "Murder is nearly always motivated by revenge, greed or convenience. One of three things. Using slightly different words, vindictiveness, avarice or fear. Inasmuch, then, as Norman lost nothing and that nobody could reasonably have been afraid of him, we are left with revenge as the one sane and sound motive for getting rid of him."

"It would seem so," agreed Pegram.

Chavasse rose from his chair, walked across the hearthrug and stood over him. "And yet," he said, "despite all the force and all the logic of that argument, there is one other possibility that we can't ignore. *And* it's one that appeals to me strongly. Have you considered it?"

Pegram began to fill his pipe again. As he worked the tobacco into the bowl with his fingers, he nodded and spoke with slow but deliberate emphasis.

"Yes. I know what you mean. If one thinks, one can't escape it. That we may be dealing with a lunatic."

"Right. A maniac! A homicidal maniac! And *that*, my dear Pegram, if you ask me, is our true solution."

Pegram thought for some seconds. He held a lighted match in his hands. "If you're right, Martin, you know what it means, don't you? And it's a pretty grim business."

Chavasse stood erect and jingled the coins in his pocket. "I do. None better. It means that before long we shall be brought face to face with another murder. A murderer of that type never stops at one. He gets the blood-lust and it grows on him."

"Or murders," corrected Dr. Pegram.

Chavasse sat down again. "Or murders. Yes—I'll accept that. Now it comes to this. If you and I are right in our conjecture, we must see Venables, and Venables, in turn, must see Sir Charles Stuart."

"Unless—" commenced Pegram.

"Unless what?"

"Unless the murderer is not a local person and simply, as it were, happened to take in Mallett on his way and in his stride. In that case there will be no more murders here or hereabouts that will cause us anxiety. When they do occur, they will occur elsewhere and we can thank Providence that the murderer has passed from our midst." Pegram puffed at his pipe.

Chavasse leant forward and looked into the red heart of the fire. "You may be right, Pegram, but somehow I don't think so. Something tells me in my bones that murder will come to Mallett again. And what's more, before many weeks are past."

"Martin," returned Pegram, "you're nearly morbid—pour me out another peg of 'Scotch' and then take another for your own benefit and comfort. Let us *not* talk of graves and worms and epitaphs."

CHAPTER III

I

THE vatication of Martin Chavasse, made to Dr. Pegram round the latter's own fireside, proved to be regrettably accurate. The prophecy was fulfilled in a most remarkable manner. And so worried and anxious did Inspector Venables and the Chief Constable of the county, Sir Charles Stuart, become, that in less than twenty-four hours after the discovery of the second body, an urgent appeal was sent through to the 'Yard' for their immediate assistance. Sir Austin Kemble, the Commissioner of Police, to whom, of course, the application was eventually submitted, turned the matter over to Chief-Inspector Andrew MacMorran, who, in his turn, immediately made contact with Anthony Lotherington Bathurst.

The result was that MacMorran and Anthony Bathurst, accompanied by the Commissioner himself, travelled down to Mallett from Paddington by the first available train. When they arrived, Sir Charles Stuart and Venables met them at Mallett station. Stuart, naturally, attached himself to Sir Austin Kemble. A big noise always held an attractive sound to his ears and afforded him grateful coolness in any heat. Anthony, semi-humorously, replied to the many statements proffered in an excess of spontaneity by Venables. MacMorran was content to assume the role of patient listener.

Venables, at first encounter, described the preliminaries of the second Mallett murder. The body of Henry King had been found at a dining-table in the saloon of the 'White Lion' at Mallett at about half-past two in the afternoon of the previous day. On this occasion, a Friday, King had dropped in for midday lunch, as he did on fugitive occasions when his wife went out for the day.

"The 'White Lion' again," murmured Mr. Bathurst when the name of the establishment was first mentioned. "Most interesting. If it's a coincidence, it's an extraordinary one."

MacMorran nodded his confirmation of the remark.

"But please proceed, Inspector Venables," said Anthony. "I am even more interested now than I was before."

Venables promptly acted upon the instruction. King, according to the Inspector's story, had arrived for lunch unusually late from the point of view of the time for service on that particular day of the week. So late, indeed, that his was the last lunch served in the dining-room that afternoon and that ultimately he was left there alone. He occupied one of the corner tables and the waitress who had been serving in the saloon was surprised to see him still there at half-past two. She then remembered that he had not settled his bill, so she approached him to that end. His order had been pea soup, boiled turbot with sauce, and raspberry flan. . . . As the sweet was a cold one, she had served him with it a few minutes after she had taken him the main dish, in order to save time. When she reached his side, she was both amazed and horrified to find that King, to all appearances, was dead. Her first reaction to the tragedy, so Venables said, was that her customer had had either a fit of some kind or a heart attack. Mr. Denton, whom she informed, immediately 'phoned for the police and a doctor, and he, Venables, had gone along to the 'White Lion' in the company of Dr. Pegram. The latter, after but the shortest of examinations, announced that the girl's opinion was a true one, and that death was due to prussic acid poisoning.

"Who was left in the dining-saloon at this time besides the dead man?" asked Anthony.

"Diners, do you mean?"

"Yes—if you like."

"Nobody at all," replied Venables decisively. "According to the girl, the last one had left the tables a good quarter of an hour before."

"What was King actually eating when he died?"

"The turbot. He had eaten about half of it. Half of the portion he had been served with. But I was coming to that. Dr. Pegram analysed the food on the man's plate and found traces of the poison in the portion of the turbot which was left on King's plate. But inasmuch as at least a dozen people had partaken of the turbot during the previous hour or so, there isn't a shadow of a doubt, as far as I can see, that King's meal had been interfered with by somebody."

"By some person or persons unknown," interjected Mr. Bathurst.

"As you say," agreed Venables with a satisfied sort of nod.

"What was this man King?" demanded Anthony.

"Baker. The biggest baker here in the district. By the term 'biggest' I mean the one with the most money and the largest trade."

Anthony smiled at the amplification. Venables went on quickly with his story.

"The whole thing is most puzzling to me. One man leaves the 'White Lion' in order to go home and is murdered on the way. A second man leaves his house to come to the 'White Lion' for a meal and is poisoned over his lunch. There doesn't seem any rhyme or reason in it to my way of thinking."

"Were these two murdered men, Norman and King, acquainted, can you tell me?" asked Anthony.

"They may have been just acquaintances," returned the local Inspector, "but as far as I know, they weren't any more than that. Norman, as you've probably heard by now, was a farmer out at a place called Forge, a few miles from here, and King, as I've just informed you, was a baker in Mallett itself. But we shall be at the 'White Lion' in a few minutes from now so that you'll be able to get a clearer idea of the place where this second murder took place than I can give you by mere description."

Within a few moments, the five men were standing in the luncheon-saloon of the 'White Lion' in the presence of Denton, the landlord. Sir Charles Stuart conducted the Commissioner of Police to the corner table where King had sat and died. Anthony, with the two professionals, attached himself to the party. The Chief Constable took it upon himself to give a somewhat lengthy explanation of the incidents that had attended King's last meal. Denton listened to the various details as the Chief Constable presented them and approved them. Anthony looked inquiringly at the Commissioner of Police.

"Go ahead, Bathurst," said Sir Austin. "Ask anything you want to ask."

Anthony at once addressed himself to Sir Charles Stuart. "According to your doctor's autopsy, Sir Charles, was King killed by a comparatively large dose of hydrocyanic acid?"

"Yes . . . yes. I understand that Pegram gave it as his opinion that a fairly large dose had been given."

Anthony nodded. "That fact should be of material assistance to us. Because this particular poison is very rapidly diffused through the body. Only a few minutes . . . or even in some cases . . . a few seconds elapse before the preliminary symptoms appear."

"What are they?" asked Inspector MacMorran.

Anthony answered. "Slowness of breathing. Slowness and irregularity of the heart's action. And then blueness of the lips and face."

"How long would it be before the man died?" inquired Venables.

"In ordinary cases," replied Anthony, "a few minutes only. A condition of insensibility sets in. Then there comes a gradual stoppage of breathing and of the heart's action. In some cases, I believe, the end is preceded by a number of convulsions."

Sir Charles Stuart nodded. "That . . . er . . . is more or less what I understood Dr. Pegram to say."

"You see where this brings us to," remarked Anthony significantly. Venables was about to speak, but before he found words, Mr. Bathurst had continued: "If all the diners had left the room an appreciable time before King died, it narrows down the issue considerably."

Stuart glanced at him sharply. "I don't altogether agree with you, Mr. Bathurst."

"Why is that?"

"For the simple reason, as it appears to me, that you don't know the exact time when King died. You are merely surmising."

"I admit that, Sir Charles. We don't know the exact moment of the death. But I consider that we may reasonably regard ourselves as near enough to knowing it."

The Chief Constable made no reply. Anthony turned and spoke to Denton. "I think it would be as well if we had a word with your waitress, Mr. Denton. What do you say, Inspector MacMorran?"

MacMorran nodded. "Ask her, will you, Mr. Denton?"

The girl came in. "You heard the conversation, Inspector," said Anthony, "between Sir Charles and me. See if you can elucidate the point for the Chief Constable, will you please?"

MacMorran advised the girl appropriately before questioning her. But when she was questioned her answers came readily and intelligently. She was certain that Mr. King was alive when Mr. Waghorn had gone out and that Mr. Waghorn was the last gentleman to leave the dining-hall. He left Mr. King dining alone. Anthony then came in with a further question.

"I understand from what Inspector Venables has told me, that you served Mr. King with his sweet course before he had finished his fish?"

"That is quite .true, sir. It was a cold sweet, so it didn't matter. I took it to him. I often do that when the sweet is a cold one and I'm busy. It saves me a journey, you see."

"And you are quite certain, I take it, that Mr. King was alive then? Be careful of your answer, because the point is tremendously important." The girl's answer came without the slightest hesitation. "I am absolutely positive of it, sir. As a matter of fact, when I took the raspberry flan to Mr. King's table and put it down by him, he smiled at me and said something. Under his breath as you might say. But I don't know what it was he did say. I didn't catch it properly. So it's no good my pretending that I did."

MacMorran made a careful note of the answer and Venables had listened attentively to the series of replies. Anthony spoke to Sir Charles Stuart.

"In view of what the waitress has just told us, Sir Charles, I still feel that we may regard the issue from the 'time' angle as 'narrowed down.' Don't you agree?"

"Perhaps," replied the Chief Constable stiffly.

"I shall feel more confident, I admit," continued Anthony, "when I've had a chat with Doctor Pegram." He gestured to the waitress. "Just a minute before you go."

The girl turned and came up to him. "How many pieces of turbot were there in the helping that was served to the dead man. Can you remember that?"

The girl looked surprised at the question. "Why, one, sir. Only one. We never serve more than one portion of fish. It was a piece of middle cut. A very nice piece it was too, sir. Fresh that morning."

"One portion only—eh?" Anthony pulled at his top lip. "In that case I shall certainly need the advice of Dr. Pegram. I wonder if—"

He paused. Venables took the point immediately. "Ill arrange that for you this afternoon, Mr. Bathurst, if that's what you're thinking. Six o'clock suit you?"

"Very well," replied Anthony. "I am indebted to you, Inspector Venables. And now I want a word with the Commissioner, if you'll excuse me."

He walked over and conferred for a moment or so with Sir Austin Kemble.

II

Sir Austin Kemble returned to Town in the late afternoon of the same day. Before he went, he arranged that Anthony and Inspector MacMorran should remain in Mallett for the next few days, at least. For one thing, Anthony wanted to interview Dr. Pegram and for another, he and MacMorran were desirous of examining closely the place where Norman's car had been found by the roadside and seeing also the burnt pellets that had been found inside the dead man's vest. The story of the death of William Norman intrigued Anthony intensely and he was not content until he had obtained from Venables a complete account of the case and all its attendant details. It still wanted a few minutes to six o'clock when Venables brought Anthony and MacMorran back to the Police-station at Mallett.

Dr. Pegram was punctual and was already there waiting for them. Venables made the two men known to the Divisional Surgeon. Anthony formed the opinion at once that Pegram seemed pleased to talk about the case. He saw that the doctor was of the type which always welcomes open discussion. He answered Anthony's questions with regard to the turbot clearly and positively.

"The turbot itself was affected, Mr. Bathurst. Definitely not the sauce. I analysed the latter with particular care. It was entirely free from poisonous matter."

Anthony nodded his approval. "Good. That statement is also going to be a great help to me. I suppose the fish portion served to the dead man was of fair size—eh?"

"Oh—yes." The doctor indicated a measurement with the fingers of two hands. "About that I should say. The dead man had naturally eaten a considerable portion of turbot before the plate came to me—but that assessment I've just given to you wouldn't be far out."

Again Anthony nodded approval. "Now tell me this, Dr. Pegram. Would it have been possible for King to have eaten *some* of the turbot without coming into contact with the poison? In other words, part of the fish may reasonably have been quite sound and good and untouched by the poison? Yes, Dr. Pegram?"

Anthony waited eagerly for the doctor's reply. "I should say so—undoubtedly. In my opinion, that's exactly what did happen." Pegram smiled as he made the statement. Then he leaned over towards Anthony Bathurst. "Now I can tell you something else, Mr. Bathurst. Something you don't know and can't, on your own, find out. The murderer wasted his time." Pegram paused.

Anthony furrowed his brow. "Wasted his time? How do you mean, Doctor, exactly? I don't know that I—"

Pegram leaned forward again. "I mean just this. If he'd held his hand and waited a little while, his design would have been achieved just the same. Without any effort from him. For the reason that King would have been dead in a few months. I found that fact out when I did the P.M. He had a malignant growth near the pylorus. Hadn't a dog's chance. Too far gone to operate."

Anthony argued. "But the murderer wasn't to know that. How could he? So I'm afraid the argument gets us nowhere."

"Very likely—but it struck me as an interesting point altogether. As a matter, of fact, I had a word with his own doctor on the matter. This afternoon. I gave him a tinkle on the 'phone."

"Local man, I suppose?" The question came from MacMorran.

"Oh—yes. Dr. Cuthbertson. Quite a character in his way. Been in practice in the district here for years."

"Was *he* aware of King's condition?"

Pegram smiled at Anthony. "I don't know quite whether I should answer that, Mr. Bathurst. Medical etiquette, you know. But I'll say this. He suspected that something of the kind was troubling King. King's symptoms were beginning to manifest themselves. There was unusual dyspeptic disturbance and derangement, and Cuthbertson had begun to think that the cause of the trouble was deep-seated and he was beginning to fear the presence of a malignant growth."

Anthony rubbed the ridge of his jaw with his fingers. "Rather extra-ordinary, I think, don't you, Dr. Pegram? I looked into the details of the other Mallett case on my journey down here and my memory tells me that Norman, the farmer at Forge, was also a man whose days were more or less numbered when he was murdered! Suggests all sorts of interesting possibilities, doesn't it?"

Anthony continued to rub his jaw. Pegram nodded slowly as the idea Anthony had projected sank into his brain. When he spoke, the words came almost casually from him:

"Looks to me like a coincidence. They do occur, you know. Nothing more than that. When you come to think of it, there must be hundreds of people walking about, apparently in sound health, but all the time they're the unsuspecting victims of incipient disease." He shook his head. "Merely a coincidence, I'm afraid, Bathurst. I shouldn't build anything on it, if I were you. If the same person killed both Norman and King, he happened to hit on a couple of people of the kind I've just mentioned, by a sheer fluke."

MacMorran looked across at Anthony Bathurst. He was wondering how the latter would receive Pegram's last statement. For the moment, however, Anthony relinquished the point.

"You said, Doctor, 'If the same person killed both Norman and King.' Am I to understand that you are not convinced of the truth that we are facing only one murderer."

There was a period of a few minutes silence before Pegram replied. "Perhaps not altogether," he said quietly. "Although a colleague of mine warned me against the probability of a second crime only about a week ago."

Anthony looked interested. "Really. And who was that?"

With a deliberate choosing of words, Pegram' told Anthony of Chavasse's effort of vaticination.

"What were his reasons for advancing this idea, may I ask?"

Again Pegram appeared to hesitate before he replied. "He is of the opinion," he said at length, "that we are called upon to deal with a homicidal maniac. In other words, that a killer of unsound mind is at large either in the district itself or in the vicinity. Though what actual grounds Chavasse has for thinking so—"

Anthony interrupted him. "That's strange. Do you know, Dr. Pegram, I was thinking much on the same lines myself. Of all the murders that I have ever been called upon to solve, these seem, on the surface, to be easily the most motiveless. That's why I find myself thinking with your friend Chavasse. Or at any rate, on his lines."

Venables was eager to contribute more support for the theory. "I know more about these two murders than anybody here."

MacMorran was unable to restrain a smile at this pompous statement. He was sitting on the blind side of the local Inspector. Venables, oblivious therefore, of the 'Yard' Inspector's smile, proceeded to make his point.

"And I'm going to say here and now, that my personal views are like-wise. The same as Dr. Chavasse's and this gentleman here. I'm glad to find myself in such good company." Venables gestured towards Anthony Bathurst. Venables continued again. "We're up against a lunatic. I feel certain of it, and if I'm any judge he's only 'batty' on occasions. What I mean is that at most ordinary times the bloke's walking about normal just the same as we are. And that's going to be our principal difficulty. To catch him and recognise him when he's got one of his mad fits on. Because at all other times he just won't *be* recognisable." Venables paused and then subsided completely.

"I'll tell you what I should like you to do for me," said Anthony quietly.

"What's that?" demanded Venables.

"I'd like a full personal history of both Norman and King, the two dead men. Don't leave anything out. Put everything in that you can think of. No matter how unimportant or irrelevant you may consider it to be. Without that detailed knowledge I'm asking you to give me, I feel handicapped. Is that all right with you, Inspector?"

Venables made a note of Anthony's requirements. "That'll be all right, Mr. Bathurst. You shall have what you want just as soon as ever I can get it worked out for you."

"Thank you, Inspector. I'm much obliged, I'm sure."

Anthony handed round his cigarette case. Dr. Pegram and the others helped themselves to cigarettes. As Anthony was replacing his case in his pocket, there came a tap on the door. Venables looked at Dr. Pegram and the latter nodded for the Inspector to answer it. To everybody's surprise, the man at the door was Denton, the proprietor of the 'White Lion.'

"Can I come in, Inspector? I've come round now purposely, because I rather fancy I've important news for you."

"Certainly," responded Venables. "You couldn't have brought your news to a better market. Most of us engaged on the case are in here now. It's a full house. Come in, Mr. Denton, and let's hear what you have to tell us."

Denton followed the local inspector into Dr. Pegram's room. Pegram offered him a chair which he seemed pleased to take. Venables then motioned to him to tell his story. Denton appeared to be somewhat perturbed.

"Well, as a matter of fact, gentlemen, I've come to correct a certain impression which I fear I was responsible for you bringing away from my place with regard to the murder of poor old King. Something which arose out of our first discussion. Much to my surprise, I now hear that there was another person in the dining-saloon with King and the waitress, after all the other diners had cleared out."

"Who was that?" inquired Inspector Venables eagerly.

"A man who claimed to come from the Mallett Electricity Supply Company to read the meters. I am informed now that he passed through the dining-saloon on his way. As this job's done by the Company every three months and at no other time he was accepted for what he claimed to be without any questions being asked. But I have since satisfied myself, gentlemen, that this man was *not* a servant of the Electricity Company. In other words, he was nothing more or less than an impostor." MacMorran cut in sharply. "What made you suddenly suspect him?"

"I didn't." Denton looked surprised as he answered.

"If you didn't suspect him—what made you inquire about him?" Anthony thought that Denton seemed a trifle shaken by MacMorran's double query. But if he had been, he quickly recovered his equanimity.

"Oh—I get what you mean. That's very easily explained, Inspector. You startled me for the minute. I didn't quite understand what you were driving at. I rang up the Company because I had a complaint to make. Not because I was suspicious of the man's *bona fides*."

Denton paused. But MacMorran was determined to concede him no breathing space. "What was the nature of this complaint?"

"Why—when I heard he'd been along—and the girl had omitted to tell me because she'd forgotten all about the incident—I protested against the job being done during the luncheon period. I think that the protest was reasonable and that I was entirely justified in making it. I told the Company that they had all day long to do the job in and that they needn't pick on that particular time of the day for it, because it was damned inconvenient." He carried the war into MacMorran's camp. "Don't you agree with me?"

The Inspector from Scotland Yard evaded the question. "I asked you what I did because of the words you yourself used. If my memory serves me correctly, you said that 'you *satisfied* yourself that the man who came into your saloon was not the man he represented himself to be.'"

MacMorran emphasised the first verb. He turned towards Anthony Bathurst for silent corroboration. Anthony nodded the confirmation. Denton appeared to think over the matter.

"Yes, I believe, on reflection, that I did say that. I see your point. But I hope that my subsequent explanation has cleared the air for you."

"Just a minute," intervened Anthony. "I don't think that you've quite finished your story, have you, Mr. Denton? You haven't told us yet, you know, what the Company's response was to your objection." Denton flushed with annoyance. "I suppose I must have been interrupted. I'm sorry. Well—I was completely flabbergasted for the Company informed me flatly that nobody had been sent to my place at all. In other words, that the man was, as I said before, an impostor. When I heard that piece of news I decided that it was my imperative duty to put you in possession of the full facts at once. So I came straight down to you."

MacMorran nodded grimly. "I've no complaints on that score. You've done the right thing."

"This," said Anthony, "looks to me like the real thing as well as the right thing. Do I understand now that your waitress saw this man, Mr. Denton?"

"Oh, yes."

"To notice particularly?"

Denton hesitated again. Anthony thrust hard. "You've already asked her with regard to this point?"

"Yes. I trust I did nothing wrong in asking her?"

"What was her reply to you?"

"That she saw the man pass through, noticed his uniform and took no more notice of him than that. Exactly as her first announcement to me had been."

"Can she describe him?"

"As to that," replied Denton with shrugged shoulders, "I'd much rather that you asked her yourself. I think it would be much more satisfactory from all points of view."

MacMorran and the local Inspector both agreed with Denton's suggestion. In response to a request from Inspector Venables, Denton promised to arrange for the further interview.

"This shouldn't be allowed to rest. Suppose you bring her along now?" queried MacMorran. "How long would it take you?"

Denton grimaced. "Well—it would be a little awkward from the point of view of my business," he said eventually. "It's getting on for our busy time now." He looked at his watch. "Right on from now to closing time. Still—if you must—"

He paused abruptly. Anthony nodded in understanding. "Yes. There is that about it. I can see your point. How would it do if we blew along after ten o'clock? Would that be too inconvenient for you? We shouldn't take too long over our business."

MacMorran and Venables waited for Denton to answer. "All right," he conceded. "That arrangement'll suit me. You come down to the 'Lion' just after ten o'clock and I'll have the girl ready for you."

Dr. Pegram smiled. "That's an invitation that has its points, I must say. How about including me in it?"

Denton looked as though the reply to that should come not from him, but from either MacMorran or Venables. The former noticed the meaning of Denton's glance.

"Why not, Dr. Pegram?" he remarked jovially. "If two heads are proverbially better than one, why shouldn't four be better than three?"

"Andrew," said Anthony Bathurst, "you're a mathematical genius. We'll all go to the 'White Lion' together, at the appointed hour."

Denton rose to go. "In that case, gentlemen, I'll expect you soon after ten o'clock."

III

Flora Douglas came in to them rather nervously. Her hands were unsteady and, generally speaking, she seemed far from confident and by no means sure of herself. Denton told her in a few short and sharp sentences why she had been requested to attend the interview.

"Now answer any questions these gentlemen ask you, Flora, just as you would if I were asking them."

"Yes, Mr. Denton," came the girl's answer.

MacMorran referred to the incident of the pseudo-meter reader. "Did this man speak to you?"

"Yes, sir."

"When?"

"When he passed by me, along the dining-saloon." The girl nodded. "What did he say to you?"

The girl hesitated.

"If you can remember them, try to give me his exact words."

"Well"—she twisted her fingers round the corners of her apron—"he just said something about having come to read the electric-light meter."

"Why? Had you inquired of him what his business was?"

"No. I—er sort of accepted him. You know. Took him for granted."

"Why? What made you do that?"

"Well—I suppose it was through seeing him in his uniform. The coats these men wear are dark blue with a sort of red braid round the collar. When he said who he was, I never thought of questioning him. That's why I forgot all about it in the first place. I do hope I've done nothing wrong."

"Don't start worrying about that. We're not blaming you for anything that's happened. What sort of voice did this man have?"

She shook her head. "He just mumbled the words at me. I couldn't tell you anything really about his voice." More finger-twisting of apron.

"And then, I suppose, he walked past you down the room and along past the tables?"

"Yes, sir. That's exactly what he did do."

"Let me ask a question, Inspector, if you don't mind," intervened Anthony.

"Certainly, Mr. Bathurst. Go right ahead."

Anthony turned to the girl. "Did you see this man again? Did he return, for instance, by the way that he came?"

The girl thought for a moment. "Yes, sir. I saw him go through the room again. On his way out, as I supposed at the time."

"Now take your time about answering this next question of mine. Was Mr. King, the dead man, eating at his table on each of the occasions that this man passed through?"

Flora Douglas shook her head again. "No, sir. The first time he went through, the saloon was empty."

"Sure of that?"

"Ye-es." The girl spoke slowly, but brisked up immediately afterwards. "Yes. I'm certain of that now I come to think of it more carefully."

"Good. Now what about the second time this man went through?" Flora Douglas knitted her brows. After some intensive thought, she produced what Anthony considered to be a most illuminating answer.

"The second time, sir, was when Mr. King was sitting at the table, waiting for his lunch to be served up to him."

Anthony rubbed his hands. "Good again, Miss Douglas! You're doing well. Now answer this. While Mr. King was sitting there waiting as you've just described to us, where was his lunch?"

The girl looked surprised at Anthony's question. "Where? I don't know that I quite—"

"Well—was it still in the kitchen?"

"It would be served from the kitchen."

"You mean that the fish would be placed on the plate in the kitchen, don't you?"

"Yes, sir."

"Well then, what I mean is this. How does the lunch come to you? What happens to it in between?"

Flora Douglas's face cleared. "Oh—I see what you mean now, sir. It's put on a shelf . . . or ledge you might call it, through the serving-hatch and waits there for me to pick it up."

"I see. How long would it remain there before you came to handle it?"

"A few seconds only, sir. As a rule that is."

"You would pick it up, naturally, and carry it to the table."

"Of course, sir. Almost at once."

"Did you, in this particular instance, observe the man in uniform anywhere near the hatch at the time?"

"No, sir."

"At the same time, from what you have already told us, he couldn't have been far away, could he?"

The girl twisted her apron again. "No, sir. You've made me realise that he couldn't have been. The way you've put it."

"What was this self-appointed electrician like?"

"Just ordinary, sir. On the tall side. Glasses and a moustache." Flora Douglas paused in her effort at description.

"No more than that?" asked Anthony.

"I don't know, sir," she replied uncertainly. "It's very difficult to say."

"I'll try to help you then. Young or old?"

"Oldish, sir. All old and wrinkled round the mouth and chin. Not a young man by any means."

"What colour was the man's hair? Did you notice that?"

She shook her head rather helplessly. At length she found the answer: "Brown. I couldn't rightly say any more than that, sir."

"The uniform that this man wore might provide us with a clue," suggested Venables, almost as though he were thinking aloud. "He must have obtained it from somewhere. I'll have inquiries made as soon as I get back to headquarters."

Anthony shook his head somewhat pessimistically. "I'm afraid you won't get much help from that direction, Inspector. Uniforms of various shades of dark blue are common enough all over the country and extremely easy to obtain. Anybody determined to get hold of one wouldn't, in my opinion, experience much difficulty."

"I agree with Mr. Bathurst with regard to that," supplemented Inspector MacMorran.

"Will you want Miss Douglas any more?" asked Denton.

MacMorran made a silent interrogation of Anthony Bathurst. The latter shook his head. MacMorran conveyed the negative to Denton in a like manner.

"I don't think so, Mr. Denton," he added. "I think that's all we shall require of Miss Douglas for the time being, at any rate." He turned to the girl. "Thank you, Miss Douglas. You can get back now. I expect there's plenty for you to do. Even after hours. If we should need you again for anything, we'll let you know."

The girl thanked him and withdrew. Denton followed her within a few moments. Anthony waited until they were out of earshot. Then he ventured his opinion.

"As I see it, gentlemen, thanks to the information which Miss Douglas has just given us, this part-playing electrician had ample opportunity to poison King's dinner when it was on the plate and placed on the shelf of the serving-hatch for the girl to collect and carry to him. I take it that you both find yourselves in agreement with me?"

MacMorran and Venables assented, albeit the latter seemed a trifle hesitant about expressing his opinion. Anthony went on:

"There's another matter, however, which strikes me rather forcibly. Which is this! Was this 'phoney' meter-reader the same man as the one the barmaid saw talking in the bar to Norman on the evening he was murdered? You will remember that this incident occurred just before Norman left to go home."

"With regard to that point," contributed Venables, "we can check up on it. We can get this girl, Douglas, and the barmaid who served Norman on that evening to compare notes for us. That should settle the matter pretty conclusively."

"Exactly," said Anthony. "I was going to suggest that myself. And the sooner we do that the better."

Dr. Pegram rose from his chair and stretched himself. "Well," he remarked, "it's all been very interesting and I'm glad I decided to come along with you. But what disturbs me chiefly is this. We think we know how Norman was murdered and how King was murdered— but has any of us the slightest idea as to 'why'? And that 'why' goes for each case. The lunatic theory looms larger than ever." He patted his coat-pockets, feeling for his pipe.

"It's rather remarkable," said Anthony, almost as though he were thinking aloud. "I don't know whether any of you others has noticed it, but most of our cogent information comes from women. Mrs. Norman, the barmaid at the 'White Lion' and lastly from the girl, Flora Douglas."

"What's your point in that?" demanded Pegram. "Do you doubt the truth of any of their stories because of their sex?"

"I don't think the girl, Douglas, was lying," put in MacMorran. "Her story sounded pretty authentic to my ear."

Anthony smiled. "May I quote to you the words of the incomparable Hanaud: 'You may take this from me, my friend, all women who are great criminals are also very artful actresses. I never knew one who wasn't.'"

"Rather sweeping," remarked Pegram with a shrug of the shoulders. "I don't know that I would go all the way with that. After all, there's always the question of motive."

Anthony smiled. "Hanaud's good on motive, too. Hark to his words of profound wisdom with regard to that: 'Motives, no doubt, are signposts rather difficult to read and if one reads them amiss, they lead one very wide astray. But you must look for your signposts all the same and try to read them aright.'"

Pegram again shrugged his shoulders at Anthony's quotations. "That sentiment seems to me to be elementary," he said rather oracularly; "and, speaking as an amateur, just what I should have expected."

"Quite so," replied Anthony, "but all the same what I said remains true. About the three women, I mean."

"I suppose it does."

"The point I emphasised struck me as being remarkable. As I said a few moments ago. In all my experience of criminal investigation, covering several years now, I don't remember a case when I was forced to rely so much on the evidence of the weaker sex." Anthony half-smiled as he spoke.

"What do you think, then, with regard to the main features? As far, shall we say, as my own theory goes?"

"The theory held by you and Dr. Chavasse, do you mean?"

Pegram nodded an affirmation.

"That we have to look for a homicidal maniac?"

Pegram nodded again. Anthony took some time before he replied. "I don't know. I'm not altogether sure. Actually—it's too early for me yet to form a judgment. I haven't been on the case long enough to satisfy myself. I'd rather wait a while before I embark on a definite opinion. For instance, I know next to nothing yet concerning the various personalities round the affair. Get my meaning, Doctor?"

"Partly—perhaps. I don't altogether know whom you refer to exactly."

"Nobody in particular, Doctor. But, for an early example, take the various men whose habit it was to dine with Norman in the 'White Lion' on the evenings of market-days. King, himself—now as dead as Norman—Marnoch, Cox, Hardwick and Waghorn, the bank manager. All local personalities about whom I know only some things, but shall certainly hope to know more. Have I made my meaning more clear to you?"

"Oh—quite. When I spoke to you just now, I wasn't thinking in that direction. So you discard the homicidal maniac theory?"

"Not altogether, shall we say. Let me put it rather like this—I'm inclined to discard it at the moment. Later on, of course, it may be that I shall be forced to change my opinion."

Pegram smiled at him. "You're frank at any rate. Which is more than I can say of some of the people the Police have brought down in their time."

"And now you're being frank." Anthony returned the smile and turned to MacMorran. "I think, Inspector, if you'll agree with me, that we'll say good night to everybody and adjourn until to-morrow. What do you say?"

"I'm with you, Mr. Bathurst," replied the Inspector. "And many thanks to all for their attendance and information."

IV

Anthony and Inspector MacMorran had deliberately decided not to put up at the 'White Lion.' They had talked the matter over very carefully between them and had been forced to the conclusion that they would find the staff of that hostelry more communicative if they only appeared occasionally amongst them, as against the conditions of what might be termed a continuous performance. The result was that they had chosen for their household and headquarters an ancient inn on the other side of the High Street to the 'White Lion,' which showed the somewhat unusual sign of the 'Laughing Angel.' It claimed to date back to the time of Bolingbroke and was said to have fallen upon evil times when the railways came, but more lately had evidently taken unto itself a new lease of life.

Before he went to bed that night, Anthony stood at the door of the inn and looked towards the lancet windows of the Early English parish church which stood about equidistant from the 'White Lion' and the 'Laughing Angel.' It was difficult to associate the old world charm of the little market town with the two carefully calculated murders which had so recently taken place within it. But there it was, it was no use denying it, or shutting one's eyes to facts, these murders had taken place and once again, he and Andrew MacMorran had the task of running the criminal or criminals to earth. He had himself already resolved to interview at least two people, no matter what MacMorran might think about it. These two people were Dr. Chavasse, whose theory Pegram had put before him that very evening, and Waghorn, the bank manager.

Chavasse, to all accounts, seemed to be a man whose intelligence was above the average, and Waghorn was a man whom Anthony desired to interrogate on at least one point. Anthony Bathurst lit his pipe—his last before turning in. He had already formed a definite theory—which fact, strictly speaking, was unusual for him. Ordinarily, he scrupulously abstained from theorising in the early stages of a case. But on this particular occasion he had come to the conclusion that the various members of the Norman family, by reason of the death of King, might reasonably be excluded from the area of suspicion. Whereas anyone of them might have harboured a motive for killing Norman, Anthony couldn't see, at the moment at any rate, how or why that one could have had a motive to murder the baker, King.

Anthony smoked his pipe, turning many things over in his mind. When the tobacco was burnt through, he stooped down and knocked out the dottle on a wall of the 'Laughing Angel.' Then he re-entered the house and slowly made his way upstairs to bed.

V

He was lucky to find Chavasse in during the early part of the following morning. Martin Chavasse greeted him genially and at once invited him to sit down.

"As a matter of fact," said Chavasse, "Pegram 'phoned me first thing this morning and informed me that I might confidently expect a visit from you. So you find me, you see, more or less prepared. Now what is it exactly that you want me to do for you?"

"All I want of you at the moment," smiled Anthony, "is a chat. Pegram put one of your theories to me last night and, candidly, I found it more than ordinarily interesting. So I thought I'd like to discuss it with you, and may be you'd care to amplify it."

Chavasse flashed a quick glance in his direction. "Hold hard a minute! Let's see where we are! *One* of my theories?"

Anthony nodded. "A-ha."

"Why I asked you," went on Chavasse, "is because I wasn't aware myself that I had more than one."

Anthony smiled again. "Oh—I see. Well—*the* one then."

"Concerning the homicidal lunatic, do you mean?"

"That's the idea."

"Well," replied Chavasse—he spoke more slowly now—"as far as I can see, that's the only possible solution of the two Mallett murders."

There was a pause. The look on Chavasse's face seemed to indicate that he was surprised that Anthony had made no immediate answer. Chavasse, therefore, followed up.

"Don't you agree with me, Mr. Bathurst?"

This time Anthony had to reply. "Only partly."

"How do you mean—partly?" Chavasse's brow furrowed.

"Well—I find a certain difficulty, when I compare the circumstances of the two crimes."

"Explain—please." Chavasse was almost impatient in his demand.

Anthony smiled at him. He had met men of Chavasse's type before. Men of strong, dominant personalities who invariably went to the heart of things, with scant ceremony and by the shortest possible route. Anthony amplified his previous statement.

"I should agree with you, I think, Dr. Chavasse, if I had only the Norman murder to consider. But when I come to the poisoning of

King, I begin to run across the difficulties concerning which I spoke just now."

"Go on," said Chavasse urgently.

"Haven't I made myself clear? Well, then, in the Norman case, surely we find a streak of almost sadistic cruelty, but with the King affair, we are brought face to face with a singularly cold-blooded but nevertheless calculating crime. The technique of the killing, to my mind, varies considerably. Perhaps I'm wrong—but if they've been perpetrated by the same person—frankly, I'm puzzled." Anthony smiled at his companion.

Chavasse regarded him intently. "You've shown me something. Do you know, I never thought of the two murders in the way you have." He stopped, and before he went on he nodded his head, as though expressing his agreement with Anthony. "Yes, I can see now that I didn't particularise enough. I was inclined merely to general-ise. I considered two callous crimes, that as far as I can still see were entirely motiveless, and classed the murderer as a homicidal maniac. When Norman died, I told Pegram what I thought about things and I made a prediction. You say that he passed that prediction on to you. And I'm afraid that since the death of King I haven't really paused to consider how it was that he did die."

He half-smiled as he turned his head towards Anthony.

"The prediction, of course, being that there would be a second murder?"

"Exactly," returned Chavasse; "and, as events turned out, I was right."

"You were! Now tell me, Dr. Chavasse. I'm interested—now that you have heard these remarks of mine of a few moments ago, have you any more predictions to make? Do you forecast yet more murders?"

Chavasse raised a leg and clasped his knee-cap between his two hands. "Had you asked me that question an hour ago, or even less than that, I should have unhesitatingly answered 'Yes.' Now, after what you've just pointed out to me, I'm not so sure." Chavasse spoke the last few words very slowly and deliberately. He paused, to go on again almost immediately: "And yet—"

"And yet what?" inquired Anthony.

Chavasse smiled. The smile was of the fugitive kind and not devoid of charm. "And yet—after weighing all the pros and cons, I'm inclined to stick to my original opinion."

"How far does that opinion now go?"

"How far?"

"A-ha. Any more predictions?"

"Oh—I see what you mean. Well—yes. If I still say 'homicidal maniac,' as I do, and that the two murders are the work of one and the same person, if I'm logical, I must go even the step further and say 'another murder.' Perhaps even 'murders.'" He turned his head and regarded Anthony gravely. "Well—I've been frank, haven't I?"

"You certainly have. And I respect your opinion. Events will show which of us is the more correct. As a matter of fact, I'm feeling a little out of my depth. More than once during my career as an investigator I've had to face a complex problem. But I can't recall an instance when the second crime came so quickly on the heels of the first and presented such an entirely different pattern from its predecessor. I find myself groping, as it were, in so many different directions." Anthony rose to make his departure. "I must possess my soul in patience, I suppose, and wait for the break to come my way."

Chavasse shook him by the hand. "Let me know if I can help you in any way. If I can, I shall be delighted."

Anthony thanked him and withdrew.

VI

Anthony Bathurst stuck his hands into his pockets despondently and faced MacMorran again.

"Not only motiveless, Andrew, but very definitely clueless in addition. Hot cinders down a man's back in one instance and poison on his fish in another. Now sit down here with me and let's try to get down to something tangible. It's high time we started. Let's take the Norman case first."

MacMorran took a seat as he had been directed. Anthony did likewise and sat facing him. Anthony began at once to ask questions.

"How long does it take in a car such as Norman's was to get from the 'White Lion' to the place where the car was found stranded?"

The Inspector furrowed his brow and made calculations. "Not a lot more than ten minutes. That is, if you go straight, of course."

"Ten minutes, you say. We'll put it at a quarter of an hour at the outside. Well, I'm not disposed to argue with you about that. So that we come to this inevitable conclusion. That, during those vital ten minutes, Norman was hailed by and picked up his passenger-murderer. And that, mark you, without a soul seeing it happen. As far as *we* know."

"Think of the night," put in MacMorran warningly. "It wasn't a night fit for a dog to be out in. You mustn't forget that. There were few abroad that night in Mallett, so they tell me. And fewer on the road to Fell and Forge."

Anthony, grew glum again. Then he nodded his head. "Yes," he conceded eventually. "I suppose the weather must have made a difference." There came a silence. It was Anthony Bathurst who broke it. "Yes . . . and the state of the weather may well have accounted for something else. On a night like this was, Norman would have been more willing to take a chance passenger! Out of sheer goodness of heart. Whereas on an ordinary night, he might have thought twice about it. We know something else, though, Andrew. Something for certain!"

"What's that?"

"Why—that the murderer was on foot. It's ten to one that he didn't have a car with him and had to get away from the dead man after the murder on foot."

"Yes—unless he had a confederate waiting for him somewhere *with* a car. There's that possibility. I'm considering that possibility very carefully."

Anthony shook his head. "Don't think that's likely for a moment, Andrew. And all this leads me to something else, too!"

Inspector MacMorran raised his eyebrows inquiringly and waited. "Yes?"

"That the criminal we're looking for lives either in Mallett itself or in the near vicinity! That's my very definite opinion. After the committal of the murder, he *walked* away from the scene of his crime quietly and quickly to his or her own home. Which, seeing the foul quality of the night, wasn't, I'll be bound, too far away."

MacMorran drew contemplatively at his pipe. "Ay! On the whole, Mr. Bathurst, I'm inclined to think you're right." The Inspector began to fill the bowl of his pipe. He pressed down the tobacco carefully—almost affectionately.

"Tell me, Andrew," started Anthony again, "about the customs of the 'White Lion,' that interesting hotel licensed for strong drink and murder! I've been wondering. What time does the usual evening dinner start?"

MacMorran explained. "Dinner in the early evening is served on market-days only. Mallett has two market-days every week. Wednesday and Saturday. On all other week-days, the 'White Lion' offers customers the ordinary lunch at midday. From twelve o'clock noon till two o'clock."

Anthony nodded. "I see. I've been wondering, as I said, but I guessed it must be something of that kind that happened."

The Inspector puffed at his pipe. "Yes. I wondered about that point just as you did. When I first heard about it. I spoke to Venables about it. Soon after we came down here. He explained it and clarified the matter for me."

"Thanks, Andrew."

There came another period of silence. Again it was Anthony Bathurst who broke it. "I still stick most tenaciously, Andrew, at the motive question. Who profited by Norman's death? As far as we can see at the moment, not a soul."

"But we don't *know*," urged MacMorran.

Anthony waved off the opposition. "Let me continue, Andrew, before you begin your campaign of devastation. Who benefited by King's death? Again, as far as we can tell from the evidence in front of us, not a living soul."

"Well," countered the Inspector good-humouredly, "that brings us back to the undoubted fact that we're careering round in circles and must confine our search to looking for that previously-mentioned homicidal maniac."

Andrew MacMorran smoked on—fiercely and aggressively. Suddenly he looked up and caught the expression on Anthony Bathurst's face.

"Unless," said the latter, slowly and contemplatively, "we regard the murders, not individually or separately, but as definite pieces of a distinct pattern which in itself is replete with motive as a—" Anthony paused and MacMorran immediately picked him up.

"As a what, Mr. Bathurst? I'm curious to know."

He waited intently for Anthony Bathurst's answer. When it came, its exact terms were a matter for surprise as far as the questioner was concerned.

"As a means to an end, Andrew. That's what I was going to say."

"As a means to an end?" repeated MacMorran with bewilderment sounding in his voice. Then he shook his head as an expression of failure to understand. "Surely the end has been reached—when we come to consider both Norman and King, the two dead men?"

Anthony nodded—a smile playing round the corners of his mouth. "Yes, Andrew, I'll concede you that point. I must. I can't possibly evade it. But I wasn't speaking from that particular point of view."

"No?" queried MacMorran. "Whose point of view were you taking, then?"

"The murderer's," replied Anthony Bathurst; "the murderer's, and the murderer's only."

The Inspector opened his eyes wide and stared at Anthony. From old he knew now that Anthony's fingers were round the first thread, brought to him by the science of deduction. "If I'm any judge—" he commenced, when a tap on the door closured the sentence.

"Come in," called Anthony.

The porter entered with an envelope in his hand.

"For Mr. Bathurst," he announced. "No answer."

Anthony slit the envelope and took out the enclosure. It was a note addressed to him by the Chief Constable.

"I'm to dine with Sir Charles Stuart to-morrow evening, Andrew. And his manners are such that you appear to be omitted from the invitation."

"Then I've an anthem for his bad manners, Mr. Bathurst, and for the blessed relief they've given me, much thankfulness."

MacMorran mopped his forehead with his handkerchief.

VII

Sir Charles Stuart's butler received Mr. Bathurst exactly as the latter knew he would be received. Every action, every gesture and every intonation were flawlessly impeccable. Anthony waited for the space of a few seconds in the lounge-hall. Somewhere, and not too distant at that, he could hear the sound of a woman's voice. Although she was talking to somebody, Anthony couldn't hear any voice in the exercise of reply. Suddenly he decided that the voice he was hearing was engaged in a conversation on the telephone. Naturally, he was paying no attention to the effort beyond the registering of the elementary fact, when his interest was abruptly aroused and enlisted almost unconsciously and entirely against his wish and will. For a stray sentence had been perfectly audible to him. He heard the feminine voice say: "Well . . . I may be able to find out something this evening. I shall employ all my well-known powers of attraction, so that if I fail, it will be entirely my fault."

Anthony was still considering the special significance of these remarks when he heard a low, musical laugh and the words, "till next time." After that came the unmistakable sound of the telephone receiver being replaced. Anthony instinctively turned himself away from the sound's direction and braced himself for the approaching encounter. He was not destined to wait very long. When Elinor Stuart came in to him with hand outstretched, he realised at once that he was in the presence of an unusually beautiful woman.

"Mr. Bathurst," she said almost impetuously, "I really had no idea you had arrived. You must forgive me. Curtis should have told me before."

Anthony murmured conventional words of under-statement. Lady Stuart patted an invisible tendril of hair.

"My husband will be joining us in a few moments. He asked me to explain. I should tell you that Charles finds it utterly impossible to be in time for anything. You may find it difficult to believe, but he was actually late for our wedding! It's perfectly true, I assure you."

Anthony smiled at her. "I am sure, Lady Stuart, that his forgetfulness on that occasion must have been engendered by a condition of feverish haste. Any other explanation would be incredible."

Lady Stuart's eyes danced at him responsively. "Now, that's very charming of you. It's ages since anybody took the trouble to pay me so nice a compliment. But tell me, Mr. Bathurst, what will you drink? A sherry or a cocktail?"

"A cocktail, if you please, Lady Stuart."

"Any particular variety? I have only to be instructed." She touched the bell. The immaculate Curtis put in an appearance almost automatically. Elinor Stuart regarded Anthony interrogatively.

"If I may—I'll have a 'Clover Club,'" said Mr. Bathurst.

"You may—and you shall," replied his hostess. She smiled brightly at him and nodded to Curtis. "Two 'Clover Clubs' and a brown sherry. Certain animal noises that I have just heard incline me to the idea that Charles is on his way," She added: "It's all a question of the trained and sensitive ear."

The noises to which she had alluded became more distinct. The lady lifted the parts of her face where the eyebrows by rights belonged.

"I was right, you see."

Anthony didn't see at the moment, but the omission was speedily rectified. The Chief Constable entered puffing and on the verge of blowing. He advanced and shook hands with Anthony.

"Ah, Bathurst—so we meet again. Pleased to see you, man." He turned to Elinor Stuart with a frown. "My dear, my dear, what on earth are we thinking about? Bathurst has nothing to drink. Good God—the situation's both appalling and humiliating."

The lady grew even colder. "Patience was never your strong suit, was it?"

He gaped at her. "D'ye mean you've ordered?"

"I most certainly have."

"Then why the devil didn't you say so! Then I wouldn't have put my foot into it."

"I think that you probably would have. If I know you! Your feet are nothing if not impetuous. Also, my dear Charles, nobody would ever mistake you for an angel."

At that precise moment, Curtis brought the drinks. Anthony, to his own curiosity, felt a strong sense of personal relief.

"Your sherry, Charles," said Elinor Stuart.

The Chief Constable took the glass of wine into his capacious hands and watched Anthony carefully. "'Clover Club'—eh? Like my wife. Not for me, thank you. Cissy drink! No offence, of course, Bathurst." He grinned and showed his large teeth before heaving himself into a seat. "How long dinner, my dear? As a matter of fact, I'm damned peckish this evening. Had a rotten day. Forgot to tell you. That woman from the fried-fish shop in Mallett High Street stopped me again with her pet grievance. You know, Elinor, that woman with the big fat red face."

"Only too well," returned his wife frigidly; "the face that launched a thousand chips. What was it this time? The same old trouble?"

"It was! No difference with the years." Sir Charles turned to address Anthony. "Woman named Clarence," he growled. "Husband's a ne'er-do-well. Always after me to give him a job somewhere. God knows where, though! Have a job to give him a job. By Jove—that's not too bad. Where he'd fit in, I mean. Mrs. Clarence has got some wretched bee in her bonnet that there's a dead set in the district against employing the man at all. That's pure poppycock! Stuff and nonsense! As I've told her on every occasion she's waylaid me."

Sir Charles Stuart disposed of his remaining sherry and looked at his watch. "Time dinner was ready. Mustn't keep Bathurst waiting, you know. Busy man! So are we all—all busy men these days. Ah—that's the stuff to give the troops."

The Chief Constable's last words were in recognition of the dinner-gong. He rose and made a sign to Anthony. "Only the three of us, Bathurst. No more. Just you and I and Lady Stuart. Can't have outsiders to hear what we shall be talking about. Wouldn't do, would it, my boy?"

Anthony murmured a polite agreement with the Chief Constable's expressed opinion. They went into the dining-room. Curtis reappeared. Anthony found him extremely interesting. Curtis's service from A to Z was smooth, effortless, and entirely efficient. The touch of the professional was obvious in everything he did, in every action performed.

The dinner itself, Anthony judged, was excellent. Smoked salmon, a perfect white soup, sole, lamb, chicken and a *soufflé*. The sherry and the claret were of indisputable merit. At the same time, there were periods of time when Anthony felt definitely uncomfortable. Sir

Charles kept up his end with a moderately easy flow of conversation, towards which Anthony assisted gallantly, but the lady, Anthony felt positive, was feeling her way with the utmost care. He thought of the telephone conversation which he felt certain he had heard while he had waited for his hostess to come to him. Elinor Stuart, indeed, was often strangely silent and surveyed plate after plate that was brought to her with an impassivity of feature which Anthony found somewhat disconcerting. The result was that Anthony fell a victim to two habits. He wondered at Lady Stuart's aloofness and admired the slick performance of the most redoubtable Curtis. The latter's adroitness and aplomb had to be seen in order to be properly understood.

Sir Charles Stuart noticed that Anthony's eyes were constantly on Curtis and translated his observation into words. "Yes . . . he's pretty good, our Curtis, isn't he? But all the credit must be given to my wife. She found him, engaged him and trained him. So now— behold the finished article."

Anthony nodded his acceptance of the statement and took a cigarette from the box offered to him. The bouquet of the liqueur brandy pleased his sense of savour and he lit the cigarette. Lady Stuart had declined to smoke. Sir Charles pushed his chair back a little from the table.

"Well now, Bathurst, I think we ought to get to business. As you may have guessed, I wanted a private word with you with regard to the 'White Lion' murders. That's what I've come to call them. Now what conclusion have you come to, yourself—eh?"

Anthony decided to finesse. The attack seemed a little too direct. And too sudden. He smiled at his host and hostess, for he had seen, directly the Chief Constable had spoken, that Lady Stuart's mechanical blankness had become less acute.

"Conclusion—eh?" he remarked, repeating Sir Charles's word. "I'm afraid that's taking a much too optimistic view of things. Of course, I'm speaking entirely for myself and nothing that I say must be taken to involve or implicate Chief-Inspector MacMorran."

He paused—obviously to obtain the assurance for which he had so plainly asked. It came. From the Chief Constable!

"Oh—of course, Bathurst—naturally! If I had troubled about the 'Yard' fellow, I should have . . . er . . . ahem . . . acted differently. Oh—yes—your point is taken. You need have no fears on that score."

Anthony inclined his head in appreciation of Sir Charles Stuart's admission. "Thank you, sir. Now that the air is cleared on that point, I can, of course, speak to you much more freely and clearly. Between ourselves, I am grateful for the opportunity."

He looked at his two companions. Stuart's head was sunk upon his chest. His wife's eyes returned Mr. Bathurst's scrutiny coldly and fearlessly.

"Yes," said the Chief Constable. "Of course—I anticipated that you would be."

A low laugh came from the lady. Anthony found it rather surprising, because as he had just looked at her, she seemed a long way from such a condition as laughter. He began to speak again when Curtis came in with the port.

"At the moment, sir," said Anthony, "I'm afraid I've made but little progress. And the main barrier to the development of a plausible theory is the complete absence of motive. Not only in the murder of Norman, but also in the case of the second dead man—King. The fact that the same hotel is concerned in each instance, may, I think, be put down to a coincidence. At least, I'm inclined to think so at the present juncture. After all, Norman had actually left the 'White Lion' premises before he was killed."

Sir Charles Stuart nodded and pushed the port decanter towards Anthony. Anthony poured out a glass for himself. While he was doing this, the Chief Constable intervened with a remark.

"I'm not sure that I agree with you, Bathurst."

Elinor Stuart went one better. "And I am perfectly sure that I don't."

Anthony countered immediately. "Why, Lady Stuart? I should be interested to hear you state your case."

For a moment or so, the lady seemed disconcerted. Her fingers played nervously with the stem of her wine-glass. Anthony's question had come too quickly for her. It took her a little time to recover fully.

"Well," she said. "I think this. Or rather I look at it like this. The 'White Lion' isn't featured by *accident*. It has probably suited the murderer's convenience. If no more than that. And if it were chosen by him deliberately, then it comes to something more than a mere coincidence, doesn't it? Have I made myself clear to you, Mr. Bathurst?"

"Yes—as far as you've gone. But if you'll pardon my saying so, you haven't gone very far."

"That depends. I've gone as far as I intend to go." Elinor Stuart set her lips firmly and primly. Anthony accepted the situation. After all, these people had invited him here. He glanced again at his hostess. She was a trifle paler, but in full control of herself. Suddenly she offered Anthony a small gold cigarette-case.

"Will you smoke, Mr. Bathurst? As a matter of fact, these are rather good."

Anthony took the olive-branch. He saw that the lovely mouth of his hostess was still set hard, as though she were in pain. Sir Charles stroked his out-thrust chin. Anthony thought that he was attempting to find something to say. Which thought was, in fact, correct. After a time the Chief Constable came over.

"I'm worried, Bathurst. Infernally worried. And I don't mind admitting it. The case has got on my nerves. I don't know where it's going—and I don't know where we're going, either."

Sir Charles stroked his chin again, having relieved himself of his confession. There was a sharp sound. It was caused by the impact of Lady Stuart's wineglass against the edge of her dessert plate.

"I really don't know, Charles, *why* you should be so bothered. As I told you when the beastly thing started, it's all so completely horrible and sordid and there's a madman behind it all! Of that I am absolutely certain! No other explanation is either possible or even feasible."

A bright spot burned in each of the lady's cheeks. Anthony turned to her with renewed interest.

"I find that opinion held by others, Lady Stuart. In fact, there's a strong weight of opinion in that direction."

"Which is only to be expected, Mr. Bathurst." The lady spoke with emphasis.

"Whose opinions are you quoting now?" asked the Chief Constable. "I should be interested to know."

"For one, Dr. Pegram's, your Divisional Surgeon, and for another, Dr. Chavasse's."

"Don't think I've met him," growled Stuart. "Know Pegram, of course, pretty well. Sound fellow, too. Good value all round."

"Well," remarked Elinor Stuart, "I've not discussed it with Dr. Pegram, and I don't think I've ever met the other gentleman you mentioned, so my opinion's entirely my own and quite unprejudiced. I am gratified, however, to think that there are other people in the locality who possess a grain of intelligence. But now, Mr. Bathurst, I'd like to ask you a question." She put her elbows on the table, held a burning cigarette between fingers of her left hand and leant forward towards Anthony. "May I?" she asked quietly.

"By all means, Lady Stuart. What's your question?"

"These two gentlemen you cited, the two doctors, may I ask if either has expressed any decided opinion with regard to the near future?"

Anthony wasn't sure what she meant. "In what particular direction. Lady Stuart?"

Her eyes held his almost imperiously. "I'll be cruelly frank with you. Does either of your friends anticipate any further murders? That's what I mean, Mr. Bathurst."

"Yes. Dr. Chavasse does. I was in his company but a few days ago—and he expressed that opinion to me. Definitely. 'Another murder—or even murders.' They were his words."

Elinor Stuart almost purred with satisfaction. She nodded her head slowly as Anthony finished what he had to say. "Thank you, Mr. Bathurst. They are my personal sentiments—absolutely. In other words Mr. Bathurst, dreadful though it may be to say so—or even admit the fact—there's a killer in our midst."

She shivered slightly. Anthony saw for the first time that she was afraid. The chill of fear had taken hold of her and she was beginning to retreat from the advance of thirsty evil. This was a condition which Anthony hadn't previously visualised and which now that he had recognised it, came as something like a shock to him. Lady Stuart went on.

"And if there's a killer in our midst, Mr. Bathurst, we are in your hands. And in my husband's! All of us. Any one of us may be the next victim, because killers of this particular brand are no respecters of persons. Pleasant prospect, isn't it?"

There was a tinge of bitterness in her voice, as she clasped her hands together. For a moment or so there was a silence. It was eventually broken by the Chief Constable.

"No need to worry yourself, my dear," he said gruffly, "or to give way to flights of imagination."

"That's not imagination," replied his wife quietly. Then she turned to Anthony. "Well—and what have you to say to me, Mr. Bathurst?" Her voice was cold and clear. "Have I been guilty of an absurd piece of exaggerated anxiety?"

Anthony was guarded in his reply. "No. Not necessarily. But I think you've given expression to an extreme view. You're exhibiting the worse side of the picture."

"Which means that you don't agree with me? And that's your way of putting it?"

"Let me answer you like this, Lady Stuart. Let us divide future contingencies into the possible and the probable. If there's a killer in your midst—to use your own picturesque phrase—it's possible, obviously, that he may seek other victims, but is it probable? That's our problem. To make up our minds between the two."

Sir Charles nodded. "Yes. I see what you mean, Bathurst."

"All right," interposed the lady. "I'll take you at that valuation. *Is* it probable, Mr. Bathurst? Give me your honest and sincere opinion. I'll be satisfied to have that."

Anthony drank the remainder of his port. "Well, Lady Stuart," he announced, "since you force me to the precipice of an expressed opinion, I must reply to you that I *do* think it's probable. Motiveless murders are horrible things to understand. The abnormal always presents unusual difficulties to the investigator. Therefore, I will admit that I am afraid that you may be right."

"Thank you, Mr. Bathurst. You have said enough."

The Chief Constable showed signs of dismay. "I'm sorry to hear you say that, Mr. Bathurst. To my mind it indicates an . . . er . . . absence of confidence in the Police authorities. My wife will never let me hear the last of this."

The lady in question eyed her husband scornfully. Anthony shook his head.

"Not at all, Sir Charles. Nothing of that nature was in my mind, I assure you. It's that factor of the apparently motiveless crime again which causes the trouble. Where are the Police to look? If the hole can't be watched, you can't stop the rat from escaping. To employ a colloquialism, the police are up against it."

"That's exactly what I tell Lady Stuart," approved the Chief Constable.

"But not the only thing, unhappily," added the lady in question tartly.

"So the point remains," concluded Sir Charles a little lamely. "Where do we go to from here?"

Anthony was surprised at the response which the question occasioned. It was supplied by Lady Stuart. "Into the lounge, if you gentlemen don't mind. For coffee."

VIII

Anthony followed Sir Charles and his wife out of the dining-room, across the warm and comfortable corridor into the lounge—a long, low room holding an embarrassment of warmth and welcome. Its furnishings, without being elaborate, were both pleasing and graceful. The room itself was soft and mellow, its lighting was clear and comforting and Anthony responded to its mood immediately and instinctively. Elinor Stuart went ahead of the two men and took a low seat near the fire. By its side stood the coffee table on which there stood spirit-lamp, cups and coffee-pot. Sir Charles Stuart offered cigarettes from a plain silver box. Lady Stuart took the coffee-pot, raised her head, and looked at Anthony. He understood the unspoken question.

"Black, if you please."

She poured out the coffee. "I expected that you would say that," she said quietly. "I can usually judge."

"Really?" Anthony gave her a smiling response. Then with a sudden impulse, for he had noticed that Sir Charles had gone to the other end of the room, he leant forward and asked his hostess a question:

"Tell me, Lady Stuart, of what are you afraid? Particularly afraid?"

He waited in patience for her answer. She looked at him disdainfully. "Who says that I am afraid?"

Anthony shrugged his shoulders.

"I don't admit for one moment that I am afraid," she went on.

"Very well, then, I will say no more. There is no need." Anthony made as though to change the subject. But the lady would have none of it. She relented a little.

"I certainly will not admit to fear. At the same time, I'll come part of the way with you, I am prepared to plead guilty in a lesser degree." She paused and waited.

"Yes?" interrogated Anthony. She saw that he was determined she should continue.

"To a feeling of anxiety, perhaps. But no more than that. You will concede me that there is a wide gulf between fear and anxiety?"

"A gulf—perhaps—but not always so very wide. Sometimes I have known the two conditions to be desperately close to each other. But never mind that. Let us face the fact. Why this acute anxiety?"

Anthony was conscious that the Chief Constable had left the farther end of the room and was walking towards them again. Lady Stuart ignored the fact. She answered quite frankly.

"It isn't acute, Mr. Bathurst. And it isn't peculiar to me, I'll swear. Look at it for yourself. There must be many a woman in Mallett and district who feels the same anxiety that I feel. Isn't it perfectly natural? There's a killing maniac at large amongst our community and, as I said to you just now, anyone of us may be the next on his list to receive his attentions. I don't find that a pleasant thought and I don't find it a refreshing thought, either. Can you blame me?" She put down her coffee cup. "So there you are, Mr. Bathurst. You have the full story. I have allowed you to peep into the deep recesses of my soul and to see perhaps more than is good for you." She laughed. It was a creditable attempt, but it didn't ring true by any means.

"Before we leave the subject, Lady Stuart," said Anthony, "what you have said disturbs me rather. You mentioned the *women* in Mallett and district. Why the women—so particularly? Am I to assume that you consider their peril greater than the men's? Because, if you answer, 'Yes'—I shall feel compelled to ask you why you think that way? Why the women, Lady Stuart?"

Anthony emphasised the question. His companion shook her head. "I don't know that I referred to my own sex particularly. Perhaps I gave you a wrong impression. I am sorry if I did. I didn't intend to. I merely looked at the general question from a personal point of view. The result was that I spoke in the terms that were uppermost in my mind and natural to me." She turned to her husband. "More coffee, Charles?"

"Thank you, my dear." The Chief Constable surrendered the small cup to his wife. Anthony watched her as she filled it. She passed it over to Sir Charles, who drank it at once.

"Well, Bathurst, I'm glad that we've got together and that I've been able to have this chat with you. You know my views. I know yours. Which is all to the good. Your Inspector, as you doubtless know, has been extremely busy all over the district. According to what he tells me, he's picked up but little. That fact alone doesn't worry me. But neither the Norman family nor the King family throws up any clue or connection which seems to have the slightest bearing on the case. From no angle can the finger of suspicion be levelled against any member of the two families. That's a fact which does disturb me just a little." The Chief Constable paused and turned directly to Anthony. "Well, there you are, Bathurst, you know nearly all that I'm thinking. I've put my cards on the table. You can pick up which ever one of 'em you like and play to it."

Anthony shook his head. "No, Sir Charles. I'm well content with what you've said to me. But I'd like to tell you this. Although I can claim to have made little progress so far, I am not entirely without hope. I can honestly say that I am toying, not without hope of success, with at least three theories. Two of them are distinctly promising. At the moment we will leave it at that."

Anthony rose from his seat and looked at his watch. "Really, Sir Charles, I must be going, I had no idea that it was so late. Let me thank both you and Lady Stuart for the warmth of your hospitality."

He shook hands with his host and hostess, and as he made his way back to his hotel, he wondered why exactly he had been favoured with the invitation. MacMorran was in when he arrived and greeted him hilariously.

"Baked meats," he gibed, "and goblets of wine. And they talk of the flesh-pots of Egypt."

"Andrew," said Anthony, "there are occasions when your levity is ill-timed."

"And this, I suppose," grinned the Inspector, "is counted by you as one of them."

"I don't say so," replied Mr. Bathurst. "And you can make what you like of that."

CHAPTER IV

I

THE 'White Lion' is the oldest inn in Mallett. It lies at the end of what is always known as the north market. Opposite to it, and almost in the middle of the chief street is the curious old Curfew Turret, surmounting a lock-up for petty offenders, long since disused. The 'White Lion' has an interesting history. Early in the fifteenth century it was purchased by a certain Archdeacon Newling, who presented it to the town of Mallett. The conditions of the donation were that its rent should be devoted to the relief of taxation for street-paving and for other uses.

In the original tap-room, now used as a lumber-room, is a famous old stone chimney-piece with the carving of a magnificent lion. Dean Swift is popularly credited with having stayed often at the inn and one of its chairs is always referred to as 'Swift's Chair.' As befits an old coaching house, its yard is cobble-stoned and stretches from the High Street itself to Saracen's Alley on the other side. Four doors open on to this cobble-stoned yard. In order from the High Street side, they are marked respectively, 'Saloon,' 'Smoke-room,' 'Kitchen,' and 'Store-room.' Outside the door marked 'Store-room' and nearest of the four to Saracen's Alley, there stands, as it has stood for generations, a large water-butt, of more recent years painted a dark green in colour. At its side stand two flowering shrubs, encased in square wooden boxes.

It was the habit of Dora Burgess, the maid at the 'White Lion,' to shake the mats outside the kitchen door soon after half-past six each morning. Three mornings after Anthony Bathurst's invitation to the house of Sir Charles Stuart, Dora, who was stout and comely, with several large-sized bees in her private bonnet, opened the kitchen door to attack several dusty mats. It was a glorious spring morning with clean, untarnished sunshine slanting down on to the cobblestones of the 'White Lion's' yard. Dora's ample heart warmed and opened to its shimmering benison. She took her first mat in her hand and poised it skilfully for the inevitable assault on the inn-wall. As she did so, she glanced from sheer force of habit in the direction of the historic, dark green water-butt. Immediately, her attention was arrested. For to Dora's eye, its appearance on this particular morning had something unusual about it. Dora looked hard at the object which had aroused her interest. In fact, she did more than look hard, she stared fixedly. Then she rubbed her eyes in astonishment. For this object, to the eye of Dora Burgess, looked exactly like a man's boot. And, which is more, a man's boot with a man's foot inside it. The sight made Dora feel strange. 'Funny' was her own way of describing it afterwards. Anyhow, the vision that she saw caused Dora to drop her mat innocent of collision, and bolt hastily back into the kitchen for the companionship of Fred Bates, the 'boots' at the 'White Lion.'

Bates was just on the point of commencing business with the knife-cleaning machine.

"Fred!" screamed Dora. "Come 'ere quick! Into the yard. There's a—there's a—" She stopped. Her vocabulary was unequal to the task of adequate description.

"There's a what?" demanded Fred. "Anybody to look at you 'ud think you'd seen a bloody ghost. What 'ave you seen? A dead cat?"

Dora Burgess patted her bosom. "Fred," she gasped. "Just a minute—I've come over 'ever so queer.' My palpitation's started. Give me a little time to get my breath and I'll tell you all about it. I shall be all right in a minute or two. Give me a breather, Fred."

Bates stared at the maid, round-eyed. For once his curiosity subjugated his natural impatience. Anyhow, Dora took her breather and began to tell her story in such a way that Bates was able to understand her.

"There's a man," gasped Dora, "in the water-butt. Down the end of the yard there." She stabbed with her finger in the direction of the butt. Bates didn't at once grasp the entire significance of what had been said to him. He opened his mouth wide.

"A man in the butt. Why? What's he in there for? Is he looking for something?"

Dora pushed him. "Don't be a fool, Fred. Of course he isn't looking for anything—he couldn't if he wanted to—he's dead! It's a dead man, Fred. That's what made me come over 'ever so queer.'" She rubbed her hand across her forehead.

"Dead?" exclaimed Fred. "In the butt? 'Ow do you know? You're seein' things. 'Ow can a bloke be dead in an old butt? 'Ow the 'ell could he get in there, to start with?"

Dora shook her head. "Not to start with, Fred! That's the wrong way round. Say to finish up with." Then the quickening force of reality seemed to assert itself suddenly within her. "Fred, we're a couple of idiots sitting about here like this—doin' nothing. Whatever's come over us? I'll take you along to the water-butt now and show you. You can see his leg sticking up a mile off. Come on, Fred."

Bates followed her into the yard. His face betrayed the queasy condition of his stomach. He kept a couple of paces behind his guide until they reached the dark-green butt. He had kept his head down purposely as he approached, postponing, as a child does, the evil minute of complete visualisation for as long as possible.

"There," said Dora, pointing upwards. "If that ain't a man's foot with a boot on it, I ain't never seen one."

Fred, open-mouthed and gape-eyed nodded, with the alertness of a village idiot. "Gawd," he said, entirely inaccurately. "What a way to do yourself in." Then he paused. "Dora," he said fearfully, "you know what this is, don't you? In relation to corpses? It's the 'White Lion's' bloody hat-trick."

"What do you mean, Fred?" demanded Dora, almost whispering her words. "What do you mean—hat-trick?"

He regarded the questioner with something akin to contempt. "Why—three dead 'uns in a row, of course! There's your blinking hat-trick. Norman, the farmer, what left here that evening to die in his car, old King the baker what eat something that disagreed with him, and now this bloke what's chosen his own bath-tub. Still, it won't do for you and me to stand here gossipin' like a couple of old house-wives. I'll pop inside the house and tell Mr. Denton. You stay out here, Dora, my love, and for Gawd's sake don't you touch nothing. Don't get fondling that there corpse while my back's turned," he added playfully. "I know what you girls are when there's a man about."

"Catch me," exclaimed Dora with a show of indignation. "I couldn't touch it—not if you paid me all the gold in the Hindies. But you get along—get along to the guv'nor as fast as you know how."

Fred Bates did as she had directed him. Dora waited by the dark-green water-butt. The morning which had seemed so bright when she had opened the door to shake her mats had now assumed a sinister character. Dora shivered. There was a corpse but a few feet away from her.

II

Denton came out with Fred Bates within the space of a few moments.

"In the butt, sir," said Bates.

Denton, who was considerably taller than either Bates or Dora Burgees, was able to look down into the water-butt with comparative ease. In the butt was the body of a man. The man was head downwards. The body was propped against the side of the butt so that one foot was stuck up grotesquely in the air. Through displacement, Bates saw that the water in the butt had slopped over the sides and subsided some inches. As far as Denton could see, the dead man was a stranger to him. He was dressed shabbily in dark clothes. The soles of his shoes were worn through and there was no sign of any hat or cap that, in life, he might have worn. Denton looked at the dead body in the water.

"I'm letting him rest, Bates, for the time being," he said. "I'm disturbing nothing. Get on the 'phone at once. To the Police-station at Mallett. Ask for Inspector Venables. Get in touch with him as soon as you possibly can. Tell him he'd better come along at once with the Inspector from Scotland Yard and also Dr. Pegram. Don't say too much. Just give him the information that there's a dead man in the 'White Lion' water-butt. Cut along now—while I stay here. You can clear off, too, Dora. Else you'll dream to-night."

The 'boots' nodded and dashed off on his errand. Dora betook herself, somewhat unwillingly, let it be confessed, to the matter of her mats, Denton looked at his watch. It still wanted a few minutes to seven o'clock. He knew that meant he had some time to wait. Bates would get through to the Police-station without difficulty, but making contact at this early hour with Inspector MacMorran or Inspector Venables would be a horse of decidedly another colour. The same conditions would apply to getting hold of Dr. Pegram.

Denton replaced his watch in his pocket with an exclamation of annoyance. He had no ardent desire to stand out here until uniformed authority arrived. What was more—he had no intention of so doing. But there was the body in the butt to be considered! Suddenly Denton had an idea. In the dining-room there was a large screen. If he got it and brought it out into the yard, he could stand it round the water-butt and its sinister burden. Denton turned on his heel and went inside the inn to fetch the screen. It would keep impertinent sight-seers from the scene of the crime.

III

A few minutes after eight o'clock, Denton's patience was rewarded by the arrival of four people. They were Chief-Inspector Andrew MacMorran, Inspector Venables, Dr. Pegram and Anthony Bathurst.

Bates's telephone message had done its work. Pegram looked in the last stages of acute irritation, Venables worried, MacMorran eager and Bathurst grave. Denton nodded his 'good mornings' and beckoned them into the cobble-stoned yard of the 'White Lion.' Anthony, as he approached, was thinking on the lines that Bates had thought. This was the third death in which the inn had been implicated.

Denton, in a few short words, explained to them what he had done and removed the borrowed screen. Venables gave vent to a sharp ejaculation when he saw the position of the body. But he surrendered the leadership to MacMorran, almost as though by instinct.

"Get the body out," said MacMorran.

Bates, who had hovered on the fringe of the company, took the order to apply to himself, so he dashed forward to give Denton and Venables an assisting hand. But there came an interruption.

"Just a moment," said Anthony. "With your permission, Inspector."

MacMorran gave a curt nod of agreement and the three men hung back. Anthony walked to the edge of the water-butt and looked in curiously. He carefully noted the height of the water.

"All right, Andrew," he said. "Go ahead."

Denton, Venables and Bates lifted out the body. It was that of a smallish man. Anthony judged him to be about five feet six inches in height and in age somewhere in the late sixties. He had a creased, puckered, wizened sort of face and as Denton and the others laid him face downwards on the cobble-stones, the water ran from his mouth and nostrils.

"There you are, Dr. Pegram," said MacMorran. "Tell us all you can about him."

The Divisional Surgeon commenced an examination of the dead man. Anthony waited silently for his findings.

"Been dead some hours," said Pegram. "Asphyxia. If you could look into his heart," he added, "you would find the right side over-filled with blood."

Anthony nodded. "In other words, Doctor, death from drowning."

"Exactly," replied Pegram.

Anthony nodded again. "Tell me, Dr. Pegram," he suddenly asked, "how long would this man have had to be under the water for death to ensue?"

Pegram answered quickly. "Complete deprivation of oxygen results in death after three to five minutes. Recovery, therefore, would be unlikely if the submersion under water lasted longer than a few minutes, though, of course, recovery very occasionally may follow immersion for a much longer period. It would depend, of course, on the nature, skill and efficiency of the treatment afforded the patient."

"I see, Doctor. Thank you very much."

Pegram got up from his position by the body. "Better get the body away, Inspector. I'll make a further examination later on."

He dusted his hands. Venables nodded. He conferred for a few moments with MacMorran and Denton. The latter said:

"All right. That will do until the ambulance comes."

He turned and gave Bates certain instructions. The 'boots' touched his forehead with his finger-tip and disappeared. MacMorran strolled towards Anthony, who was still looking at the water-butt.

"Before the body goes to the mortuary, Mr. Bathurst, Venables and I are going to give it the once-over. Come along over with us, will you?"

"With pleasure, my dear Andrew. Well—what is it, suicide or murder? Or death from misadventure? How will that suit you?"

"Not a doubt," replied Andrew. "Murder—every time. You agree, don't you?"

"Count me in, Andrew. As you said yourself—not a doubt. Not the merest suspicion of one. But we'll get along to Venables and Denton. I want to know who this fellow is. Rather badly, between ourselves, Andrew. To tell you the truth—I'm even more bewildered than before. From the look of this chap in the butt, he doesn't seem to me to fill the picture at all. That is, as I've been inclined to paint it."

The Inspector accompanied Anthony across the yard to an empty shed where the body of the drowned man had been taken.

"Nobody could have got in that butt to commit suicide," declared MacMorran. "It's not possible, and nobody could convince me that it was. Here we are. Mind your head, Mr. Bathurst."

Anthony ducked at the Inspector's warning. The door opening of the shed was lower than he had judged it to be. Venables beckoned to them as they entered.

"Not much on him," he announced, "but we've established identity."

"That's the stuff," said Anthony. "And who is he?"

"According to a post-card in one of his pockets, his name is George Clarence. His address is 22 West View Terrace, Hammeridge."

"Where's that?" put in MacMorran.

"Hammeridge is a village about five miles from Mallett. Not in the Forge direction. The other way."

Anthony nodded. "I've heard of it. I saw the name on a local map the other day. Who sent the post-card, Inspector?"

Venables examined it closely. "Meet me in the public-bar of the 'Gardener's Arms' on Thursday evening at 7.30. I hope to be able to make you a good offer for what you want to sell. A. Smith." Venables stopped after reading the message. "That's what it says."

"Interesting," remarked Anthony. "And kindly note, gentlemen, that to-day happens to be Friday. Thursday evening therefore, was only as long ago as last night. Any address on the card, Inspector? Sender's address, I mean?"

Venables shook his head.

"What are you thinking, Inspector? That I'm asking for jam on it?"

Venables remained humourless. "Well, as a matter of fact, I was."

"Thought so," returned Anthony, glancing towards MacMorran.

"I'm wondering," said the latter, "what it was that Mr. George Clarence was desirous of selling. Seems to me that to know that might tell us a lot."

"Anything else of importance on the body, Inspector?" inquired Anthony.

"A knife, a small length of string, an empty tin probably used for carrying tobacco, a cheap bowl-pipe, a box of matches with five matches in it and cash to the value of eightpence halfpenny."

"Highly illuminating," remarked Anthony. "What do you say, Andrew?"

"I was thinking much the same thing, Mr. Bathurst."

Anthony went closer to look at the dead man. "Can't make it out," he said, almost to himself. "Type all wrong. Wrong to blazes." He turned to Inspector MacMorran. "What would you say this chap did for a living, Inspector?"

MacMorran joined him by the body. After a little time he shook his head. "Shouldn't like to be too positive about anything. If you want my real opinion, he and hard work weren't on much more than nodding terms."

"My opinion, too. Then what the hell did he have to sell that was valuable? As you indicated just now! Problem, Andrew—very much so. Still, we shall have more definite news of him, no doubt, after Venables has got busy. Ask him to let us know anything important, directly he gets it. In the meantime, you and I, Andrew, will go back to our car, I think, and discuss a little matter of breakfast."

IV

Anthony was in the company of Inspector MacMorran at the inn where they were staying when Venables came to them.

"Sit down, Inspector," said Anthony, "and then tell me what you'll drink."

Venables chose beer and Anthony saw to the supply. "What news," he said curtly. "I presume you have some for us. Otherwise—"

Venables cut in at once. "I've just come back from Hammeridge. Been to Clarence's house for the second time. Interviewed his wife and then brought her here to identify the body. Poor old girl—over sixty, so she tells me. Clarence lived on what he could pick up here and there. In her words—an odd-jobber. Probably wasn't above a spot of housebreaking if it suited his book. But naturally, Mrs. Clarence didn't open out too much in respect of that."

"I don't expect so. How old was Clarence?"

"He would have been sixty-three on Christmas Eve. To the best of his widow's recollection. She's not too strong on detailed information, let me tell you."

"Go on, Venables, fill in the picture as completely as you can. You'll have me interested all the time."

"There are two children, both married and neither of them living in the district. Moved away years ago. When they married—naturally." The local Inspector stopped. Anthony waited for him to continue. Venables looked at him.

"On that particular score, I don't think I've much more to tell you."

"Pity. I could have borne a lot more. What about Alf Smith?"

"Alf?" queried both Venables and MacMorran, almost in the same breath.

"Hundred to one it was meant for Alf," smiled Anthony. "Did you pick up anything about him?"

"Well—I did and I didn't. I'll tell you all about that angle."

"Who is he?"

"Mrs. Clarence had no idea."

"H'm. Good start! She'd never heard of him?"

"Only in the same way as we have." Venables produced the post-card found on Clarence and tapped it with his finger-nail. "From this card here. She knew Clarence had it. She put it into his hand at breakfast, she says, when it was delivered. But she hasn't (or she says she hasn't) the slightest idea as to who Smith is."

"Don't tell me she says she thinks she's heard the name before, will you, Venables?"

"It's not quite as bad as that, Mr. Bathurst."

"Go on, then," said MacMorran. "Let's have it."

"Well what I mean is this. Mrs. Clarence knew *something*. She knew what it was that Smith wanted to buy." Venables paused again. This at least was going to be his moment.

"What was it?" inquired Inspector MacMorran.

"A stamp collection."

"What?" declared Anthony.

"It's true," repeated Venables. "Clarence's stamp collection."

Anthony's face twisted into intensive thought.

"I thought that would surprise you," said Venables with a certain degree of satisfaction.

Anthony scratched his cheek. Then he looked at Andrew MacMorran and smiled whimsically. "The decline and fall of crime, Andrew. From death by red-hot cinders to a stamp-collection."

Venables leant forward with finger outstretched. "Just a minute. Mightn't a collection be extremely valuable? A collection of a certain kind?"

Anthony shrugged his shoulders. "In Clarence's hands, do you think?"

"He might have stolen it. Remember what I told you about his *penchant* for housebreaking."

Venables's French accent was not all that it should have been. Even MacMorran noticed the fact. Anthony looked serious. Suddenly he turned to Venables.

"Tell me, Inspector. When Clarence went out last night, did he take the stamp collection with him?"

"He did, Mr. Bathurst."

MacMorran whistled. "He did, did he?"

"He did," replied Venables; "and we know that it wasn't on him when he was fished out of the water-butt. Looks pretty obvious, doesn't it?"

Anthony began to pace the room. MacMorran relapsed into silence. Venables sat and watched them. After some minutes had passed, Anthony looked at MacMorran and then turned to Venables.

"Inspector Venables," he said, "you're going to Hammeridge for the third time. And this time MacMorran and I are coming with you. Where's your car?"

V

Mrs. Clarence looked even more scared when she opened the door to her three visitors than she had when she first saw Inspector Venables. The last named explained matters to her and the three men followed her into the best room of the heriditament known as 22 West View Terrace, Hammeridge. The term is a euphemism. Mrs. Clarence produced three chairs and invited her audience to sit down.

"These gentlemen want to ask you some questions, Mrs. Clarence," went on the local Inspector. "Try to answer them to the best of your ability."

Mrs. Clarence nodded nervously.

"What time did your husband go out last evening?" inquired MacMorran.

"A few minutes before seven, sir."

"Did he tell you where he was going?"

"Yes, sir. To the 'Gardener's Arms.'"

"How far away is that?"

"It was never far enough, sir. For my liking. Not much more than ten minutes walk from here."

"So that there was nothing unusual about him going there then, Mrs. Clarence?"

"It would have been unusual if he *'ain't* gone there. More than unusual, sir. It would ha' been more like a perishin' miracle."

Anthony resisted an inclination to smile. "And that was the last time that you saw your husband alive?"

"Yes, sir." Mrs. Clarence wiped her eyes with the corner of an apron she was wearing.

MacMorran nodded to Anthony Bathurst. The latter understood the significance of the nod.

"Mrs. Clarence," he said quietly and persuasively, "when you saw Inspector Venables in the earlier part of the day, you mentioned to him something about a stamp collection. Will you please tell me as much as you can about it?"

"My husband took it out with him when he went to the 'Gardener's Arms.' He was going to sell it."

"He told you that?"

"Yes, sir. He'd been talking about it for a day or two."

"How long had he had this stamp collection?"

"I don't know, sir. Honestly, I don't."

"Have you ever seen it?"

"Yes, sir. Once, I'm sure. About a week ago. Perhaps twice."

"What was it like?"

"A big book. Something like one of them old-fashioned family photo albums."

"You never looked inside it?"

Mrs. Clarence shook her head. "No, sir."

"Have you any idea how much your husband expected to get for this stamp collection."

Mrs. Clarence thought over the question. "I think 'e said, 'A quid or two.'"

"You don't know who 'A. Smith' is?"

"No, sir. Only somebody George was going to meet in the 'Gardener's Arms.' Nothing more than that, sir."

"He wasn't a friend of your husband?"

"No, sir. Well—if he was, George didn't talk about him. If you ask me—"

Mrs. Clarence stopped short suddenly. Anthony waited for her to go on. He was disappointed. Mrs. Clarence showed no sign of continuing. Mr. Bathurst, therefore, prompted her.

"Well," he said, "suppose we do ask you? What about it?"

"Well, sir. What I was going to say is this. If you ask me, this Smith was a chap what George picked up with in the 'Gardener.' It wouldn't be the first time—not by a long chalk. And well I know it."

But Anthony was loth to leave the matter where it was. "Tell me, Mrs. Clarence," he said, "was your husband generally interested in stamp-collecting?"

"No, sir."

"He didn't talk about it?"

"No, sir."

"You never heard him discuss stamp-collecting prior to this occasion we've been talking about?"

"No, sir. Never. Beer, tobacco and money were my husband's stock-in-trade as far as conversation went. Oh—and 'orses. 'E loved 'orses—on paper. Turned by instinct to the 'orse page."

MacMorran seemed suddenly seized by an idea. He leant forward to the woman whom Anthony had been questioning. "Mrs. Clarence, you mustn't mind my asking you this question. Seeing that your husband's dead—and dead in such a manner. But, as far as you know, had your husband ever been in prison?"

Mrs. Clarence began to cry. The corners of her apron again came into play.

"Well?" persisted MacMorran. "You haven't answered me! Had he?"

Mrs. Clarence nodded slowly. The answer came. "Yes, sir."

"When?"

"About five years ago."

"What for?"

"Stealin', sir."

"Where?"

"At Marriton, sir."

"What did he get?"

"Twelve months 'ard, sir."

"I see. Thank you, Mrs. Clarence." MacMorran made certain notes in his note-book. He nodded to Anthony and Venables. "I think," he said, "that our way lies in the direction of the 'Gardener's Arms.'"

VI

The landlord of the 'Gardener's Arms' was by no means a man of the ordinary type. For one thing, he had a wooden leg. For another, he was unhappily (so many thought) the complete antithesis of the ideal Boniface. He was a man of sour, curdled visage and he rejoiced in the name of Benjamin Woodmason. Had there been an active opposition to his house of call within the village of Hammeridge, Woodmason's personal banking account would have been nothing like so flourishing as it was. Benjamin Woodmason sold the only beer to be had in Hammeridge. Hammeridge therefore drank it and Woodmason prospered.

When he saw Venables approach him accompanied by Inspector MacMorran and Anthony Bathurst, he was, at first, inclined to adopt a truculent attitude.

"Look here," he said, his cadaverous face working nervously, "I'm a busy man. And I don't know what you chaps, barging in here like this, expect a busy man—"

This was too much for MacMorran. "Just a moment," he said curtly. "Let's get this straight. I happen to be Chief-Inspector MacMorran of the C.I.D. If you want my credentials, here they are."

Woodmason looked MacMorran straight in the eye. And then altered his mood and manner. "Well, that's all right, Inspector. You're a man of the world, no doubt, the same as I am. And business is business—even when the Police come ferreting round. Still—that's O.K. by me, Inspector."

"Very good," MacMorran remained curt and to the point. Woodmason beckoned the members of the party. "Come along inside, gentlemen. We can talk more comfortably in the parlour behind the bar."

They followed the landlord into a small but comfortable room, well-furnished and generally inviting. Woodmason gestured them to their seats. MacMorran came to the point without further ado.

"We are inquiring into the death of a man named George Clarence, a native of Hammeridge. He lives, or, rather, lived, at Number 22 West View Terrace. Can you tell us, Mr. Woodmason, whether Clarence was in your house at any time during last evening?"

"He was."

"What time would that have been?"

Woodmason considered the question before he answered it. "Soon after seven o'clock. And he was here, gentlemen, until just on closing time. As far as I can remember."

MacMorran glanced towards Anthony. "Alone?" he asked Woodmason.

The landlord shook his head. "No. Decidedly not. He was on his own for about a quarter of an hour. Then he was joined by another man. These two remained together until just before closing-time, when the place was crowded. And what's more, I rather fancy they left the bar together. But I'm not sure of that."

Anthony leant over to Venables and MacMorran. "Notice the similarity to the conditions just before Norman met his death? Most remarkable."

MacMorran nodded and got to grips with the main point. "Any idea as to who this man was?"

"No, Inspector."

"Ever seen him before?"

"Yes, Inspector."

"Where?"

"In the bar here. But he's a recent customer at this house. I can't recall ever having seen him before about a month ago. Since about then he's been a fairly frequent visitor here."

"Did you know his name?"

"Not really. But I've heard him called 'Smith.' Usually by George Clarence himself."

"H'm." MacMorran was noncommittal. Woodmason became emphatic. Almost, thought Anthony, as though he were defending himself against a challenge or an accusation.

"Remember this, Inspector," he said vigorously. "I had no call to question him. Either about his name or anything else. He came into my pub, ordered his liquor, paid for it without any argument, drank his liquor and generally behaved himself like a decent citizen. That was all that concerned me. I'd like you to make a note of that, Inspector. In common justice to myself."

Woodmason sat back and thrust out his chin. Anthony came in with his first question.

"Any idea, Mr. Woodmason, as to where this man Smith lived?"

"No, sir. Not the foggiest."

"Not in Hammeridge?"

"Not as far as I know. Never seen him knocking about the village."

"I take it, then, that he came to the 'Gardener's Arms' by car. Yes?"

"Again I couldn't say. I don't stand here watching out for all the people that come to my inn by car. Got too much to do, if you ask me. But I should think that in all probability he *did* have a car."

"Where do the cars that come here park?"

"Outside in the clearing. You must have noticed the approach when you came in."

"How many cars do you have there of an evening? Average, say?"

Woodmason frowned. The question appeared distasteful to him. He avoided Anthony's eye when he answered him. "I couldn't be certain.

As I said just now. I don't keep count of them. The place gets crowded. But I should say, on an average, about a dozen. Folk come out here from Mallett and a few from Forge and Fell. Especially when the better weather comes."

MacMorran took another hand in the inquiry. "Did you take good stock of Clarence and Smith last night?"

Woodmason frowned again. He was beginning to get rattled. "More or less," he muttered. "Chiefly less."

"And that means?" demanded MacMorran.

"I saw them together. At one of their tables. They always chose one of the two tables in the corner."

"Were they alone together all the time?"

"As far as I know."

"You didn't see anybody else with them?"

"I did not. But that doesn't mean a lot. I keep telling you the bar was crowded out. They always kept themselves to themselves. Gave me the impression they were talking business all the time."

"I see. Now give me a description of this man, Smith, will you?"

"Tallish. Middle-aged. Horn-rimmed glasses. Always wore loud plus-fours. At least I'd call 'em loud. Big checks. And always walked with a bit of a limp."

"Which indicates," said Anthony, "that in all probability he must have come here by car."

"Not a doubt about that," supplemented Venables.

"Just a minute," said MacMorran. "Let's have a few more details with regard to Smith. Physical. Hair! What colour was it?"

Woodmason shrugged his shoulders. "Nothing distinctive about it. Call it brown—that's as near as I can get to it."

"Eyes? What about them?"

Woodmason shook his head. "Couldn't see 'em well enough to describe them fully. I told you he wore horn-rimmed glasses."

MacMorran made suitable notes. He then closed his book and looked at Anthony. "Well, Mr. Bathurst? Any more questions that you want to ask Mr. Woodmason?"

For a moment Anthony didn't answer. Eventually he came from his reverie. "Yes. There is one. When Clarence and Smith were together at this particular table of theirs, did you notice if, at any time, they were looking at anything special? Anything like a book, for example?"

Woodmason replied to the question at once. "No. I couldn't say that I noticed anything of the kind. If they were looking at a book, I didn't see it. But why do you ask? Is it important?"

"It might be," replied Anthony. "I can't be sure yet." He rose from his seat and gestured to the Scotland Yard Inspector. "I don't think we shall serve any good purpose by remaining, Andrew. Mr. Woodmason has probably told us all he knows."

He paused for a momentary period. Then as though giving expression to an afterthought: "Concerning the actions of the late Mr. Clarence in the bar yesterday evening."

VII

"Dr. Pegram," said Anthony Bathurst on the following morning, "what have you to report *re* Clarence? Anything exciting or even unusual?"

Pegram shook his head. "He'd been in the water about six hours. That's as near as I can say. I should be inclined to assert too, that he was drunk—and well drunk at that—when he went in the butt. There was an unusually large quantity of alcohol in the stomach."

"When he *went* into the butt?"

Pegram smiled at the emphasis on the question. "All right. If you want me to be absolutely precise. When he was shoved in. By person or persons unknown."

"He would have been an easy victim, I take it?"

"Oh—quite. Very comfy. No trouble at all. Money for old rope. Apart from the state he happened to be in, he was of poor physique and in wretched condition. T.B. for a cert, I should say. One lung was in very bad shape. Clarence wouldn't have made old bones. There's not the slightest doubt about that."

Anthony fell to reflection. What possible connection could there be between Norman, Henry King and George Clarence? One burned to death in a car, one poisoned at dinner, and the third drowned in a water-butt. One had left the 'White Lion,' one had been in the 'White Lion,' and the third had come to the 'White Lion,' or, better still, had been brought there.

"What are you thinking?" inquired Pegram.

Anthony shook his head. "That I can't make head or tail of any of it. I can fit nothing whatever into anything like a reasonable pattern."

"Right," returned the Divisional Surgeon. "Don't move from there. Hold on to that thought and concentrate. Then pay me the compliment of remembrance. I still assert that we're looking for a homicidal maniac."

"Very likely—but—"

"Wait a minute." Pegram waved an admonishing finger. "Let me continue for a moment or so. A man who kills anybody! Anybody without the slightest individual significance. In other words, a criminal who kills simply for the sake of killing. He's not particular. He doesn't mind. When the time is ripe, the coast clear, and the conditions convenient, he emerges from the security of his house, which serves as his natural hiding-place, runs into an inevitable victim—and kills."

There was a silence. "Well?" persisted Pegram. "How does it go? Does it appeal to you?"

"No," returned Anthony.

"Why not?"

"Just because!"

"Just because what?"

"Well—using your own word—it doesn't appeal to me. It doesn't satisfy my reasoning. Can't tell you why—exactly. Yet awhile. But I shall be able to. Give me a little time longer." Anthony smiled at Pegram.

The latter still argued: "Will you mind if I call you obstinate?"

"I shan't lie awake at night and worry over it, I assure you."

"I don't suppose you will—for a moment. But you'll never convince me by just denying my suggestion. You talk of your reasoning, but you don't actually produce any reasons." Pegram grinned. "That's fair criticism, isn't it?"

Anthony took the shaft with good humour. "Yes, I must admit that. But as I said just now—give me time. At the moment you'll have to content yourself with my bare rejections. Sorry and all that—but it's the best I can do for you."

Pegram shrugged his shoulders. "All right. I understand. If you can't say any more, you can't, and I must abide by your decision."

He paused and took his pipe from his pocket. "But I will do this," he added as he packed tobacco into its bowl. "I'll give you a piece of additional information."

Anthony looked at him curiously. Pegram grinned at him again.

"I held it back from you as a *pièce de résistance*. I must have a flair for dramatising myself."

"What is it?" asked Anthony slowly.

"Why this! Wouldn't it interest you to know that Clarence wasn't drowned in a water-butt?"

"What do you mean, Doctor?"

"What I say."

"But I saw the body taken from the—"

"Butt—exactly. But a water-butt should contain water."

"Well—what did this one contain, then?"

Pegram smiled at Anthony's anxiety. "Not only water, Bathurst."

"Not only water? What was the other constituent, then?"

Pegram's eyes twinkled. "Wine, my dear fellow. Wine. Such as maketh glad the heart of man."

"Wine?" Anthony became almost incredulous. "What sort of wine?"

"Ah—that's the rub, isn't it? But if you must know—port."

"Port?" Anthony wrinkled his forehead in his surprise. "How do you know?"

"Well—I suspected something of the kind. So I analysed a sample. I should say, from the results that I got, that at least one bottle of port—rich old tawny—had been poured into the water-butt."

"But why, Pegram, why? Why in the name of conscience, pour port into a water-butt of that kind when it also houses a dead body?" Anthony paced the room—his hands thrust deeply into his trouser-pockets. He swung round on to the Divisional Surgeon with an almost fierce insistence. "Why, man—the case grows crazier than ever. Burnt cinders, poisoned turbot and now wine mixed with water to drown a man! But just a minute, Doctor. The wine may have been in the butt all the time. It belongs to the 'White Lion'—remember. We may be chasing a red herring. Denton will be able to tell us. We must find out."

Pegram shook his head. "I don't think so. From what I found by my analysis. If my opinion's worth anything, the wine hadn't been in the butt overlong."

"What caused you to suspect its presence there?"

Pegram rubbed the corner of his chin. "I noticed the faint tinge of colour showing. At first glance I had the idea that it was blood. Probably, I surmised, coming from the corpse. But it wasn't. I proved that beyond any doubt. Upon analysis, I found that it was port. Yes, my dear Bathurst, the wine of Oporto. Neither more nor less."

Anthony gestured with his head towards the telephone. "Get on to Denton and ask him if there should be any wine in that butt. From the 'White Lion' point of view. It's vital that we should know that from the start."

Pegram nodded. He walked to the telephone and dialled. Anthony listened to him. "This is Dr. Pegram speaking. Is Mr. Denton there, please? . . . Thank you. . . . I'll hang on." "He's coming." he whispered to Anthony with his hand over the mouthpiece of the receiver. Anthony nodded understanding. He heard Pegram speaking again. "Good-morning, Mr. Denton. I've an important question to put to you. . . . Yes. . . . I'm afraid it is. . . . That water-butt in your courtyard . . . has it ever been used for storage of wine? Wine—yes. WINE. No. W—W for Walter. That's it, Never as far as you are concerned? You couldn't account then, for the presence of port wine in the water it contained? Thank you very much, Mr. Denton. We may speak to you again about it."

Dr. Pegram put the receiver back into place. He looked at Anthony. "There you are, Bathurst. You heard that. No wine of any kind should have been present in that water-butt. Now what do you make of that."

Anthony shook his head. "Candidly—nothing. It's crazy—all of it. I can only describe it as drowning *de luxe*. What do you make of it, Pegram?"

"Twice as much as you—and the answer's still the same. But there you are. I thought that you ought to know about it."

"Oh—of course. It must mean something. Our job is to find that something."

"I agree. But take the case as we see it. As it appeals to us in its broad lines. Or, if you prefer it, in the only lines of it that we can properly see at the present time. The murderer, intending to drown his victim in a water-butt, either prepares the water by pouring wine into it or pours the wine in *after* the body has been deposited. Touching consideration—if you like. Murder by chivalry."

"You don't *know* that's how it happened."

"I know I don't," returned Pegram good-humouredly, "but I'm willing to listen to your idea of what took place. Point is—have you a better story than mine?"

"That's only fair. But I'm afraid I can't help you. All I would say is this. That the wine has been added to the water for a definite reason. It's not meaningless. It's not gratuitous."

Pegram shrugged his shoulders again. "Does a maniac reason? Isn't the far more likely explanation that it's yet another tangent of a dis-ordered brain? Or *must* you discard the probable and seek the impossibly abnormal?"

Anthony knocked the ash from a cigarette. "Ignoring the cynicism for a moment, I don't *have* to. But if the explanation which you call the ordinary one fails to satisfy my reasoning and my intelligence, then surely I am not bound to accept it." He smiled at Pegram and went on. "On what compulsion must I? Tell me that."

Pegram made no reply. Anthony continued, therefore:

"You asked me just now whether a maniac reasoned. Perhaps not—as you and I understand reasoning power. But very frequently a maniac possesses an inordinate sense of what you and I would probably term 'low cunning.' As an example of that, I'll cite the case of Harold Jones, the Welsh boy who, some years ago, murdered a number of little girls in the same village and who for a considerable period went entirely unsuspected. More than once, after having murdered his victim almost under the eyes of a number of people, he joined with them in the search for the body."

Pegram nodded. "I think I remember something of the case—but I'm far from convinced. Conditions in a Welsh village, as I know them, are very different from conditions in this district. I stick to my maniac."

"And I—with equal confidence in my judgment—reject him. Unequivocally. I can't give you a chapter and verse, but I reject him, nevertheless. And before long, my dear Pegram, I hope to prove you wrong."

Pegram smiled at Anthony's challenge. "Good. In the meantime, though, how about the old question?"

"Which one do you mean?"

"Do you anticipate any more murders?"

Anthony took some time to reply. "That's a difficult question to answer. But I'm afraid the reply must still be 'Yes'. For this reason. That I don't think we can see the definite *plan* behind the murders yet awhile. For that there was a definite plan, I'm absolutely certain."

"Then it's your duty, Bathurst, to stop it. Or them."

Anthony stared at him. "My dear Pegram, you may rest assured that I shall do my best. Don't make any mistake about that."

"And even then, you may not be successful."

"Even then, as you say, I may fail." Anthony looked grave. "My job, you know, is extremely like looking for a needle in a haystack. So you must make allowances."

"I'm willing to do that. But, all the same, I shall expect you to deliver the goods."

Anthony shook him by the hand. "I promise to do my best not to disappoint you."

VIII

Anthony mixed with the occupants of the bar at the 'White Lion.' He had not, on this particular evening, made any contact with Denton. The conversation from almost all the knots of people concerned the latest Mallett murder. After a time, Anthony found himself talking to Richard Cox, one of the men who had been in the dining-saloon of the 'White Lion' on the evening that Norman had walked out to his death. Cox was a farmer with a small farm near Conniss.

"So there's been the third murder, sir," commented the farmer. Anthony noted the description. "Why so definite, Mr. Cox?" he asked. "Why 'the' and not 'a'? One might almost imagine, judging by what you have just said, that you have been waiting for the closing figure of a series?"

Cox's heavy features broke into a smile. "Perhaps I have—in a way. Let me explain myself. I'm country-born and country-bred. Perhaps because of that, I'm inclined to cling to many of our rural beliefs, sayings, and even superstitions. I've always had the idea that things do go in sets of threes. That if you hear of two deaths, you're almost bound to hear tell of a third. There you are, then. When I heard of Bill Norman and after him of King, the baker, I surely said to my missus, 'Mark you, Peggy lass, there'll be a third yet—for sure.' And a third there has been, mister—and it wasn't long in coming, neither."

"I see," responded Anthony. "You weren't particularising. You were just speaking generally. Expressing your own individual ideas."

"That's the ticket, mister; that just about sizes it up."

"You called out 'Good-night' to Norman, didn't you, when he left here on the evening he died?"

"I did that. As I told Inspector Venables when he questioned all of us."

"Yes. I've seen the notes on the case. It was Waghorn, wasn't it, who saw Norman's companion in the bar?"

Cox nodded. "You're quite right. Waghorn reckons he went out to the lavatory and saw Norman in conversation with a stranger in the bar. He described this fellow to Inspector Venables. I can't remember all he said, but I know Waghorn said he wore a gold ring on his left hand."

Anthony nodded. "That's so. You all put him down as a stranger because not one of you knew him."

"It's not a bad reason," put in Cox quietly.

"No, perhaps it isn't. Still perhaps you aren't looking at it in the same way as I am."

"I can't reply to that," said Cox, "because you know more about it all than I do."

"You live at Conniss, don't you?" inquired Anthony.

' 'Yes. Born there and lived there all my life. Like my father and my grandfather before him. I should be lost if I went anywhere else. I love the place and I love my farm. I wouldn't change with anybody."

"I like to hear a man talk like that. How far is your place from Hammeridge?"

Cox took his pipe from his mouth. "Thinking of Clarence?" he said.

"Yes. To a degree."

"Conniss is about four miles from Hammeridge. If you come from Mallett, you pass through Hammeridge to get to Conniss."

"Did you know Clarence, the third dead man, at all?"

Cox shook his head. "No, I was seldom in Hammeridge—except to pass through it—and I don't think that Clarence was a genuine local man. It's not a Hammeridge name."

Anthony raised his eyebrows at the statement. "You're sure of that?"

Cox laughed. "Perfectly, mister. Most of the people in the village of Hammeridge have lived there for generations. And they nearly all spring from about three original families. The Aspinalls, the Hillmans, and the Stennings. You can take it from me that Clarence wasn't a real Hammeridge man. Not a native. I ought to know." His eyes twinkled. "My wife comes from Hammeridge. She was a Hoad. But her mother was an Aspinall. There you are. Now you know why I feel so certain about it."

Anthony put a further question to him. "Do you know Woodmason, mine host of the 'Gardener's Arms'?"

"By sight and reputation. The latter isn't too good, by the way. The name of the 'Gardener's Arms,' Hammeridge, isn't what it might be. From hearsay, of course." He looked at Anthony intently. "Did Clarence use the 'Gardener's Arms'?"

"Yes. So our information goes."

"I suppose he was bound to, when you weigh it up. The other inn, the 'Drum and Monkey,' which is a couple of miles outside Hammeridge, is even worse than the 'Gardener's Arms.'" Cox shook his head. "The whole business bewilders me, mister. I knew Norman as an acquaintance who dined fairly regularly in the 'Lion' here, and I knew Henry King even better than I knew Norman. King was a baker in Mallett ever since I've been farming at Conniss. But I'm darned if I even knew this fellow Clarence. And what Clarence had to do with the other two, God alone knows." Cox repeated the business of shaking his head.

"I agree with you entirely," said Anthony. Cox evidently waited for him to go on. But he was destined for disappointment. For instead of continuing with the opinion that he had just expressed, Anthony countered with another question: "Something you might be able to answer for me, Mr. Cox. Do you happen to know of anybody in the district who is interested in stamp-collecting?"

Cox regarded him curiously. "Well, as it happens, I do."

Anthony felt a little tremor of excitement. "Who is it, Mr. Cox?"

"Waghorn, another old chum of mine. You've met him yourself, Mr. Bathurst. Like me, he was with Norman on the night he was murdered."

"Of course. I remember. Waghorn is the Manager of the Mallett branch of the Western Counties Bank. Is he a keen collector?"

"Very. Sometimes I tell him it's the only thing he ever thinks about. But I'm wondering, mister. Why do you ask? What's the point behind your remark?"

Anthony noticed how bright Cox's eyes had become. He laughed lightly. "Well, to tell the truth, I'm a rather keen philatelist myself and I wondered if I could run up against anybody in the district with a kindred taste."

Cox looked thoroughly unconvinced. "For the moment," he said bluntly, "you made me think you had something on your mind concerning the murders."

"My dear fellow," remonstrated Anthony, "I take a rest from my duties occasionally. Does that fact surprise you?"

"I imagined you fellows were always on the job—so to speak. On the look-out for anything that comes your way."

"That's different," rejoined Anthony.

He looked across the bar and saw Denton talking to Martin Chavasse. The latter caught Anthony's eye and waved cordially to him. Anthony spoke to Cox. "If you'll excuse me, I'll have a word or two with Dr. Chavasse. I rather fancy that he has some news for me."

"Very good, mister," remarked Cox; "and thank you for your company."

IX

Anthony joined Chavasse and Denton. Chavasse shook hands. "Good evening, Bathurst. Well, how are things? I'm sure you'll extend your forgiveness if I say, 'I told you so.'" He laughed. "On second thoughts, I won't say it. I'll merely hint at it."

"Clarence, you mean, Doctor?"

Chavasse nodded. "I said the list of victims wasn't complete, didn't I?"

Anthony smiled. "That was only one of your predictions, Doctor."

"A-ha! Still unconvinced and argumentative—eh? 'Pon my soul, you professionals do take some wearing down."

His tone was so good-humoured that Anthony was incapable of feeling resentment. He riposted, however: "On a point of order— I'm not a professional—I'm what I believe is usually and popularly referred to as a 'bloomin' amateur.'"

"That's a good one, Bathurst. Still—I deserved it. What are you drinking?"

Anthony ordered a beer and, with Denton and Chavasse, went to a quiet table away from most of the crowd in the bar.

"What do you know about the Clarence affair?" asked Anthony.

"Only what Pegram has told me," replied Chavasse. "And don't be surprised at that," he added, "it has been his habit for years to pour his troubles and worries into my receptive ear."

"Have you seen MacMorran?" queried Anthony.

"Good Lord—no! Actually I've been exceptionally busy. Been running quite a glut of quinsy cases. I came over this evening to meet Pegram. He asked me to meet him here, as a matter of fact." He looked at his watch. "I'm a trifle early for him."

"What, then, do you think of the Clarence affair, Doctor?"

"You already know," replied Chavasse with dogged imperturbability. "Same as Pegram, only more so. I say that because I think that my idea influenced him a little in the first instance—when we discussed the Norman case—the Hot Cinders murder. Homicidal maniac! Personally, I don't harbour the slightest shred of a doubt." He lit his pipe.

"I argued that out with Pegram."

"Don't I know! I heard nothing else." Chavasse turned to Denton. "Extraordinary thing, Denton—how your 'White Lion' keeps coming in the picture. I've an idea, by the way, about that."

Denton smiled ruefully. "I'd be interested to hear it. Another murder and I may be out of business."

Anthony, rather pointedly looked round the bar. "I don't notice any particular diminution of devotion, Denton. The faithful appear to be present in rather impressive numbers."

Denton waved the remark to one side and addressed himself to Dr. Chavasse. "Anyhow, Doctor, as I said, I'm interested to hear your theory of the 'White Lion' being mixed up in these affairs. What is it?"

Chavasse laughed. "Only an idea of my own. Entirely my own." He laughed again. "What I believe is this. The murderer, whoever he may be, has a definite grudge against somebody here. Somebody, if you like, closely connected with the establishment. Say yourself— just as an example. To do with some grievance—in all probability a purely imaginary one. This, allied to his unstable and disordered mental condition, has caused him to vent his spleen as it were upon these four walls. Like a child, who in deliberate and malicious anger, vindictively destroys something or messes something up. To show his power and, at the same time, to denote his contempt. Burglars of a low type, have, I believe, a singularly objectionable habit of leaving behind most unpleasant evidences of their visit. Each time our murderer murders, he either commences or comes back as one might say, to sully the 'White Lion' doorstep."

Chavasse turned to Anthony. "Well, Bathurst, and what's your reaction to that?"

Anthony shook his head. "I don't know that I agree with you. Once again."

Chavasse's eyes held the light of banter. "Why not?"

"For this reason." Anthony chose his words carefully. "That if our murderer held the grievance that you have depicted, I should expect him to wreak his anger upon *people* connected with the 'White Lion' and not upon the place itself. Upon the animate and not upon the inanimate. Upon the living entities who he imagines have injured him, whom he can see and hear. Not in a soulless revenge directed against an edifice of bricks and mortar."

Chavasse broke in upon him impatiently. "But the man's mad, I tell you. He's not normal. You're describing what a *normal* man might be expected to do. You wilfully blind yourself to the almost certain fact that the man's off his mental balance. Which makes every bit of difference."

Denton closured the discussion with his next remark. "Here's Dr. Pegram and Waghorn with him. It's a gathering of the clans this evening—and no mistake."

The Divisional Surgeon and the bank manager made their way to the table which Anthony and the others were occupying. Denton provided chairs for them.

"I've been waiting for you, Pegram," said Martin Chavasse. "What's the news?"

"I've got some," replied Pegram, "but it will keep."

Anthony's eyes met his and he thought that he understood. In the meantime, Anthony studied Waghorn. The latter smiled at him cheerfully. "I wanted to see you, Mr. Bathurst," he said with disarming candour, "because I've just had a word with Dick Cox. He tells me that you fancy yourself a little in the realm of philately. Is that true, or have I been misinformed?"

Anthony was instantly on his guard. This opening had come over suddenly and was almost, as he whimsically put it to himself, too true to be good.

"Only a little," he admitted defensively. "I'm afraid my enthusiasm outdistances my knowledge."

Waghorn nodded eagerly. "If we admit the truth, that applies, I expect, to most of us." Then he winked prodigiously, leant forward to Anthony and in a stage whisper said jocularly, "I suppose your collection doesn't house the 'Blue Mauritius' or the 1-cent British Guiana of 1856?"

Anthony knew just enough to shake his head and say, "I should say not," before Chavasse intervened with scant ceremony:

"You and your pansy stamps! Why the hell don't you grow up and put away childish things? You'll be discussing Hornby trains next."

Denton rose and left the table. Waghorn turned on Chavasse good-humouredly. "Have you ever heard me gas about my stamps? Because I'll say you haven't. I never obtrude *my* personal idiosyncrasies. I never let myself get that far out of hand. Now be fair and admit the truth of what I say."

Chavasse laughed and said rather boisterously: "All right, my dear chap—have it your way." Then he caught Anthony's eye across the table, partly understood what was required of him and subsided into silence. Waghorn came back to Anthony.

"Now, Mr. Bathurst, I'll pass on to you a morsel of most extraordinary news."

"What is that?" inquired Anthony.

Waghorn smiled enigmatically. Waghorn pushed his face a little nearer. It exuded beatific self-satisfaction.

"What do you think happened to me yesterday?"

"I haven't the slightest idea."

"I had a complete stamp collection given to me! Worth quite a bit, too, if I'm any judge."

Anthony's finger-tips tingled. "Who gave it to you?" he asked with casual nonchalance.

Waghorn slapped his hand on his thigh. "Well—that's the most remarkable part about it! I don't know!"

"You don't know?"

"No. The affair was sent to me by post."

"Who sent it?"

Waghorn shook his head. "Don't know, I tell you. It came anonymously. No clue at all to the sender. In a brown-paper parcel with a piece of string round it. Now what do you make of that! Nearly as mysterious as these murders—eh?"

Waghorn sat back and almost chuckled. Anthony was nonplussed. He temporised.

"And you've really no idea from whom or whence it came?"

"Not the foggiest. All I can say is that it's very charming of somebody to remember me in such a fashion. For, believe me, I'm thoroughly grateful."

"Must be somebody you know, surely. Somebody living near here who knows your particular interest. What was the post-mark, Mr. Waghorn?"

"Oh—that was local, I admit! Mallett!"

Anthony kept himself well in hand. He spoke to Chavasse. "Unknown benefactors now appear to be at large. Dispensing philanthropy far and wide. Did you hear Waghorn's story?"

Chavasse who had been talking to Pegram, looked up when he heard Anthony's voice. "What was that you said, Bathurst? I'm afraid that I wasn't listening."

Anthony induced Waghorn to repeat his story of the anonymous donation. The two doctors listened with great interest. But when the bank manager had reached the final point of his story, Pegram shook his head. The gesture appeared to be somewhat critical. Anthony soon saw in which direction the criticism was implied. Pegram spoke:

"I think that the explanation of what you've just told me will prove to be eminently simple. It will turn out to be this. That the person who sent you the gift of the stamp collection forgot to enclose the necessary letter. Which it's pretty certain will arrive later. It must be a friend of yours residing in this district."

Anthony kept quiet so that Waghorn. might reply., "Do you think so?" said the bank manager with doubt in his tone.

"Ten to one on it," responded the Divisional Surgeon. He turned to Martin Chavasse. "What do you think, Chavasse?"

"I don't know," rejoined Chavasse. "It depends. How many people in the district knew of this gentleman's hobby? Was it well-known? Seems to me it depends largely on that."

"I think it was pretty well-known," said Waghorn. "I've a fairly large circle of acquaintance."

"There you are," said Pegram triumphantly. "You'll find I'm right—I haven't the least doubt."

Anthony looked at his watch. "Well, I shall have to be leaving you, I'm afraid. I want a word with MacMorran before I hit the hay tonight."

He spoke pointedly and Pegram sensed his meaning. After Anthony had left the table, Pegram rose with a muttered apology and came over to join him.

"I can't let you go, Bathurst, without passing on certain information to you. I gave you an inkling that I had some when I joined you this evening. But I wasn't spilling it over there—I 'spied strangers,' as you might say."

"Yes. I knew you had something for me," said Anthony. "Is it about Clarence?"

Pegram smiled and nodded. "It is, Bathurst. And it's damned interesting—say what you like about it. You listen. I did a P.M. on Clarence this afternoon. I noticed something which made me inordinately curious. What do you think I found, Bathurst? Fancy yourself at guesswork?"

"It won't be guesswork," replied Anthony slowly. "Anyhow, I'll have a shot at it. You found that Clarence was in an advanced stage of tuberculosis. Well—do I get my penny back?"

Pegram whistled under his breath. "You do, by George! One of the worst cases I've ever seen. Much too far gone even for an A.P. But I'm dashed if I know how you did it."

"Two reasons," said Anthony laconically. "One—I expected something of the sort, and two—I thought he looked as though tuberculosis was his likeliest malady. In addition, you hinted at it yourself."

"Well—you're right—never mind how you arrived at your conclusions. But it's all darned peculiar. Three of 'em murdered in a row. And no insurance company would as much as have looked at one of 'em. Coincidence? I wonder. Well—you want to get away. Tell MacMorran what I've just told you."

Anthony shook hands with him before turning to wave as he walked up the road.

X

Anthony found Andrew MacMorran at the inn where they were staying.

"Andrew," he said quietly, "I want a talk with you. Behold in me the bearer of news."

"Good,?" inquired the Inspector curtly.

Anthony shook his head. "Can't honestly give it 'good,' Andrew. Call it 'important' and I'm with you."

"What is it?"

"Listen, my super-sleuth! What do you know about the Clarence stamp collection?"

"No more than you. Only that Clarence was out to sell it. And probably did—to the man who murdered him. Whom he met at the 'Gardener's Arms,' Hammeridge. You'll give me full marks for that, won't you, Mr. Bathurst?"

Anthony grinned. "I don't know about that. Anyhow, I know the man who's got the stamp collection in his possession at the present moment. What have you got to say to that, my not so merry Andrew?"

"What?" cried MacMorran. "What's that you say? Out with the story, man, before I lose all my patience." '

"See here, Andrew, and listen here in addition. Remember Septimus Waghorn?"

"Ay—very well! Bank manager, working in Mallett. Uses the 'White Lion.' What about him?"

"Only that he has the Clarence stamp collection."

MacMorran whistled. "Has he now! And how do you come to know that, may I ask?"

"A simple answer yet again. Waghorn told me so."

"Told you so himself?"

"Ah-ha! Not more than an hour ago."

MacMorran stared at him incredulously. "What explanation did he give you?"

Anthony shrugged his shoulders. "Merely—that it had been a gift to him."

"From whom?"

"That information he can't give."

"Can't give? What do you mean by that?"

"Exactly what I say, Andrew. Waghorn states that the gift was forwarded to him by post and that the donor was anonymous."

MacMorran whistled again. "Pretty thin story—to my way of thinking. Don't know what you think about it."

"Don't quite know what to think. I'll admit, though, that I'm disturbed."

"Why?"

"Well—I was talking to Cox, the farmer member of the 'White Lion' contingent, during the earlier part of the evening. And, during the conversation we had, Cox told me that Waghorn was interested in stamp-collecting. Naturally, I pricked up my ears at that morsel of savoury information. It was exactly what I was looking out for. Imagine my interest, therefore, when Waghorn blows along a little later, tells me first of all about his hobby and then spills the amazing box of beans that he has the Clarence stamp collection. In the circumstances that I have just described."

MacMorran held his breath. "Let me get this straight. If Waghorn told you that he had the Clarence collection—"

"But he didn't! I'll make a clean breast of it. He said, 'A complete collection has been sent to me.' But don't worry, Andrew. It's the Clarence collection all right, never fear."

"Sure of it?"

"Positive. It's a thousand to one on it."

But MacMorran was persistent. "But why? What makes you so certain of it?"

"My dear Andrew, consider it for yourself. Take the time-question alone. It's so absolutely and psychologically sound. Rings true all the way. I don't ask any question of it! Clarence—'White Lion'—Waghorn—there's the undoubted sequence for you. Logical, complementary and entirely coherent. Clarence goes to the 'Gardener's Arms' to sell a stamp collection. Clarence's body is found in a water-butt on the premises of the 'White Lion' at Mallett. The stamp collection which must have left Clarence gets to Waghorn, who uses the 'White Lion' and who used it on the days when both Norman and King were murdered. *And* the parcel which contained the collection has the Mallett postmark on it. Why, Andrew, man, there isn't the vestige of a doubt about it. Any other idea would be positively unthinkable."

Anthony, having unburdened himself thus, lit a cigarette and offered the case to the Inspector. The latter kept silent for a few minutes.

"Waghorn," he said at length. "Waghorn, the bank manager! I can't make it out." He turned to Anthony. "You say that Cox told you about Waghorn's interest in stamps?"

"Quite right."

"What happened after that?"

"I lied, my dear Andrew. Say rather I tinkered with the pellucid truth. I assumed an interest and a knowledge of the art of philately which, alas! honest confession forces me to admit I don't possess. But it was enough to convince Cox."

MacMorran nodded. "I get you. Go on."

"Some little time after that, Cox and I parted company. But not for long. For when I was sitting with Pegram and Chavasse, Cox turned up again. Note carefully, Andrew, with whom he arrived. He was accompanied by Waghorn."

More nodding from MacMorran. "What came next?"

"Ah—now we come to grips with it. Waghorn immediately opened out on stamps, stamps—and still more stamps. Imagining, of course, from what Cox, the famer had told him, that I was a similar devotee and in like condition. From that point the transition was excessively simple. He leant over and announced to me that he had just been the recipient of a gift of a stamp collection. Which fragment of news intrigued me immensely, as you may guess. There you are, Andrew— there you have the score to the fall of the last wicket. In proper sequence and order. Now it's up to you to make what you can of it."

MacMorran smiled ruefully. "Sounds all right. Ve-ry tasty. Ve-ry sweet. But I'm not jumpin' to any conclusions. Same as you, if I'm any judge, Mr. Bathurst."

He looked at Anthony as though inviting either a denial or an agreement. Anthony grinned at him—but said nothing. MacMorran tossed away the stub of his cigarette and took out his pipe. Anthony let him fill it before he spoke again.

"In addition to all that, Andrew, I have this piece of news for you."

"What—more of it? Have a heart, Mr. Bathurst—or you'll have me running round in circles."

"Listen, Andrew. According to information passed on to me by Dr. Pegram, the dead man Clarence was in an advanced stage of tuberculosis."

"In other words—his number was up?"

"Very much 'up', if you ask me, Andrew."

Anthony lit another cigarette and drew at it steadily. MacMorran shot at him a quick, quizzical glance.

"As per the previous samples—eh?"

"Exactly. Three in a row again! *Hat tricks de luxe.* Three deaths. All violent. Three 'White Lions.' Three men all ailing—almost to the point of an imminent decease. Anything strike you about that conclusion, Andrew?"

"Anything!" MacMorran audibly snorted. "I should find it difficult to pick out *one* thing! Much more like three bags full—surely?" Anthony spoke reminiscently. "Diseased heart, malignant internal growth and this time—just ordinary T.B. What shall we call it, Andrew—euthanasia in reverse? For that's how it almost strikes me."

MacMorran shook his head. "The more I see of it, the more I find myself coming round to Dr. Pegram's idea. That we're up against a homicidal maniac. The crimes are purposeless. They lead nowhere. Nobody gains anything as a result of their commission."

"Just a minute. As far as you know, Andrew," remonstrated Anthony quietly. "And that makes a hell of a lot of difference."

"I agree. But what we don't know—we *don't* know. And it's no use running about conjecturing things."

"Again—that's only true up to a point. What we don't know—it's our business to endeavour to know. And that's another matter of difference."

MacMorran smiled ruefully. "Tearing me off a strip—eh?"

"Not quite that. Merely attempting to guide the ship a little." Anthony pressed out the stub of his cigarette in the ash-tray. MacMorran spoke again: "I can't get my mind off that Waghorn business. I'm inclined to think that he tried to pull a fast one. Took the war deliberately into your camp, as it were. Came over all innocent and artless. He realised the significance of the Clarence stamp collection and played a piece of sheer, unadulterated bluff. What do you think of my idea, Mr. Bathurst?"

"Don't know! Not decided. Got to weigh up several matters I'm not yet certain about. But I'll tell you what I would like to know, Andrew."

"What's that?"

"The real value of the Clarence collection. In terms of hard blatant £ s. d." His eyes held a far-away look as he spoke.

MacMorran gave him another side-long glance. "Why—do you think it's worth a lot?"

"It *might* be, Andrew! For all we know. It's on the cards, I suppose, that it's worth the dickens of a lot. The job is how to find out. Proves how limited knowledge is always a handicap. Unless we can get a third party interested, we're in Waghorn's hands. He can declare it's worth a couple of thousand quid—on the other hand, he may say it isn't worth a box of kippers."

MacMorran nodded. "I agree entirely. But, as I see things, there's another possibility which it would be unwise for us to disregard."

"What's that, Andrew?"

"That the murderer, whoever he may be, *planted* the collection on to Waghorn. Knowing, of course, that Waghorn was interested, and that directly he got it, the finger of suspicion would at once point towards him."

Anthony screwed up his forehead. "You may be right, of course. But somehow that doesn't make sense, Andrew. Why steal it—or buy it, if you like—assuming that the transaction with Clarence was all fair and above-board—to dispose of it immediately? I don't know that I can get the point of that."

MacMorran scratched his chin. "Does seem dopey, I admit. But there you are. Criminals—especially murderers—often do senseless things."

"Yes," murmured Anthony drily. "Including the murder itself."

"Well—there you are," supplemented MacMorran with a shrug of his shoulders. "It's an idea. You can please yourself about it—take it or leave it."

Anthony made no immediate reply. MacMorran watched him closely. He saw that a different expression had come over Anthony Bathurst's face.

"Well?" he inquired, as though prompting him. "Got something?"

"Not sure, Andrew; but as you said, it's an idea, and maybe there's something in it. I may even come round to your way of thinking. And I'm forced to remember this, also. We've recently touched both Cox and Waghorn. But five people were wont to dine with Norman, the first man to be murdered. The remaining three were Marnoch, King and Hardwick. Of them, King has travelled the same road as Norman. Leaving again, for our consideration, Hardwick and Marnoch. Birds of strongly dissimilar plumage, you will note. Hardwick's Deputy Town Clerk of Mallett and Marnoch's, I believe, a retired Inspector of Police. That's down your street, Andrew. Know anything about him?"

MacMorran shook his head. "Can't say that I do. Name's not famil-iar to me. But I can easily remedy that. I can make discreet inquiries."

"I am sure," said Anthony with a smile, "that the adjective is redundant. But I shall be obliged if you will—and pass on to me whatever you pick up. As soon as you like. For I find myself interested in *all* that the 'White Lion' has to offer me. And that goes for both dining and wining personnel."

MacMorran frowned. "Yes. I agree again; but there's one point we mustn't forget. When King was poisoned in the luncheon-room of the 'White Lion' and the 'phoney' electrician came into the dining-saloon to do his stuff, Cox, Waghorn, Hardwick and Marnoch were all present. I've checked up three times on that. It looks as though, from that fact alone, that they're let out."

"I wonder," replied Anthony, walking towards the Inspector. He grinned ruefully. "Seems to me, Andrew, that I'm being guilty of the very misdemeanour of which I heard you complain a little time ago."

"What was that, Mr. Bathurst—may I ask?"

"Running round in circles! Large and ever-widening circles. And it don't please me, Andrew! In fact I might almost say that it definitely depresses me."

Anthony stopped suddenly in his tracks and faced MacMorran.

"But to-morrow is also a day, Andrew—and to-morrow is certain to be here—whereas yesterday has both come and gone."

CHAPTER V

I

IT MUST be recorded with some degree of criticism, possibly, that the 'White Lion murders' case was the first in the whole of Anthony Lotherington Bathurst's career as a criminologist which he was forced to relinquish. And it is more than probable—indeed, it is almost certain—that had not the fourth murder taken place, another man would have died, the murderer would have remained undetected and the case written off by Anthony and Andrew MacMorran as a lamentable failure.

Anthony left the case during the second week in May. Nearly two months since Norman had screamed in the death car and Constable Wragg had heard him. He abandoned it for the stark reason that not a satisfactory clue came to him during the time that he spent in Mallett which supported substantially any one of the theories he had regarded as even temporarily attractive. Several likely clues raised their heads and received his attention, but every one petered out, and eventually Anthony returned to Town and left the problem for the time being to the tender mercies of Inspectors MacMorran and Venables.

But on the eighth day of June, Anthony returned in haste to the West-Country town of Mallett. On an urgent call from Sir Austin Kemble, Commissioner of Police, New Scotland Yard, who asked Anthony to return to MacMorran, Venables and Mallett, *statim*, *pronto*, post-haste or what you will.

MacMorran and Venables met Anthony on the platform at Mallett Station, and he could tell at once from the expressions on their faces that the news was grave and that he had not been recalled merely for the purpose of eating a lunch in the saloon at the 'White Lion.'

As Anthony stepped from his compartment on to the platform, a thought came to him which almost caused him to hold his breath. Clarence! Now why the devil hadn't he thought of that angle before? He ought to be kicked from Dan to Beersheba for crass negligence and idiotic forgetfulness. He must repair at once the appalling—but MacMorran's voice put an end to his self-castigation and brought him back to earth again immediately.

"Good afternoon, Mr. Bathurst," the Inspector was saying. "Here's Inspector Venables with me. We're downright glad to see you, believe me; but, to come to the point at once, we've damned bad news for you."

"Thank you, Andrew. Good afternoon. Inspector. Now tell me the worst and get it over. Who is it this time? Anybody I know?"

Venables shook his head. "No, Mr. Bathurst. It's a lad murdered this time."

"Where?"

"His body was found on a settee in the smoke-room of the 'White Lion' this morning."

It was MacMorran who answered, and he spoke with a quiet deliberation and gravity which impressed Anthony directly he heard the words. "How was the lad killed?"

"Of that we are not sure," replied MacMorran slowly.

"Why? How do you mean exactly?"

"Dr. Pegram's at work now. Some method, in all probability, of asphyxiation."

"How old was this boy?"

"About eleven, I believe."

"Local boy?"

"Don't know yet. Venables doesn't think so."

"How did he get into the smoke-room of the 'White Lion?'"

"Again, we don't know. From what I've seen of the case so far, his body must have been brought there."

Anthony knitted his brows. "It's the same old 'White Lion,' you see. This is the fourth in succession."

MacMorran shook his head with gloomy despondency. "The whole thing beats me. Beats me to a frazzle."

"What was the name of the murdered boy?"

"Richard Yorke."

"Healthy?"

"As far as I know—up to the moment. Pegram, no doubt, will tell us more about that later on."

Anthony thought over things. "If you don't know where he lives, how did you find out the boy's name?"

MacMorran grinned and Venables smiled. "Been expecting that question," exclaimed the former. "But the explanation is simple. There's a picture postcard in his jacket pocket. Which isn't addressed and hasn't been through the post. On it is scrawled in a childish hand: 'To Dickie Yorke—many happy returns of the day—May 26th.'"

Venables chimed in: "I've told Chief-Inspector MacMorran, Mr. Bathurst, that the dead boy may have been intending to *send* the card. To another boy. In other words, that he'd written the message—himself—but Scotland Yard doesn't agree with me."

Anthony gave him a sharp glance. "I agree with MacMorran's view, Inspector Venables."

"I formed my conclusion by consideration of the date," said MacMorran.

"I agree," returned Anthony. "The weight of odds is that, seeing the date is past, the card was sent to this dead boy and that his name is Yorke. If he were intending to send the card, the date would certainly be a future one."

"Exactly as I figured it," added MacMorran drily.

"Who found the body?" demanded Anthony.

"A maid. By name of Burgess. She was concerned, if you remember, with the body in the water-butt."

"First on the scene of things, of course. And the body was on a settee, you say, in the 'White Lion' smoke-room?"

"You've got it."

"Fully dressed?"

"Absolutely."

"Any news been received by the Police, Inspector Venables, in relation to a missing boy?"

"Not up to the time when I came away from the station. We shall probably hear more when we get back there."

Anthony relapsed into silence. Norman, King, Clarence and now a boy. About eleven years of age. It seemed, more than ever now, that Chavasse's theory must be the correct one. A farmer, a baker, an unemployable, and now a boy. What was the common factor underlying the four crimes? Clarence! Anthony thought of the stamp collection again and of his interview by invitation with the Chief Constable. This reverie was interrupted by their arrival at the Police Station at Mallett. At this moment, by a coincidence, Police-Constable Wragg made his second entry on to the stage of the particular drama.

"Information through about the dead boy, Inspector," he said addressing himself to Venables. "From the mother. His name's Richard Yorke all right. Been missing since five o'clock yesterday afternoon. Lives in a village about ten miles from here. Beyond Hammeridge, North Zelly."

MacMorran and Anthony listened with the local Inspector to what Wragg had to tell them. "Good," said MacMorran. "Now we know and we've done surmising. Another village implicated now. Will you contact Mrs. Yorke, Venables?"

Venables nodded. "I'd better, I suppose. But first of all, let's hear what Dr. Pegram has to say."

Anthony was a little uncertain as to what action he had better take. Venables soon reassured him. The local Inspector beckoned to

MacMorran and to him to follow. Anthony and Andrew MacMorran went in his wake and entered the mortuary, where Anthony could see Pegram standing at a few yards' distance. The Divisional Surgeon gestured to the others to come forward to join him. The three men moved forward into the apartment. Pegram's face was a trifle flushed as he advanced to meet them.

"Well, Doctor?" inquired MacMorran. "And what have you got to tell us?"

Pegram's mouth twisted into a crooked smile. "Wasn't a difficult matter—this latest job. I found in that dead boy over there, the exact condition which I expected to find when I started the P.M. I'll be very frank with you. I anticipated finding status lymphaticus—lymphatism."

MacMorran nodded rather impatiently. "All right, Doctor. Go on, please."

Anthony listened intently. Pegram continued:

"He was a pale, weak, rickety child and he died suddenly. I should say from an apparently moderately trivial cause. Which I'll discuss with you a little later if you'll be patient with me and hear me out."

His three companions nodded. Pegram went on again.

"There is great enlargement of the thymus and of the lymphatic glands throughout the interior of the boy's body. I doubt very much whether he would have stood up to the slightest of operations or taken even an ordinary anaesthetic." Pegram spread out his hands. "So there you are, gentlemen. There you have my findings in a nut-shell."

There was a silence of a few seconds' duration. Eventually Anthony came to the most important point. "And assimilating all that, Dr. Pegram, what in your opinion was this moderately trivial cause which brought about the lad's death?"

Pegram showed some hesitation before he answered. "Well," he said quietly and steadily, "I think he was smothered by something like a cushion or a pillow."

It is an understatement to record that Anthony and the two Police Inspectors were surprised at Pegram's opinion.

"Little violence, I suppose, need have been used—judging by what you have just said, Doctor?"

The question came from MacMorran.

Pegram was emphatic. "Very little indeed, Inspector MacMorran. The shock and even just gentle pressure would, in my opinion, have been enough."

Anthony became practical. "What was it exactly, Doctor, which brought you to that opinion? With regard to a cushion? I presume that you are doing something more than merely guessing?"

The Divisional Surgeon smiled again. "Your presumption's right, Bathurst. Look at this and you'll understand."

Pegram walked over to a shelf in the corner of the mortuary. He came back with a small something lying on the palm of his left hand. The others looked closely at it. Anthony saw a tiny, flimsy strand of pink silk.

"I took this," continued Pegram quietly, "from a corner of the dead boy's mouth."

Anthony and the two Inspectors examined it carefully. "I think you're right, Doctor," declared MacMorran. He swung round to Anthony. "What do you say, Mr. Bathurst?"

Anthony took the tiny piece of silk between his fingers. "Yes, Andrew—like you, I'm inclined to agree with Dr. Pegram."

He handed the silken particle on to Inspector Venables. The local Inspector examined it and quickly expressed his agreement with the others. Pegram took the wisp of silk and proceeded to demonstrate.

"A silk cushion, in all probability, was pressed on the boy's mouth and he was smothered. And as I said to you just now, it didn't require much violence or pressure on the boy's mouth, seeing his condition, to cause his death. There you are gentlemen. I can't tell you any more." MacMorran thrust his hands into his pockets and shook his head despondently. "As far as I am concerned," he said almost lugubriously, "the case goes from bad to worse. It holds neither rhyme nor reason. It is motiveless. It grows more—"

Anthony interrupted him. "Out of pattern—eh Andrew?"

"I should say so. A medley. A hotch-potch. Norman burnt in the car, King poisoned, Clarence drowned in the water-butt and now this boy smothered by a pink silk cushion. It won't piece together at all. There's only one solution to it. And you've heard it before. A homicidal maniac. I can make no other suggestion."

He turned away, a touch of impatience. Anthony and Inspector Venables remained silent. The former would have found it difficult to demolish Andrew's contention. Venables was thinking that it was up to his duty to get into touch with Mrs. Yorke of North Zelly as speedily as possible. When the experts of Scotland Yard spoke as they did, who was he to enter into argument? Anthony spoke to MacMorran.

"I'd like to see the boy's body, Andrew. Take me along to it, will you?"

"Over here, Mr. Bathurst. Come while Dr. Pegram's still in session." The two men went over to the Divisional Surgeon. Pegram turned down the sheet and Anthony found himself looking at the features of the dead boy. He saw a pale, thin, frail, under-nourished child. Pegram saw what Anthony was thinking.

"Yes. He's not a robust specimen, is he? Afraid he doesn't come of sound stock. Parents in poor circumstances. Little doubt about that. Have a look at his clothes over there! Boots and stockings as well." Anthony followed the direction of Pegram's gesture and saw a heap of clothes hanging over the back of a chair. The suit was of poor quality and had been worn threadbare. The cheap, multi-coloured tie was ragged in places, stained and creased. The boots needed repairing badly. The shirt and pants had been patched many times in an almost abortive attempt to add to the length of their lives. There were holes in the stockings both in legs and toes. Anthony felt that it was unnecessary for him to take a second look. Pegram's remarks were entirely justified. "Anything in the pockets?" he asked of MacMorran.

"The card I told you about, two coins—a penny and a ha'penny—a soiled handkerchief, a penknife—blades broken—and a fairly long piece of string."

"For his age," remarked Anthony, "a collection that may be termed moderately representative."

"I agree, Mr. Bathurst." MacMorran showed a tendency to hang about. Anthony noticed it. He translated his observation into words. "What's particularly worrying you. Andrew?"

"Particularly?" asked the Inspector in return and not without heat. "Rather ask me what in hell isn't? Candidly, I don't know which way to turn. As it is, I think I'll wait until Venables comes back from North Zelly before I take my next definite step."

He looked at Anthony as though inviting either approval or disagreement. Anthony gave the former.

"All right, Andrew. You wait for Venables. In a way, you're almost bound to. I'll see you later. With regard to what Venables picks up at the lad's home."

MacMorran nodded. "That's O.K. by me. What's your personal programme, though, in the meantime?"

Before he replied, Anthony rubbed his chin reflectively with his fore-finger. "I'm going over to Sandals."

MacMorran's glance was interrogative. "Why? What for?"

Anthony grinned. "I was afraid you'd ask me that. And my answer's going to be, 'I don't quite know.' But I do know this—it's to do with Clarence, the corpse in the 'White Lion' water-butt."

MacMorran looked surprised at Anthony's answer. "Clarence?"

"Ah-ha, Andrew."

"What's the Chief Constable to do with Clarence?"

"Don't know again, Andrew. But I'm going to try to find out."

II

Anthony was fortunate enough to find Sir Charles Stuart at home. After appropriate inquiry, he was ushered into the presence of the Chief Constable. Sir Charles rose to greet him. Anthony could see at a glance that he looked grey and grave.

"Hallo, Bathurst—didn't know I was due for this pleasure."

Anthony smiled at him. "I didn't know it myself, sir, until about an hour ago."

"Really? Well—that's an eye-opener. But I presume you've run into something important. What's it to do with—the fourth murder?"

Anthony shook his head. "No, Sir Charles. I haven't been on that much more than a couple of hours."

Stuart made a gesture of dismay. "Nasty case. Very nasty. From some—er—angles, the worst one possibly of all. But I'm digressing. I haven't heard about you yet."

Sir Charles walked back to the seat he had been previously occupying. He waved Anthony into a chair facing him. "Now, Bathurst, let's have it. What's your inquiry?"

There came a slight interval of silence. Eventually, Anthony found relevant words. "I've come to ask you about Clarence."

Sir Charles looked up—a little startled. "Clarence?" he repeated. Anthony nodded in confirmation.

"Yes, Sir Charles. In the first place, I must confess to a piece of appalling negligence."

Up went the Chief Constable's eyebrows. "Negligence? I'm afraid that I don't quite—"

Anthony raised his hand. "Your patience, Sir Charles. Even though there are no cards to shuffle. Bear with me, please, for a moment or so. I will endeavour to explain to you wherein my negligence lay. It was a fault of omission."

The Chief Constable stared at him wonderingly. Anthony went on: "It occurred in this way. When the body was taken from the water-butt in the courtyard of the 'White Lion' and it was identified as the body of George Clarence, for some reason which is still obscure to me and for which I am flagrantly culpable, the name made little or no impression upon me. Or rather upon my memory. It may have been that the circumstances of the crime were so unusual, and if I may say so, remarkable, that my mind was occupied with them, to the entire exclusion of almost everything else."

Anthony paused. The Chief Constable waited for him to continue. "But eventually—I regret the dimensions of the delay—a wave of memory brought a wisp of fact back to me."

"And er . . . what was that . . . Bathurst, may I ask?"

"A remnant of conversation that we had together, Sir Charles, upon the occasion when you were kind enough to extend an invitation to me to dine here. With you and Lady Stuart."

As he finished the sentence, Anthony noticed that Sir Charles's face was clearing. And though he was annoyed with himself to admit it, the fact somewhat disconcerted him.

"Of course," came in Sir Charles. "I know exactly to what you are about to refer. I mentioned the name 'Clarence' to you. Before we went in to dinner, wasn't it?"

Anthony inclined his head. "I rather fancy it was. You mentioned that a woman had made certain representations to you earlier on that same day. You expressed some degree of irritation at the incident."

Sir Charles coughed. "I did. The woman is an old offender in that particular respect. But what's all this got to do with the murder of the other Clarence? 'Pon my soul, Bathurst, I don't know where all this is leading to."

"I am merely seeking information, sir. It's possible, of course, that I'm entirely on the wrong track. But I've been toying with the idea that there may be an entanglement somewhere."

The Chief Constable shook his head decisively. "Forget it. Dismiss the idea. You are barking up the wrong tree. My Mrs. Clarence—if I may describe her in that way—keeps a fried-fish shop in Mallett High Street. Her husband is named Albert Clarence. As I previously indicated to you, Albert is a bad egg. A backslider. Work-shy! Hates the sight of it, the thought of it, or even the sound of its name. Some two or three years ago—I'm not sure as to the exact date—I was influential in getting him a job with the Mallett Council. Painting white lines on the main roads as a help to traffic. But he failed to hold the job down. He was late—regularly—slack with his work and more than once, I understand, he painted a side line with the middle brush."

Anthony grinned. Stuart continued: "So they sacked him, on the recommendation of the Highways foreman. With this sequel. Mrs. Clarence convinced herself that Albert was the victim of a persecution and that all, the employers in the town were allied in a sinister sort of conspiracy to keep him out of employment." Sir Charles laughed in immoderate gusts. "At least that was how she put it. And of late she has conceived the idea of waylaying me at every presentable opportunity and pleading Albert's cause and case. There you are, Bathurst—there you have the Clarence story as far as I know Albert Clarence."

Anthony pondered over the information the Chief Constable had given to him. At length he translated his doubt into words.

"And is there no possible connection between the Clarences of Mallett and the Clarences of Hammeridge?"

Sir Charles Stuart pursed his lips. "Well—that's asking me to answer something, isn't it? As far as I know—there is no connection. What induces you to think there is?"

Anthony shook his head. "I don't think there is. I merely thought that there might be. I was forced to consider the possibility. You see,

Sir Charles, it would be criminal of me to neglect anything, no matter how trivial it might appear to be!" He rubbed the ridge of his jaw.

"I agree," assented the Chief Constable. "I agree with you entirely. But I'm afraid there's nothing for you out of the Clarence coincidence. For that's all it is—I assure you, my dear Bathurst."

Anthony seemed unconvinced. "Tell me, Sir Charles, is Clarence a territorial name in this neighbourhood? Are there many of them?"

Sir Charles looked a little lost at the question. "Well—I don't know as to that, Bathurst. I don't know that there's such an almighty lot of them—come to that! I've certainly run across the name once or twice in the district and the vicinity, but that's about all. These people we're discussing may be cousins of one another and all the time oblivious of the fact. That's a condition which often appertains with members of the same family. I've often found it to be so."

Anthony felt that he must concede the truth of this statement. "Yes. I suppose that's so, Sir Charles. And that, after all, I've journeyed over here on a wild-goose chase."

"Never mind. Your voyage hasn't necessarily been a wasted one. At any rate, you're clear on a point now—concerning which you were previously not clear. And that's all to the good. You must admit that. Good-bye, Bathurst." Sir Charles Stuart extended his hand.

"Good-bye, Sir Charles—and many thanks for your help. I'll retrace my steps—both physical and mental."

Anthony grasped the Chief Constable's outstretched hand. Sir Charles nodded sympathetically. On his way back to Mallett, Anthony fought desperately with his brain for the elusive clue. So far he had toiled long and caught nothing. He cudgelled and castigated his wits to discover the essential indication which would ultimately lead him to the light. Years afterwards, when he viewed the case in retrospect, he marvelled and almost shivered at his own blindness. "Far from," he was wont to say at these times, "one of my happiest cases."

III

MacMorran and Venables came to him that evening in the comfortable room at the 'Laughing Angel.' Anthony pushed chairs towards them. The two Inspectors seated themselves. MacMorran gestured to the local man to open the proceedings. Venables was quick to accept the situation.

"I'm back from North Zelly. The home of the Yorkes. You'd better hear the details that I picked up over there. Mrs. Yorke, the mother of the dead boy, is a widow. There's another child besides the dead boy. A girl—aged six. People in extremely poor circumstances. And all of them in bad health. I should say that the mother is tubercular and both the children have spent a considerable time in different hospitals. On the day of the murder, the boy, Dickie, was sent out by his mother on an errand. To the baker's. I've been to the shop—it's at the extreme end of the main street in the village of North Zelly. Dickie Yorke called there with his basket for the family loaves about a quarter-past five in the afternoon. He was served with three large cottage loaves. After that, he seems to have vanished from mortal ken. Because I can find no trace of him anywhere—either in North Zelly or outside it. After a time, when he didn't return to his home, the mother went to the Police. You know when she was able to gather any information, because I think you were there when the news came through."

Anthony nodded. "Quite right, Venables, I was there."

The Inspector addressed shrugged his shoulders. "Well, there you are. I'm afraid I can't offer you any more."

"Well," rejoined Anthony, "that's not too bad—when you consider everything. What do you say, Andrew?"

"I agree," said MacMorran tersely. Anthony went on.

"You've certainly established one thing," he declared. "And that's this. The boy Yorke was picked up by his killer somewhere between the baker's shop in the street at North Zelly and his own home."

The two Inspectors nodded. "Now, Venables," said Anthony, "what do you make the distance between these two points?"

Venables thought over the question. He put his reply into words. "The main street at North Zelly is deceptive. As regards its length. It's not like a street in a town, say, like Mallett here. It's long and straggling. Considerable stretches minus little shops or houses." He paused and thought again. "On second thoughts, I should put the distance at close on a quarter of a mile. All of that."

"That fits very well," responded Anthony. "It gives both time and space in which the killer could have worked. And there's no doubt either, I should say, as to the way in which he worked."

The Inspector from Scotland Yard put a match to a packed bowl of tobacco. "Little doubt indeed, I should say. In a car."

"That's what I meant, Andrew. He found the boy he wanted, got him in the car under some pretext or the other and drove off with him. When the time came that was convenient for him, he drove off again. But on this second occasion, without the boy. Because he was on the settee in the smoke-room at the 'White Lion.'"

"There would be an interval of some hours on that showing," observed MacMorran.

"There would, Andrew. I'm not denying that."

"The boy was hidden indoors somewhere, I should say. In a house—in all probability. Until the time came for the murderer to sally forth with the victim for the purpose of 'dumping' the body. Unless you've anything better to suggest, Andrew."

The man addressed shook his head. "No. I think myself, that's about the size of it. I certainly can't put up anything better."

Venables leant across towards Anthony with a question in his eyes. "Just a minute, Mr. Bathurst—if it's all the same to you. But you and Inspector MacMorran are travelling a shade too fast for yours truly. There's one point I'd like to make before we leave it too far behind to be able to retrace our steps."

"What's that, Inspector Venables?"

"I'm wondering about something you said just now. The words you used. I'm not at all sure whether you used them deliberately or not." Venables smiled as he concluded. "You see, Mr. Bathurst, I don't know you quite so well as Inspector MacMorran does."

Anthony smiled back. "Which were the words, Venables?"

"It was when you were describing how the criminal worked from a car. You used the term, 'He found the boy he wanted.' No doubt you'll remember saying that. Did you mean that exactly as you put it?"

Anthony smiled again. "I did, Venables. I meant it exactly as I put it."

Venables wrinkled his brows. "Found the boy he wanted! Do you actually mean that the murderer was on the look-out for this particular boy? Had him already marked down, as it were?"

MacMorran watched Anthony's face intently for the reply. "Yes, Inspector, I do. Although I've only very recently begun to think so."

The reply was forthcoming briskly and emphatically.

"Then he knew him?"

"He knew him in so far as he was Richard Yorke. He had made it his business to find that out. I wouldn't go as far as to say that they were anything like personal acquaintances."

"Where had he met him, then?"

"Oh, come, Inspector. Don't tax me too highly. At this stage of the case. I can see that I mustn't make too many definite assertions. Because I can't produce chapter and verse for all of them yet. Although I hope to be in that happy position later on."

Venables's face still bore a look of bewilderment. "What was important about this boy being Richard Yorke?"

"Nothing—I should say."

"I'm sorry, then, Mr. Bathurst," replied Venables a little curtly; "but I don't get you."

"That's all right," returned Anthony. "But as I see things, another boy, similar to Yorke, would not have suited the killer's purpose. Completely! The virtue lay to an extent in him being named Richard Yorke. If I failed to imply that to you before, I apologise for not making myself more clear."

Venables clinched the argument by shrugging his shoulders. "I suppose I shall have to wait a little longer before I see where we're getting to. But with regard to the meantime—"

Anthony intervened. "With regard to the meantime, Inspector Venables, we'll fill it up by having some beer. Andrew, press that bell, will you, please."

IV

It was a matter of three days after his talk with the two Inspectors that Anthony discovered against whom the menace of the 'White Lion,' as he called it in his own mind, was directed. He had been turning over the various features of the four murders, in his mind, almost idly, and his last conversation with Venables, when suddenly part of the truth blazed up at him. As often happens in relation to mental excursions, an idle, ephemeral, fugitive thought led to the truth where intensive mental concentration had signally failed so to do.

When the realisation hit him—and it hit him hard, it must be confessed—Anthony almost held his breath. William Norman, King, George Clarence and the boy Yorke had all died—been murdered, to admit the hard black truth—as part of a set pattern and definitely sinister purpose. Which had for its ultimate purpose the death of yet another person, before the grim circle of crime would be completed! Anthony was in his room at the 'Laughing Angel,' Mallett, when this fearful realisation came to him. He sat in his chair and wiped the perspiration which had broken out on his brow. His first thoughts, naturally, were as to the best plan to combat the evil that must, by now, be hovering perilously close to the intended victim. He thought the matter over coolly and carefully. After a time, he decided to enlist the help of the Chief Constable himself. This, he considered, would be his best move in the scheme of defence which must, of necessity, be speedily set up, if the worst were to be averted. He resolved to telephone to Sandals immediately and put that resolution into effect.

The Chief Constable was at home and Anthony was speaking to him over the telephone within the space of a few minutes. It was at once obvious that Sir Charles was surprised to hear from him again so quickly after their previous encounter.

"What's that, Bathurst? You want to see me again? When? Over here? Why—man—what's happened? It's scarcely five minutes ago that you were over here talking to me. What? What's that? You think you're on to something? Oh—well—if that's the case—"

Sir Charles began to listen attentively to what Anthony Bathurst had to say. After Anthony had spoken, and it must be said that he spoke at some length, there ensued an interval of silence. Anthony waited for the Chief Constable's response. When it came, Anthony was able to detect an unmistakable note of agitation. The condition of suspicion almost seemed to have wrapped itself round Sir Charles's tones. This time it was Anthony Bathurst's turn to listen.

"If this is the goods, Bathurst, and I must say you appear to be convinced of it, you'd better come over here at once. You mustn't mind if I insist on your putting all your cards on the table. After all you know—what you're asking of me—"

The Chief Constable stopped before he finished the sentence. But before Anthony could get in again, he had gone off on another tack. "By the way, Bathurst, is MacMorran in with you on this? Does he know of your latest conclusions?"

"No, sir."

"Does Venables?"

"No, sir. I thought it so immensely important that I 'phoned you at once about it."

Anthony heard the Chief Constable clear his throat at the other end of the line.

"I see. Perhaps you've done the right thing. Anyhow, I shall be expecting you this evening. You'd better come to dinner again. Lady Stuart's away—unfortunately. She's been called to Town—one of her aunts is ill. Likely to shuffle off this mortal coil—so I'm given to understand. But you mustn't mind that."

"I shan't, sir," replied Anthony; "especially as I haven't had the pleasure of the lady's acquaintance."

The Chief Constable frowned, although Anthony couldn't see him. "I didn't mean that, man. I was referring to the matter of Lady Stuart's absence."

"Oh—I see, sir," said Anthony. "In that case, I'm sorry, and I beg your pardon. Expect me to dinner this evening."

Anthony smiled and replaced the receiver.

V

Sir Charles Stuart's mood at dinner that evening was a strange admixture of emotions. At one minute he would appear to be optimistic and in the best of spirits. At another, he would seem to be almost sub-merged by an undulating layer of depression and arrant pessimism. Anthony noticed particularly that he drank sparingly. When they sat down at the dinner-table, the Chief Constable had waved his hand as though he were warding off or waving away an invisible enemy agent.

"Let's enjoy our grub, Bathurst, for the love of Mike. Leave your grim story off the menu—to please me. When we're finished with the replenishment of the inner man, we'll get down to it and discuss it fully and freely. Till then, desist—as dear old George Robey used to say in the good old days." Sir Charles heaved a heavy, large-sized sigh. "I hate spectres at the meal table, my dear Bathurst. Hate 'em like poison. They're like skeletons. And ought to be treated in the same way. No place found for 'em at feasts—should be shut up in cupboards."

Sir Charles drank a little Hock. Anthony noticed that the fingers round the stem of the wine-glass were unsteady. So out of regard for more than one consideration, he fell in with his host's wishes. The meal ran its course. When it was over they adjourned to the lounge where Anthony had drunk coffee previously. Sir Charles shook off his mood of depression and brought his courage to the sticking-point.

"Now, Bathurst, I feel fortified. Bring up your heavy battalions and tell me the worst."

Anthony, thus encouraged, gave the Chief Constable the full story of the conclusions to which he had recently arrived. Sir Charles listened attentively and gravely. Anthony came to the end of the revelation.

"Now, sir—you see what the position's like. I felt it incumbent on me to acquaint you with the entire facts as far as I feel certain of them."

Sir Charles Stuart sat still in his chair. Suddenly he began to drum on his knee-caps with nervous fingers. At length, he found words.

"Bit of a facer—eh, what? Unnerved me a bit. Suppose it's only what you might expect. Not so young as I was. Makes a difference. Despite what some people say. But they don't tell the truth! I know."

Anthony waited for him to continue. Sir Charles began to sift details.

"I don't know any of the men who were close to Norman. I don't know, speaking without the book, that I've ever had any conversation with a single one of them. King, the baker, of course, is dead himself. That only leaves Cox, Hardwick, Waghorn and Marnoch. A farmer, a Deputy Town Clerk, a bank manager and a retired Police Inspector. The more I look at it all, the more it all leaves me wondering. Where is my mortal enemy—and why?" Sir Charles Stuart shivered a little. "It's an unpleasant thought, Bathurst—say what you like about it."

Anthony offered sympathy. "I entirely agree, sir. But whatever it is, you and I have to resist the adversary and outwit him. That's primarily the object of my telling you and of my visit here this evening. In short, I must ask, Sir Charles, for your closest co-operation."

Stuart nodded. "I see that, Bathurst. It must be so."

"You must maintain close touch with the Police and me from now onwards. All day and every day. You mustn't allow yourself to be induced to take the slightest risk. Every offer which comes to you, every suggestion which is made to you, every line of action which is presented to you—they must all be referred to us. We must know all about all of them, Sir Charles. No matter how attractive the guise may be in which anyone comes to you. Or no matter how innocently simple. See what I mean?"

"Yes. Only too clearly. This is what it comes to. I must do nothing really—unless you and the Police know all about it." Sir Charles laughed scornfully. "Nice, comfortable situation for a Chief Constable! Highly dignified, I must say."

"Dignity and comfort, Sir Charles, are 'also-rans' compared with your life and personal safety. And you can't argue that they aren't."

"I suppose you're right," assented the Chief Constable gloomily. He lit a cigarette and tossed the burnt match into the ash-tray.

"In addition to all I have said to you, Sir Charles, about co-operating with the Police and with me, you will have to do your own part."

Sir Charles frowned heavily. "My own part? In what way, exactly, do you mean, Bathurst?"

"In this way, sir. You will have to be on the watch yourself all the time. You mustn't relax for an instant. You must always be on your guard."

"On the *qui vive*—eh? Is that the idea?"

"If you prefer it that way, sir—well—yes."

Sir Charles nodded acquiescence. "Right. I'll do my best to fulfil all the obligations. Is there anything else?"

"Yes, Sir Charles. I'm afraid there is."

The Chief Constable shot a shrewd look at him. "What is it? Out with it man, for Heaven's sake. I abominate beating about the bush."

"What I say, I want taken absolutely literally. I want you to trust no one. And when I say no one—I mean no one."

Another shrewd look came from the host. "Damn it, man—*don't* beat about the bush—I say!"

Anthony smiled at his vehemence. "Surely, sir, I should find it difficult to be more explicit."

Sir Charles Stuart made a noise that sounded like a growl. "Perhaps not," he muttered. "But no one's a pretty tall order."

"I agree. Tall, perhaps, but not too tall."

Sir Charles shivered a little. He clasped and unclasped his fingers. "'Pon my soul, Bathurst, you've succeeded in giving me the jitters. Here I am reacting to your forebodings like some wretched little pip-squeak."

"You must pull yourself together, sir. Otherwise you can't help us to the fullest extent. We want you at a hundred per cent, fighting fit."

"When do you think the attack will be made, Bathurst? Quickly from now?"

"That's a very difficult question to answer, Sir Charles. If I say 'comparatively quickly,' I don't want you to deduce from that that I expect the attack to take place to-morrow. It's mere conjecture, of course, but I don't think the attack will take shape for a week or so."

Sir Charles regarded him anxiously. "Have you grounds for that view? Sound grounds?"

"Yes. To my way of thinking, I have."

"Thanks, Bathurst—you've given me some slight measure of relief. I may have time to look round, as it were. I feel that I need time. Your news this evening has been in the nature of a shock to me. It would be useless to deny that. I need time to recover from that shock. If I am called upon to face this attack right away—I've no confidence in myself. I feel that I may crumple up. But a respite—I use that word, although it isn't the right one—if it's only for a week or two, will give me time to husband my strength a bit." He laughed nervously and jerkily. "See what I mean, Bathurst?"

"Quite clearly, sir. And as I said, I think you'll have your week or two all right. If I'm any judge of our killer's technique! Now, if you don't mind, I'll go over the ground again. We can't afford to leave the slightest margin of risk. Listen carefully again, Sir Charles."

Anthony leant forward eagerly in order to make his points. The Chief Constable bent his head to listen

VI

It was on the next evening that Marnoch, the retired Inspector of Police, called upon Anthony and Chief-Inspector MacMorran. He came, entirely of his own accord to their room at the 'Laughing Angel.' The 'boots' brought Marnoch's card up and was told by the Scotland Yard Inspector to show the visitor up to the room immediately.

Marnoch in person arrived about three minutes later. Anthony who had, of course, seen him before, took good stock of him as he entered. Marnoch, by this time, was a man probably between fifty-five and sixty. He was tall, of good physique, with grizzled hair and a lean cast of features. He looked very fit. Anthony judged that in his prime he had been a powerful fellow and well able to take care of himself in a rough house when actions spoke a great deal louder than words. His voice was a little harsh but not unpleasant to the ear.

"Good evening, gentlemen," he opened. "I suppose I might have telephoned to you earlier in the day and fixed up this appointment. As a matter of fact, it never occurred to me to do so until I was on my way here this evening. But seeing that I've found you in and you've invited me up here, it doesn't seem to matter. So that's O.K. by all three of us."

MacMorran gestured him to take a seat. Marnoch thanked him and did so.

"You and I, Chief, may regard ourselves almost as colleagues, I take it. Although you're still in harness and I'm put away in the stable. Yes?" He laughed pleasantly.

MacMorran nodded. "I suppose we can, Mr. Marnoch. And you can include Mr. Bathurst here in that. Now to what do we owe the pleasure of this unexpected visit?"

Marnoch's eyes twinkled. "Ah, so we get to business quickly—do we? Well there's nothing like it. I was never one to stand still and let the grass grow under my feet. Well, to cut the cackle and come to the 'osses, I've breezed over here this evening because I fancy I've got some information for you."

"In that case," said Anthony, rising and speaking for the first time since Marnoch's entry, "we'll send for some appropriate liquid refreshment." He rang the bell. "What will you drink, Mr. Marnoch?"

The ex-inspector of Police smiled at the invitation. "Well—that's very nice of you, Mr. Bathurst. As it's warmish this evening, I'll have a gin and ginger-beer, if it's all the same to you."

Anthony gave the requisite orders and the drinks were brought in on a tray. Marnoch sampled some of his before continuing his story.

"Now my information, gentlemen, is this. It's to do with the murder of the boy Yorke. I understand he was found on the settee in the smoke-room at the 'White Lion.'"

There was no answer. Marnoch looked at the faces of his auditors. "At least—that's what I find according to the Press. That is to say, the local Press."

MacMorran nodded. "That's all right. Go on."

"Very good, then. Now listen to this. I left the 'Lion' on the evening before the body was found just before closing time. Say at twenty-five minutes past ten. That time would be almost exact. Now, I live about twenty minutes' walk from the house. Down Nag's Head Lane. I actually turn down the lane, and it's pretty dark down there, let me tell you. I turned down there on that particular night about twenty minutes to eleven. Perhaps it would be a minute or two later, I can't be sure. But I met a car. It was coming down the lane—towards me. I was going up. My bungalow is about a quarter of a mile up on the right-hand side. Now, it's a most unusual thing to see a car in that lane. Not only at that time of night. At any time! For one thing, it's an appallingly bad road and, for another, it's all ups and downs. When I met the car it was travelling downhill and moving pretty fast. Now this was such an unusual occurrence, gentlemen, that I paid particular attention to it. And now comes the most interesting part of my story. As it passed me, I heard a child crying inside it. Not a baby—mark you—a child! There's a difference. I know it. And this was a child all right. In view of what we know, it strikes me as highly significant."

Marnoch sat back and drained his glass. Anthony spoke to him.

"Let me have your full story then, Mr. Marnoch, do you mind?"

For the moment the retired Inspector of Police looked startled, but the condition was short-lived. "As you wish, Mr. Bathurst. My idea's this. The boy was taken to the 'White Lion' in a car. Some time after they closed—of course. The window of the smoke-room was pushed up from the outside. It's easily accessible from the yard. The boy's body was dropped through on to the settee. That's the theory that I'm inclined to hold."

Anthony nodded. "I don't think you're very far from the truth, Mr. Marnoch. I'd come to much the same conclusion myself."

"If there's anything in your story—" began MacMorran.

"What do you mean exactly by that?" demanded Marnoch. His tone, Anthony thought, bordered on the truculent. But it passed, evidently unheeded by MacMorran.

"I mean this. That if the car you saw was in any way connected with the murder of the boy Yorke, everything in your story, if value is to be extracted from it, comes back to that car itself. What description of it can you give us?"

Marnoch laughed drily. "Ah—that's a different story. And I'm afraid that you're relying on a broken reed when you apply to me for that. All I can say is 'a car passed me.' Beyond that phrase I regret that I can say nothing. You want to be in Nag's Head Lane about eleven o'clock on a moonless night such as this was. Besides, the sky was clouded over with heavy, sullen rain-clouds. It would be useless for me to attempt, even, to describe the car. So I'm not going to make that attempt. I bring you help, you see, but the effort is but stinted."

Marnoch leant back in his chair and folded his hands across the knee-cap of his raised left leg. His right foot remained on the floor. For once MacMorran seemed a trifle nonplussed.

"No help to identify the car at all?" he queried lamely. "No fragment of description? Size? Colour? Anything?"

Marnoch shook his head—almost patronisingly. "You can wash out the idea of my telling you the colour of the car. With regard to its size, I might be able to produce something. Let me think a moment. My distinct impression is that the car was on the large size. Certainly 'large' rather than 'small.' There you are, Inspector MacMorran. That's the best I can do for you in that direction."

Marnoch abandoned his easy attitude. MacMorran accepted the inevitable. "We are not ungrateful, Mr. Marnoch, for your assistance and information. What you can't tell us—well, you can't tell us! So it's no good my pressing you."

Anthony offered his cigarette case to the retired Inspector of Police. "One little point, Mr. Marnoch, that I feel I should like to ask you. With regard to the crying of the child in the car which you say you heard. Of what sort of crying was it? If you were asked to describe it more fully, how would you do that?"

Marnoch seemed as though he failed to understand. "I don't know that—"

"Well—let me put it to you like this: did the child suddenly cry out—for instance?"

"Oh—no. Nothing hit my ear all of a sudden. There was no cry or scream or anything of that nature. Or was it a mere whimpering. No—decidedly neither of those. Much more like a continued sobbing—as though the child were thoroughly afraid of something that had either happened to it—or was going to happen to it. I'm fairly confident with regard to that."

"Thank you, Mr. Marnoch. You've answered that just as I wanted you to answer it. And by so doing you've told me exactly what I desired to know."

Marnoch showed pleasure at Anthony's words. "Only too pleased, Mr. Bathurst. When I hear you talk in that fashion I tell myself that my errand hasn't been wasted and that I did right to come over here. I only hope that the chief here thinks on the same lines as you do." He looked towards MacMorran in an invitation to compliment.

"Certainly," contributed the Scotland Yard Inspector. "And now here's a question for you from me that I'd very much like to have answered."

"Let's have it, Inspector," said the satisfied Marnoch. "Give it a name as soon as you like."

MacMorran smiled at the man's effervescence. "This Nag's Head Lane that you've mentioned once or twice in your story this evening—do many people make use of it?"

"In daytime, do you mean?"

"Not altogether. Generally, say."

Marnoch repeated the word: "Generally—eh?"

"Yes—in the ordinary course of events."

"I see. Well—certainly a fair number of people use it. Not many, though, late at night."

"Where does it lead to? Anywhere in particular?"

"Oh—it's on the way to Hammeridge and North Zelly. But I was under the impression that you knew that."

"No. I wasn't sure," replied MacMorran. "I've never actually used the lane myself to get anywhere."

"And you say that few cars use it?" inquired Anthony.

Marnoch nodded his head. "Very few. And practically all that do, do so in the daytime. You scarcely ever see a car in the lane at night-time." Marnoch stood up. "Well, gentlemen, I don't think I can tell you any more. You've had the sum and substance of my knowledge. And now you must allow me to return the compliment of your hospitality. What will you drink, Inspector? And you, Mr. Bathurst?"

Anthony thought that MacMorran seemed disinclined to accept the invitation. His eyes caught MacMorran's and conveyed the message that he wished to convey. MacMorran understood. Marnoch said: "If you'll ring, then, gentlemen, this round is on me."

Anthony rang the bell and as before gave the necessary orders. When the drinks came, Marnoch showed in the best of spirits. "Let me give you a toast, gentlemen. I'll undertake to make it appropriate." He raised his tankard. "May you, Inspector MacMorran, soon get your hooks in the 'White Lion' murderer—whoever he may be. And when you've got him—may he swing—say I."

He tossed back his drink and laughed. "Seems like old times to me! When I was hot on the trail myself." He sighed. "It hurts you sometimes, you know, when you realise that certain times will never come again. Leaves a bitter taste in the mouth."

Anthony smiled and glanced at Marnoch's empty tankard. "Well," he said quietly, "I don't know that you can grumble at that."

"Eh?" said Marnoch suspiciously. "Oh—I see! Well good-night, gentlemen—and thanks for the cordial reception."

VII

Anthony told MacMorran of his interview at Sandals with the Chief Constable. The 'Yard' Inspector listened attentively. Halfway through the story, he scratched his chin. From the look in his eyes, Anthony felt that criticism would be immediately forthcoming.

"Bit far-fetched, Mr. Bathurst, isn't it—if you'll allow me to say so?"

Anthony was emphatic. He had realised that if he failed to convince MacMorran early he wouldn't convince him at all. "It may be far-fetched, Andrew, as you call it, but I'll stake my oath it's the truth for all that."

At the prompt intervention, MacMorran subsided a little. "All right. Perhaps I was wrong to criticise your idea before you'd finished. Say the rest of your piece."

Anthony proceeded with his narrative. This time MacMorran heard him right through to the end. "There you are, Andrew," remarked Anthony as he reached his conclusion. "That's the lot. Pick the bones out now—if you like."

MacMorran sat silent.

"Well," said Anthony. "I'm waiting for you."

MacMorran found inadequate words. "I can't say much more than I said just now. Sounds pretty wild-eyed to me."

"So it may. But test it! Try its links. They'll stand it, Andrew— wild-eyed or not. Great Scot, man, it must be so! The sign-posts of meaning are all there . . . in a row . . . ticketed and labelled with something appallingly like precision. If I'm wrong and my theory's unsound, the long arm of coincidence has the sky for its limit."

MacMorran sat and pondered over Anthony's reply. "I take it," he said at length, "that you've said nothing of this to Venables?"

"Of course not. I shouldn't approach him before I spoke to you, naturally."

"He ought to know."

"I agree. I'm with you entirely. We'll tell him together at the first opportunity. But I'm going to make one stipulation with regard to that, Andrew."

"What's that, Mr. Bathurst?"

"That I tell him only my conclusions. I don't want to give him all the details that I've just handed on a plate to you. I don't want to— and I don't think either that I need to. All the same, I'd value your opinion on that."

MacMorran thought it over. "No—perhaps it isn't vitally necessary that he should know all the details. At the moment. As long as he thoroughly understands what's expected of him at the Stuart end, he should be all right."

"That's just what I think. We'll agree on that procedure, then. I suggest we stroll down to the station first thing in the morning and spill these particular beans to Venables when we get there. Yes?"

MacMorran nodded. "Right-o, then, Mr. Bathurst. That will suit me. In the meantime I'm going to run over your theory again and see if I can find any holes in it." The Inspector smiled and then flew another kite. "Seems to me it stands to reason there must be some."

"And I suppose if there aren't," grinned Anthony, "you'll find some. It's the old Adam in the old Andrew!"

MacMorran caught his mood. "I'll do my best to. You can bet your bottom dollar on that."

"Now there's another thing I want to say to you. After we've seen Venables in the morning, I'm going to make another special contact. I've had it in my mind some time now."

MacMorran raised his eyebrows. "What's that?"

Anthony tossed away the stub of a cigarette. "Hardwick. Horace Marsden Hardwick, Deputy Town Clerk of Mallett."

"And why—particularly?"

Anthony was some time before he replied: "It's difficult for me to explain, perhaps, but let me put it like this. Take the men close to Norman on the evening that he was murdered. There were five of them: King, Waghorn, Cox, Marnoch and Hardwick. Remember the quintet?"

MacMorran nodded, but spoke words: "Agreed. I remember them. But I don't know that I can see where you're getting to."

"I've been thinking things over very carefully. Come along with me now. King! Number One. When alive, he was a baker. He's dead. Murdered, without a doubt, as Norman was. Number Two, Septimus Waghorn, bank manager in Mallett itself. In a way and to a degree touches the third murder, that of the drowned Clarence. Through the medium of a stamp collection and the hobby of stamp-collecting. In addition to that, has encountered me socially and shows, generally, a general disposition and an overwhelming desire towards captivating conversation. Number Three—" Anthony broke off with a quick smile. He had noticed that Andrew MacMorran was listening eagerly. "Why, what's the matter, Andrew?"

"Nothing. Only that you've got me keenly interested."

"Good. Number Three, Cox, the farmer. Hasn't appeared quite so much in the central picture as his two immediate predecessors. But, like Waghorn, must be found guilty of same cheerful disposition and tendency towards the elocutionary art. Also quite inclined to discuss Waghorn, for instance, and possibly some others. Which brings me to Number Four, Marnoch. That same Marnoch whom we have so recently entertained. Marnoch, the retired Inspector of Police who brings us the news of the crying child in the car travelling by night. Who brings it to us *sua sponte*—sorry, Andrew, 'of his own accord'—and takes the trouble to walk over to us by night to deliver his message. That leaves us with Number Five—and only Number Five. The before-mentioned Horace Marsden Hardwick. And, to repeat myself, Deputy Town Clerk of Mallett. This 'ere Mallett in whose boundaries we eat, drink and sleep. Don't you think I might line him up *avec les autres*? So that we may be able to survey the complete collection?"

"Putting it the way you have—my answer's 'Yes.'"

Anthony rose and slapped him on the back. "Good for you, Andrew. That's settled, then, and we're in agreement with regard to the next moves in the campaign. First, for both of us, that which is Venables, and afterwards for me, that which is Hardwick."

VIII

Anthony came to the unpretentious building which did duty as the Public Offices to the Borough of Mallett, and almost immediately felt a certain measure of disappointment. Having visited other Public Offices and Town Halls, Anthony was naturally not unduly optimistic as to the manner of his reception, and on this particular occasion his lack of roseate optimism was more than justified. For the Public Offices at Mallett had neither quality nor distinction. When he entered, Anthony found himself confronted by a narrow and distinctly shabby-looking staircase. An arrow on the right-hand wall said tersely "Rates." Anthony looked round for further detailed information. Then, to his left he saw a door marked "Town Clerk's Dept. General Office." "This," he said to himself "is more like it." He walked over to the door and tapped on it. A voice from inside called upon him to "come in." He availed himself of the invitation.

A lank-haired, pasty-faced local government officer came forward to meet him.

"Whadjerwant?" asked the legal image.

Anthony produced his card. "I should like, if possible," he said courteously, "a few words with Mr. Hardwick."

"We don't want any temp'ry clerks," said the youth.

"I should hate," said Anthony, "to think of becoming a permanent one. But rest assured, I have no designs on your establishment. All I want is the pleasure of a few words with your Mr. Hardwick."

The scion of local government pushed his fingers through his untidy hair. "I'll see what he says, then, if you'll just wait a minute."

"Thank you," said Anthony. "I shall be delighted."

The youth disappeared through another doorway leading out of the room with Anthony's card between his fingers. Anthony waited in patience. After a few moments he was joined again by the same young man.

"Mr. Hardwick's in, sir. And he says he'll be pleased to see you. Come this way, please."

Anthony followed him into the presence of Mr. H.M. Hardwick. The youth closed the door behind him, prior to disappearing again. The room occupied by the Deputy Town Clerk of Mallett was not, in appearance, inhospitable. The carpet was warm in colour and the furniture solid and comfortable-looking. Hardwick was sitting at a roll-top desk. When Anthony was shown in, he rose and walked towards him. He gave Anthony his hand.

"Good morning, Mr. Bathurst. It was quite a surprise to me when your card was handed to me a moment ago. You were almost the last person I expected to see in this room of mine."

"I trust," smiled Anthony, "that I am none the less welcome because of that."

Hardwick became boisterously effusive. "Of course not—and you know it. Now sit down in that chair and tell me what I can do for you."

"Well," said Anthony, "we've met before—at the 'White Lion'—so you can readily guess what I've come about."

Hardwick's mood changed. He immediately assumed the defensive. "I don't know that I can tell you any more than I have told you.

You know when I mean. When you came to the 'White Lion' and Denton was there with us."

Anthony agreed. "Oh—yes. I remember that. But let me explain myself more fully to you. I owe it to you, perhaps, to do that. I haven't come so much to gather information. If by the word 'information' we simply mean more facts, more details of those facts, more accounts of occurrences and so on. Let me say that I'm more concerned with essentials. Essentials of character. Psychologies. And you knew—I may even say 'know'—the men round Norman on the evening he was killed as well, if not better, than anybody."

Hardwick shifted uneasily in his chair.

"Do you see what I mean, Mr. Hardwick?"

"Yes. I suppose I do."

"Good. Then I'm asking you to help me all you can."

Hardwick's fingers played nervously with his top lip. "I shall be only too delighted. But—er—how would you like me to start?"

"Take the men whom Norman knew—and tell me about them. If you like—if the idea appeals to you—you may commence with Norman himself."

There ensued a short period of silence. Anthony waited for Hardwick to set his own pace.

"H'm. Norman himself. I—er—didn't know too much of Norman himself. But just a minute, Mr. Bathurst. Before I really get on with the job, perhaps you wouldn't mind answering me a question. Why do you come to me for this? Why, for instance, haven't you gone to one of the others?"

"My dear sir"—Anthony simulated a certain astonishment—"surely the reason for that is very obvious."

Hardwick's face wrinkled into an unspoken question. Anthony answered it.

"Your professional experience—naturally. Your legal knowledge. Your position in Mallett. You are a trained observer. Whereas the others can scarcely be placed in that category."

Hardwick nodded. "I see. Putting it that way, of course—" he paused.

"Norman," repeated Anthony. "You had begun on Norman."

"Yes. Well, as I said, I didn't know a tremendous amount about Norman. He was a farmer. His main—almost his sole interest in life lay in farming. He was sound. A man you could trust. A man, I should say, who had known both adversity and comparative prosperity. And rather more of the former, probably, than the latter."

"What makes you think that?"

Hardwick weighed his words. "From the expression on his face. His habitual expression. And from certain remarks I heard him drop from time to time. I formed my own judgment of him—to a certain extent. Of course, this may not be—"

Anthony cut in. "Don't worry! You're telling me just the things that I want you to tell me."

Hardwick flushed at Anthony's words. "Oh—thanks. That's—er—satisfactory to know. I wasn't feeling too sure." He leant forward and took a cigarette from Anthony's proffered case. "Thank you again."

"He wasn't what you would call a happy man?"

"Happy in some directions—perhaps! But definitely a man who had been at some times during his career at odds with fortune. A strong-minded man, stronger in spirit than in physique. But a man who lived in himself and for himself. And by 'himself,' I mean, naturally, his wife and family. I should say he had no vices and few weaknesses."

"That," said Anthony judicially, "is where you enter the realm of conjecture, isn't it?"

"I suppose it is when you come to weigh it all up. But I was only trying to help."

"I know. And you are helping. Any more Norman projections?"

"No-o, I don't think so. I think I'll pass on to King."

"That will suit me."

"King, as you know, was a baker. Different altogether from Norman. One of the 'successful business type.' Social mixer. Self-assertive man rather. Boisterous. Freemason. Liked the 'flesh-pots of Egypt.' Was Mayor of Mallett a few years ago. On that account, I knew him better than I knew Norman. He was stout—rubicund—jovial. But the joviality wasn't normal. To me, it always seemed to emanate from a sense of self-importance, highly developed, rather than from a genuine quality of loving his fellow men. He was round, dark—a bouncing little man. Born probably, with an inferiority complex, which he determined to transform by external appearances, at least, to one of the superior kind. In America, I suggest, he would have been called 'slap-happy.' How am I doing?"

"Excellently. Go on. I assure you I'm a most attentive audience."

"I know," said Hardwick, as though under the influence of a sudden inspiration. "I've a photo of King here, when he was Mayor of the Borough. That was about seven years ago."

He pulled open a drawer on the right-hand side of his desk and took out a number of photographs. He began to look through them. "Here you are. Here's Alderman King, to give him his title of those days. In full Mayoral regalia—robes, chain and gloves on his lap. Have a look at it for yourself."

Anthony saw a smiling, round-faced man, who, as Anthony himself would have put it, "looked extremely pleased with himself and in the true lineal descent of the late John Horner, Esquire."

"Added to what you've already told me about him," he said aloud to Hardwick, "I get an excellent picture of the man. Many thanks!"

He handed back the photograph to the Deputy Town Clerk. Hardwick took it and replaced it in company with the others he had taken out, within the drawer. Hardwick continued his analysis.

"Unlike Norman, King had been on good terms with the fickle jade all his life. The bakery business had come to him down many generations and he had by far the biggest trade of that particular kind in the whole of Mallett. When the terms of his will are made known, I venture to predict that Henry King will be found to have died an extremely wealthy man. Certainly five figures! I wouldn't be surprised if it weren't six, even. In a decidedly different category from Norman—you see."

"How long have you been Deputy Town Clerk, Mr. Hardwick?" Anthony noticed that Hardwick flushed a little. "Ever since I was demobbed. Early in 1919 that would be." Hardwick went on speaking much more quickly than he had before. "I had an advantage you see, when I applied for the job. After the appointment had been advertised in the public Press."

"Which was?" smiled Anthony.

"I had served in the Glebeshire Yeomanry. So I was able—to be perfectly candid—to pull a string or two."

"I expect you're indulging in an exercise of modesty." Anthony smiled at him again.

"No—really. I must be frank with you. Whom shall I take next?"

"I'm in your hands. Any one of the remaining three will suit me. Suppose, though, that we nominate Waghorn."

Hardwick's face clouded momentarily, but soon cleared again. "Waghorn! H'm. The man who knows most of our secrets. Of a certain kind, that is. Well, I've known Sep Waghorn for a good many years now. He's a strange bloke in several ways. Been a highly successful manager since he took over in Mallett. When old Bob Buxton retired. Waghorn, I should say, handles every decent account in Mallett and its vicinity."

"Does that include King's and Norman's?"

"I should say there's little doubt on that point, Bathurst. Waghorn's a mixer, and this quality of his is a great asset to him in his business relationships with the men and women of Mallett."

"Yes. I see your point there. He's a man with a hobby, too, isn't he?"

Hardwick raised his eyebrows. "Eh? Oh, I understand what you mean. I didn't connect for the moment. Yes—he's a philatelist. Keen as mustard too—when there's anything about that he thinks is worth picking up. I'm not misjudging him—I'm going entirely on things that he's told me himself. He'd talk stamps with anybody who'd let him, until the cows come home. He's a Freemason, too, same lodge as King. Bit of a lad as well, I fancy, if you could see right inside him. I don't know that I can say a lot more. I've only met him on social occasions, outside the daily round of having lunch with him. But, summing up, I'd call him a decent bloke, and I dare say he'd run an overdraft for me, if I asked him nicely."

Hardwick laughed and continued: "I don't suppose Septimus Waghorn tears his hair or tosses on his nightly couch because some of his accounts are showing up red-ink figures on some days of the month." Hardwick grinned. "Don't forget you're in a country town, Bathurst. Everybody knows everybody else's business. And if it doesn't come to them easily, they make up their minds to go after it and get it."

"I can't say that I'm surprised. My experience had taught me to expect something of that sort."

"But, despite all that I've said, it must be conceded, if one is fair, that Waghorn is far removed from the ordinary type of bank manager. He possesses undoubted qualities, and they have helped him towards the success he's obtained. He's used them judicially and has attained in Mallett a genuine degree of personal popularity. As a result of this, his successor—and I don't care who he may be—will find a smoother road to travel than Septimus Waghorn found facing him when he first came here."

Anthony nodded. "Thanks a lot. Now let's hear about Cox."

Hardwick shook his head. "That's my vulnerable suit. I know next to nothing about Cox. He's a small-way farmer. I do know that. Out at a little place called Conniss. Towards Hammeridge. The only place where I've ever run across him is the 'White Lion.'"

Anthony intervened. "Norman also farmed. So we can't look on Cox as the intruder within the circle."

Hardwick nodded. Rather slowly. "That's true. I see what you mean. I hadn't looked at it in that light before."

"Never mind," remarked Anthony. "Go on, please."

Hardwick hesitated. "I don't know that there's any more for one to say. Cox doesn't spill a lot when you're with him. He's not a talker by any means. For instance, that little knot of us used to have a special Christmas dinner on our own in a private room at the 'Lion.' Usually about the Friday before Christmas. Denton used to do us very well, too. Three or four different kinds of wine he'd serve, during the dinner. Well—what I'm getting to is this. Cox used to come. He's been present, I feel certain, on each occasion for the last three years—he'd eat and drink and you'd see him there—and he'd join in the laughter and stand his corner, and then, when the show was over and you went home and thought it all over in your mind—you wouldn't be able to recall a single remark that Cox had made! That's what I mean. There *are* men like that, you know. They don't pull much of an oar in the social boat."

"I agree. How is he placed financially? Any idea?"

"I should say he's pretty comfortably breeched. As far as I know. But he's a man you can never get really near. Just as King was quite different from Norman, and Waghorn from both of them, so Cox is almost entirely one on *his own*. In character and in relation to the life he leads. But—and I'd emphasise this—I know nothing whatever against him, or to his discredit in any way. He's taciturn, but, as far as I know, straight. He never wore *his* heart on his sleeve, I assure you."

"That goes for Cox, then. Only one left now. Marnoch. What can you tell me concerning him?"

There was no hesitation about Hardwick now. He spoke with confidence and emphasis: "I can tell you a great deal more with regard to Marnoch than I was able to concerning Cox. As you already know, Marnoch is a retired Inspector of Police. He's been resident in this district for some years now. And I've seen him and met him pretty frequently. As a rule, I'm willing to admit, in the precincts of the 'White Lion.' Usually, as you may expect, either at lunch there, or in the saloon bar of an evening. Marnoch"—Hardwick began to speak much more slowly—"is by no means an ordinary sort of chap. He's very much of an x as an unknown quantity. Indeed, of the whole 'White Lion' crowd, Norman and Marnoch were the only two, in my opinion that is, who could be regarded as being like each other. Each was reserved. Each always seemed to me, a trifle morose. Wrapped up in himself. Smouldering fires banked up inside somewhere. But you'll know what I mean, without my developing the theme any more. Marnoch is always alone. He walks alone. He'll go to the cinema alone. I know that, because he's told me so. He'll even drink alone. And I'm a man, Bathurst, who cherishes the notion that a man who drinks alone isn't too nice a piece of work."

Anthony smiled. "What is he—a widower?"

"Don't think so. Never heard of a Mrs. M. No—I'm pretty sure he's a bachelor. Dyed-in-the-wool at that! As far as I can judge, women don't interest him, have never interested him, and almost certainly never will."

More smiles from Anthony. "Perhaps he's been crossed in love! And, that being so, has remained faithful to the one girl in all the world. It has happened, you know."

"Maybe. But I should require a good deal of convincing on that point, I'm afraid."

"I'm not stressing it. You know the man. I don't."

"Exactly. Another thing about him. He's a man of uncertain temper. I believe that's the phrase customarily employed to fit the bill. I'll tell you more details."

Hardwick leant forward in his chair with a certain amount of eagerness. "Marnoch keeps a dog. An Airedale. His neighbours assert that he thrashes it unmercifully. That story's been extant for years. I can't confirm or deny. I know nothing about it. But I can add this reminiscence. You listen! You may find it illuminating. Two or three years back, Marnoch was knocked over by a bike. Ridden by a lad of about sixteen. He wasn't hurt. Actually, he staggered back after the impact, for a considerable distance, before he really fell to the ground. The boy was much more scared at the incident than Marnoch was. It was a hired machine. You know—bob an hour from a cycle-shop. Poor brakes and bell not in proper working order. If you get back to the shop after your day out and the bike hasn't fallen to pieces, you're dead lucky. Well, Marnoch picked himself off the ground in a towering rage. He advanced towards the lad, kicked the bicycle out of the way, seized the boy by the shoulders and threw him over a hedge into an adjoining field. Luckily for Marnoch and, of course, the boy himself, not much harm was done. The kid landed in a patch of good thick grass and no bones were broken. So the affair blew over. For some time the boy's father went about talking of taking action against Marnoch for assault, but he couldn't make up his mind, and eventually it all ended in smoke, which drifted into oblivion. Except, naturally, that people talked. You can't stop people talking, especially in a place like Mallett, and talk they did. Marnoch's ears must have burned most days for many weeks."

"How long ago did you say that this incident took place?"

"I think I said two or three years back, but if you give me a moment to think, I can tell you exactly. Wait a minute and I'll work it out for you, from certain associations."

Hardwick leant back in his chair and closed his eyes. "It was two years ago last May. Just over two years. I can tell that because they'd just started building in the next field to where Marnoch flung the boy who had knocked him over. One of our Council's housing estates. Well—what do you think of it? Now that I've told you?"

Anthony shrugged his shoulders. "You haven't told me much more than that Marnoch is a man of ungovernable temper. I mustn't begin to build bricks from pieces of straw of that calibre. Still—what you have told me of all these Norman acquaintances is most useful, Mr. Hardwick, and it's up to me now to do a spot of sifting. That must be my next task. And I mustn't delay in starting it."

Hardwick rose. "I'm glad to have been of some assistance to you. When you first came in, and announced what you wanted, I harboured strong doubts as to whether I should be equal to the task. I'm only too delighted to think that I haven't failed ignominiously." He rather ostentatiously glanced at his watch. "And now, if you'll excuse me, Bathurst, I've some minutes to prepare for our next Council meeting. Any other time that you care to—"

He held out his right hand to Anthony. As he did so, the telephone bell rang on Hardwick's desk. Turning aside from Anthony, he went back to answer it. Suddenly he looked up.

"Excuse me, Bathurst, but the Town Clerk wants me. You can let yourself out, can't you?"

Anthony intimated that he could, and Hardwick disappeared into an adjoining room through a connecting door. Anthony picked up his hat preparatory to taking his departure. On his way out he noticed a photograph standing at the back of the mantelpiece. Anthony saw that it was a regimental group. He stooped down a little so that he might obtain a better view of it. The description at the foot of the photograph told him that he was looking at the Second Company of the Glebeshire Yeomanry, taken in January, 1918. In the forefront of the picture he was able to pick out Hardwick himself, mounted and in the uniform of a trooper. The set of the head and the strong line of the jaw were unmistakable. Anthony looked at *la toute ensemble* with definite approval. There was an atmosphere about the whole thing which appealed to him. He was just about to turn away, when another figure in the group attracted his attention. Surely there was no mistaking the face of this man! Again he bent low to make assurance doubly certain. Yes—he was right. The man whose face his eyes were now searching was King, the ex-Mayor of Mallett, and the man who had been found dead in the 'White Lion' as a result of eating poisoned turbot. The likeness between this photograph and the one which Hardwick had only a few minutes ago shown him was too obvious to be missed.

Anthony straightened himself and thoughtfully ran his finger along the ridge of his jaw. King, here, in the ranks of the Glebeshire Yeomanry! Alderman and Deputy Town Clerk of Mallett! Strange! No—not strange in itself, perhaps, but strange that Hardwick, in all his confidence and analysis, had omitted to mention it. Anthony, thinking hard, passed out of the room of the Deputy Town Clerk of Mallett. He made his way again to the foot of the squalid-looking staircase and then into the street. His thoughts rioted. Now, why hadn't Hardwick told him that the dead man, King, the second dead man in the 'White Lion' tradition, had served with him in the ranks of the Glebeshire Yeomanry?

Anthony walked for some paces—a victim to the relentless probing of this question. For some distance, he was unable to find any answer which brought him even a measure of satisfaction. Then suddenly, and without preliminary warning of its approach, a ray of light burst upon his intelligence.

"Of course," he muttered to himself, "that must be the reason. Now why the devil didn't I think of that before?"

CHAPTER VI

I

MARTIN Chavasse sat in a chair by the bedside and watched a patient with troubled eyes and anxious lips. Chavasse cupped his chin in one hand and his eyes sought the time from the watch he wore strapped to his wrist. From what he read there his eyes appeared, to take to themselves an added gravity. Chavasse shook his head slowly. The man in the bed moaned a little in his disordered slumber and tossed his body wearily from one side of the bed to the other. Chavasse shook his head again as he watched the sick man's restless efforts. The patient had an unruly shock of black hair, which sprawled almost across the whiteness of the pillow as he lay there. Every now and then, he muttered something—always, as far as Chavasse was able to tell—unintelligible. Several times Chavasse had lowered his head nearer to the pillow and to the sick man's lips, in an abortive attempt to catch some glimmer of meaning in what he was trying to say.

Suddenly, on this last evening, Chavasse heard words which approached sense and coherence merge from the condition of delirium and come from the dying man's lips:

"Only one more now. And then, that will be the end. The end of all my striving and of all my pain. But I haven't signed. The paper isn't signed. I must sign the paper. Bring it to me—the paper. I must sign."

After this lapse into something like comparative sanity, the lips drooled again and the words themselves blurred again into a murmured medley of meaninglessness. Chavasse continued to watch him and shake his own head from time to time.

Eventually he pushed his chair from beneath him with one foot, and walked across to the door of the room. For some few minutes he stood at this door, still inside the room, and watched the restless figure in the bed, now with one arm thrown at its full length across the pillow. Chavasse rubbed his eyes wearily, turned, made his way from the sick man's room and walked to the foot of the staircase, which continued its way of ascent but a few yards from the bedroom door. Chavasse halted at the foot of this staircase and called in a loud voice to somebody on the floor above.

"Mrs. Logan! Mrs. Logan!"

An answering voice called back to him almost at once. "Yes, Doctor. Are you wanting me, then?"

"I am wanting you, Mrs. Logan. At once please! Come down here. Do you mind?"

Chavasse, having got this off his chest, returned to the sick man's bedroom. In a few moments he could hear the buxom, good-natured Scotswoman, Mrs. Logan, the tenant of the rooms upstairs, descending the staircase towards him. She was heavy and breathed hard, but her face indicated the kindliness of her nature. She came into the bedroom. Chavasse was now back in his chair by the patient's bed. As Mrs. Logan entered, he leant forward and wiped the sick man's lips.

"Evening, Doctor," gasped Mrs. Logan; "and how is he to-night, the poor fellow? It's not more than the half-hour since I left him.

He was asleep then—but not a nice easy sleep. I watched him. The District Nurses had gone not so very long before."

Chavasse was curt. "He's dying, Mrs. Logan. But he'll go at least another twenty-four hours. In my opinion, more like forty-eight. Perhaps even more than that. It's hard to tell. But his lungs are rotten with disease and worn out! They're finished—and if he were Croesus himself, he couldn't buy himself a new pair. Note that, my good Mrs. Logan, and ponder on the relative values of health and wealth."

Mrs. Logan continued to breathe heavily. But for all that, she liked listening to Martin Chavasse. In her own words, "Doctor Chavasse was such a *one*." Mrs. Logan propelled herself nearer to the bedside.

"He looks bad, poor soul."

Chavasse laughed mordantly and bitterly at the old woman's platitude. "So will you probably when you're waiting at the brink for Charon to ferry you over. For that's the last journey any one of us will ever take."

"Who?" demanded Mrs. Logan.

"Charon," flashed back Chavasse. "The Ferryman of the Styx."

"I've never met him," declared Mrs. Logan stolidly. "I was never one for the water. I like my two feet on good solid ground. My old mum was just the same. I take after my old mum in lots of ways."

Before Chavasse could enlighten her further concerning her immediate problem, the sick man began to mutter and mumble again. Mrs. Logan looked disturbed. She had evidently been able to hear some of the words he had muttered.

"What's he want to do, Dr. Chavasse? About signing some paper? It's on the poor soul's mind. Can't we help him?"

Chavasse smiled his bitter smile again. "He's got to journey alone, Mrs. Logan. With nobody's hand to hold. With nobody's shoulder to rest his head on."

"But this paper—what do you think he wants?"

Chavasse bent his head to listen. "I rather fancy, Mrs. Logan, that he wants to make his will. But he's too far gone for anything of that kind to-night. He'll probably regain consciousness some time to-morrow. It may be the last time. You'll stay with him through the night?"

"Oh—yes, Doctor. I've made arrangements to do so. I promised the nurses I would."

"If you want me, send for me," returned Chavasse, curtly.

"Yes, Doctor. I'll use the 'phone-box at the corner. I've got your number on a piece of paper upstairs. How long is it since he first called you in?"

"Three months, almost to the day. And I gave him three months to live the first time I examined him."

The man in the bed coughed badly and a bloody foam flecked his lips.

"When he wakes," said Chavasse, "give him a dose of the medicine. It may relieve him for a little while. I shall be back some time to-morrow unless you send for me before then."

Mrs. Logan nodded. The sick man began to speak again. But his eyes were closed. "The paper. You've seen it. Bring it to me."

"I think he's coming to a little," said Mrs. Logan, almost fearfully.

"It's getting dark," replied Chavasse. "Switch on that light; it won't trouble his eyes. I'll have another look at him." Chavasse, who had been preparing to go, walked to the bed again. "I don't think so, Mrs. Logan. He won't be conscious for some hours yet."

Suddenly Mrs. Logan saw him lean a little nearer to the prostrate figure and a quick, suspicious look come into his eyes.

"What's the matter, Doctor? Has he passed over?"

Chavasse shook his head impatiently. "No—of course not. Something I've seen worries me. You wouldn't understand if I told you."

Mrs. Logan stood round-eyed and wondering. "Shouldn't I, sir? I've had seven of my own, sir, and brought 'em all up."

Chavasse hardly heard her. He kept his eyes fixed on the dying man. "Even that stupendous performance, Mrs. Logan, won't make any difference. Ah, well—I must think this over—and don't forget the instructions I gave you."

Martin Chavasse left the bedside and put on his hat. "Good night, Mrs. Logan." Then he made his way out carefully. Almost at the front door, he thought of something and again turned back. A light tap on the bedroom door brought Mrs. Logan to him almost immediately.

"Just to remind you again, Mrs. Logan. The medicine. On no account fail to give him the proper doses of the medicine. It may make all the difference."

"Very good, Doctor. I won't forget. Every four hours."

"That's the idea. Good night again, Mrs. Logan."

Chavasse walked up the street. The man's condition puzzled him intensely. Three times now, during the last month, he had given every appearance of dying within the next twenty-four hours and three times he had rallied remarkably. Indeed, on one of these three occasions, so he had told Chavasse, he had got up, dressed and even gone out. "The candle," murmured Chavasse to himself; "the candle that invariably flickers into brighter and stronger flame, just before its end." As he thought this, he saw a big car pass him, with another, a smaller one, just behind it. "The Chief Constable's car," thought Chavasse and then realised that Sandals was something less than a mile distant.

II

Chavasse went straight from the bedroom of the man, Frederick Jordan, to the house of Dr. Pegram. Pegram, always glad of his company, welcomed him almost effusively on this occasion.

"Sit down, Martin," he said waving his guest to a chair with the stem of his pipe, "and tell me where the hell you've been these last ten days or so. And the explanation, my dear chap, when it is submitted, let me impress upon you, must be in triplicate. That will give it the hall-mark of authority. In addition to all that—help yourself." He indicated the drinks on the ample sideboard.

Chavasse grinned at the manner of his reception and took advantage of the invitation.

"My dear Pegram," he said, "for one thing, you've been busy on the 'White Lion' holocaust—Norman, King, Clarence and Yorke, farmer, baker, burglar and boy—and I've been in close attendance on a rather unusual patient. As a matter of fact, it's to do with that latter matter that I'm here to see you at this late hour of the evening."

Pegram looked up, surprised. "He must be unusual for you to talk like that."

Chavasse turned on him. "How did you know my patient was male?"

Pegram grinned sarcastically. "I didn't! I guessed! Or, rather, I used my powers of deduction. The science of deduction, my dear Martin. Ever heard of it?"

Chavasse shook his head. "All very pretty—but really I don't know that I get you."

Pegram's grin broadened. "You don't? Verily, verily, then I taste the sweets of triumph. Do you want me to explain?"

"Yes, I certainly do."

"My dear Watson—it's excessively simple. I know only too well your somewhat—if I may say so—peculiar and individualistic ideas with regard to the sex. I've heard you remark on several occasions that nothing ever done by a woman can be truthfully accounted as 'unusual.' That was point number one which influenced my judgment. My second point was this. With women, or rather to do with matters connected with women, you're most certainly inclined to be over-secretive. You don't talk about them much. You keep your *affaires* strictly to yourself. You don't parade them. All to the good, of course, and, to my mind, all in your favour. Therefore, when you came in just now and made that preliminary announcement of yours, I knew that the patient of whom you spoke was a man. *Voilà!*"

Chavasse's mouth twisted with a hint of cynicism. "Many thanks, Pegram, for the masterly analysis. I had no idea that you had held me under a microscope so minutely. Anyhow, I won't boggle over it. You're right. My patient is a man."

"I was sure of it," returned Pegram. "Now get on and tell me about him."

Chavasse helped himself to another whisky and soda. Pegram did likewise. Chavasse sat down and crossed his legs.

"I will enunciate my problem. The patient's name, so far as I have been able to gather, is Jordan. Frederick Jordan. Age? Say somewhere in the middle forties. That's near enough. He sent for me just over three months ago. Lives near Sandals. And as I realised this evening when I left his bedside, quite near to Sir Charles Stuart's place. I examined him and found a sarcomatous growth which had taken its origin in the space between his lungs. I thought at first there might be hydrated cysts in the lungs, but this is not so. The tumour is of long standing. I can do nothing. An 'op' is unthinkable. There is intense difficulty of breathing from the pressure of the growth upon the lungs and on the bronchial tubes. Well, I won't weary you with any more details. That was that. Interested?"

"Rather. I'm wondering what's coming—where the snag is."

Chavasse laughed. "You would! Jordan lives by himself, but a decent old Scots body by the name of Logan 'does' for him. I leave him in her charge. He's *in extremis*. A matter of forty-eight hours or so. Maybe a little longer—not much, though. Well, you're still wondering—I can see that—here comes the kernel! He has most extraordinary periods of strength! From time to time he has rallied in a most remarkable manner. In fact, on one occasion, I taxed him on my next visit, with having been out! In the street, I mean. Anywhere, in fact, for all I know."

Pegram stared at him—his eyes full of interest. "That's extraordinary. What did he say?"

"He admitted it. To deny it again later on! *In Toto!* But his denials didn't satisfy me, and, frankly, I didn't believe him."

Pegram nodded. "Did you tell him as much?"

"No-o. Not altogether. In so many words, that is."

"What did he say to that? How did he take it?"

"He just denied everything, wouldn't budge from that position. It's difficult to argue against a blank, unyielding wall of denial. When I pointed out his previous admission, he said his mind must have been wandering."

"H'm—I see. Something you didn't tell me. What made you think he'd been out? That's what I find most interesting about the whole thing."

"Oh—come to that—several things. Mrs. Logan implied as much when she let me into the place on that particular morning. I think he'd been talking. I checked up as well as I could. Watched his clothes, the state of his shoes, his own condition, took his temperature and his blood pressure. The evidence that I was able to accumulate satisfied me that Mrs. Logan was a long way from being wrong. But, as I said, that was as far as I was able to get. Jordan now won't hear of it. Admits nothing. Repudiates everything."

Pegram smoked vigorously. "How many times did this happen? Or rather—did anything similar occur again?"

Chavasse nodded. "It did. In my opinion, that's the funny part about it."

"Did Mrs. Logan tip you off as before?"

"No. After the first occasion, of course, I kept my eyes open. More open. Similar evidences presented themselves and I was somewhat reluctantly forced to similar conclusions."

Pegram heard this and smoked hard. When he spoke, he said: "Martin—how many times altogether?"

"Three or four, I should say, without the book. I don't know that I've troubled particularly to remember."

"Martin—be exact if you can! Think! How many times exactly?"

Chavasse considered the question. There came a few seconds' silence. It was eventually broken by Martin Chavasse. "To be exact—four. I thought first it was three—but on second thoughts I put it at four."

"Very strange," declared Pegram. "And, candidly, I don't know what to make of it."

"I'm not so much worried over the part I've told you," continued Chavasse. "It's something else that's causing me concern."

"Oh—what's that? I'm all ears."

"On my last two visits to him, Jordan has babbled about a paper. A mysterious paper that he wants taken to him as he lies there in bed so that he may sign it. When that has been done, he raves in his delirium that he's more or less prepared for the end to come. Now I deduce from all that that he's made his will, but he hasn't signed it and it's hidden away in the room somewhere. Do you think, Pegram, that I should search for it next time I go there?"

It was some time before Pegram replied to the question. "Why do you think it's a will that the fellow's worrying about?"

"For the simple reason that I think a will is the most likely matter to be troubling him. That's all." Chavasse waited. Then he followed up: "Don't you?"

"I wasn't sure. Perhaps you're right." Pegram paused.

Chavasse rallied him: "Well, you haven't answered my question yet."

"*Re* the will and looking round to see if you can find it?"

"Ah-ha! That was the course that suggested itself to me. But I felt that I should both like and value your opinion."

"Well—this is how it strikes me. You're his medical bloke—you aren't his lawyer or yet his father confessor."

"Agreed every time! But one feels, I think, that one should try to help a bloke in this condition, as much as is humanly possible. At least, that's how it appeals to me."

"I don't see, though, weighing all the pros and cons, why you should worry your fat about it."

Chavasse shook his head. "Don't get me wrong, Pegram. I'm not worrying about it in the sense that you appear to be thinking. I merely want to help a wretched human soul whose on nodding terms with Admiral Death. I'm a doctor. You're a doctor. But I'm not as case-hardened as some of our noble profession."

Pegram struck a match and tossed the burnt stick into the ash-tray on the table. "I've been wondering, Martin, all the time that you've been telling me this, whether I'm reading something into it that doesn't seem to have reared its ugly head in front of you."

Chavasse stared at him curiously. "What the devil are you hinting at?"

"No idea?"

"No. Not the slightest. But let me have it, whatever it is. Don't keep it stored up, for the love of Mike."

"All right. I will. Seeing as 'ow you've asked me to. On how many occasions did you say that Jordan may have walked abroad?"

"Four." As Chavasse spoke his face showed unmistakably that he had realised the significance of his words. "My God, Pegram," he whispered, "what are you thinking?"

Pegram shrugged his shoulders. "Well—there you are. You can see the road that my thoughts have been travelling. Maybe there's nothing in it. Maybe it's fantastic! But the murders themselves are fantastic! They've taken place, though, for all that."

Pegram ceased talking rather abruptly. Chavasse sat in his chair as though his features had been petrified. Once he whistled softly under his breath.

"Good God! And my mind was centred on him so thoroughly as a patient, that I never gave the other possibility a thought." Then suddenly his face cleared, "No Pegram. It's absurd. I refuse to believe it. I refuse even to entertain it for a moment."

Again Pegram shrugged his shoulders. "Well—that's up to you, but it's perfectly obvious what we can do. Check up on the times.

We know when the murders took place. Can you vouch accurately as regards the occasions when this bloke went prowling round?"

"I don't know that I can give the exact dates, but I can tell within a little. Have you the dates of the four murders?" As he spoke, Chavasse took his diary from his pocket.

"I have," returned Pegram. "Wait a minute and I'll turn them up for you."

Pegram rose and took a pile of papers from the top of his bookcase. He brought them back to the table and began to turn them over.

"Norman was the first. Norman was killed on the eleventh of March. How does that go for the theory?"

Chavasse flicked the pages of his diary. Pegram saw the agitation come into his face. "I visited Jordan on the thirteenth of March. That was the first occasion that I conceived the idea that he had left his bedroom somehow. By Jove, Pegram, it looks as though you're on to something! Take the next one."

Pegram referred again to his official file. "The King death. Half a minute, and I shall be able to give it to you." Chavasse waited. "Here we are." Pegram gave the date.

Chavasse nodded his acceptance and went to his diary again. Pegram watched him anxiously. After some few minutes' searching, Chavasse shook his head. "This is against me. I'm going to let you down. I don't appear to have made any record of the second incident. At any rate, I've no entry round about that date that you give."

"Make sure! Make sure you haven't it somewhere else. Which would prove conclusively that we're on a 'stumer.'"

"Yes, I agree. I must do that." Chavasse ran his finger down the pages, meticulously. "No. I've nothing. And what's more, I *think*—mind, only *think*—that that date of yours wouldn't be a lot out. Anyhow, check up on the third murder. We may have better luck."

"I don't know that 'luck' is the right word to use. Still—we'll see! Clarence was the third, wasn't he?"

"Yes—Clarence."

Pegram flicked the files and gave the date of the Clarence murder. Chavasse went to the pages of the diary again. When he looked up, Pegram saw that his face was drained of colour.

"I visited Jordan the day after that date—and my opinion was that he had been out. God, Pegram, where are we getting to?"

"We'll clinch it if we can. Let's take the Yorke affair. That took place during the first week in June. I'll give you the actual day. Hold on for a second while I turn it up." Pegram found the date and gave it. Chavasse shook his head.

"Haven't got it. No record! But my memory tells me it's as near as damn it to the last occasion when I fancied Master Jordan had played truant."

There ensued a lengthy silence. Pegram broke it. "I feel," he said, "that we're facing a problem that is almost insoluble." His voice was grave.

"How exactly do you mean?" enquired Chavasse.

"Isn't it obvious, Martin?"

"Well—before I can answer you, tell me what you mean."

"What to do. What to do for the best. You and I merely suspect. We haven't a scintilla of proof. We're building an edifice of accusation in our minds and hearts, which is foundationed solely on certain coincidences of time. Beyond that we have nothing."

"I agree—but the idea emanated from you, Pegram. And you've convinced me that there may be something in it. Those dates—they've frightened me. You can't get away from them!"

"I know, Martin. They're so—sinister! And because they're so sinister, they frighten me, too. But—think of all the attendant circumstances, Martin. That's where my worry starts."

"You mean his illness, I presume?"

"Exactly. The man's a patient of yours. He's suffering, as you know only too well, from an incurable disease which has reached the stage when his death is just round the corner."

Chavasse nodded. "Again I agree. With everything that you've said. Yes, Pegram—it's all damned difficult. And then, after all this, there's the—" Chavasse stopped. Pegram took him up.

"There's the what?" he demanded.

"Why—the business of that will. The question with which I started the ball rolling this evening. I still have to consider that. And I'm no nearer knowing what to do with regard to it than I was at the outset. Am I?"

Pegram shook his head, "No—I suppose you aren't." Then an idea seemed suddenly to strike him. "There's one thing, Martin. This theory which you and I are considering at the moment upsets that pet idea of yours, doesn't it?"

Chavasse furrowed his brows. "Which one?"

"The one *re* the murders. The homicidal lunatic theory."

Chavasse shook his head vigorously. "No—not for a moment. You're wrong if you think so. I don't concede that, Pegram. It's all in the same gallery. And in the *right* gallery, too. How do you know the condition of Fred Jordan's mind? *Mens Sana*, Pegram, and don't you forget it! How do I, his doctor, know the condition of the man's mind? Who've had him under my care for months? I tell you frankly I *don't* know it. For the simple reason that I've never looked into that particular question. I've been looking after his body, Pegram. And the malignant growth on the poor devil's lungs."

Pegram's eyebrows went up. "Poor devil? After what we've come to—"

Chavasse cut in. "*Yes*. Poor devil! Who are we to judge the reactions of a mortally stricken man?"

Pegram made no reply. He had heard Martin Chavasse in this strain before and he knew that all the forces of argument he might employ would be useless. Chavasse realised the advantage he had gained and went on almost at once:

"Another thing. What possible action can one take? No proof—mere suspicions—and a man sick unto death? Now, I ask you, Pegram!"

Pegram still remained silent. Chavasse found a measure of impatience. "The only thing I can do, Pegram, is to see that he's not allowed to perpetrate any more mischief. And that I propose to do." He rose and paced the room.

"It's deuced awkward," muttered Pegram. "I can see that just as plainly as you do. And I'm damned if I know the best course to advise or even the best thing to do."

"I know what I'm going to do. I made up my mind a few moments ago."

"What's that?"

"I'm going to pursue a policy of masterly inactivity. In other words, I'm going to wait and see what happens. Because, frankly, I don't think the fellow can possibly leave his bed again. I'm positive that he's reached a stage when he doesn't possess the strength." Chavasse was emphatic in his statement.

Pegram, against his better judgment, it seemed, accepted the situation. "All right," he conceded. "We'll see what the future brings forth. I say it against my will—but it's about all we can do. In the meantime, I propose that we sleep on it."

Chavasse nodded. "That's never a bad idea, Pegram, no matter how complicated the problem may be. We'll both act on your suggestion."

Pegram grinned. It was the first sign of levity that he had shown for a considerable time. "Before you leave, Martin," he said with much of his usual complacency, "let me help you to another spot of Scotch."

"That, Pegram, is a suggestion that meets with my unqualified approval."

III

Martin Chavasse had never been a man to let the grass grow under his feet. When he left Pegram, he came away with the inflexible intention of getting to Jordan again at his earliest possible opportunity. He translated the intention into actuality early on the day following. Mrs. Logan met him at the door.

"I'm right glad you've come, Doctor! Never has a face been more welcome to me than yours on this day that ever was."

Chavasse smiled kindly at her. "And the reason, Mrs. Logan?"

"Why? Why on account of that poor soul in there, to be sure. He's that poorly, to-day, you can hear the wings of the Angel of Death—you can!"

"Did you give him his medicine in the night, Mrs. Logan?"

"I did, Dr. Chavasse. Went in there twice to him, I did. And much good did it do him."

Chavasse shot a quick glance at her. He saw that his suspicions were unfounded.

"I'll take you in to him now, Doctor," said Mrs. Logan. "And you can see for yourself the turn for the worse that he's taken."

Chavasse followed Mrs. Logan into Jordan's bedroom. He soon saw that the man was sleeping. He was breathing heavily. But as Chavasse looked carefully at him, the Doctor's expert eye told him that he was in disagreement with Mrs. Logan with regard to Jordan's condition. To the doctor's eye, the patient looked a little better. Certainly no worse, as Mrs. Logan had it. Chavasse shook his head.

"On the contrary, Mrs. Logan," he said, "he's a lump better than I anticipated he'd be. He's a bit flushed, but I'm not worrying over that. I'll stay with him until he wakes. So if you want a spot of rest, you can go and take it at once, Mrs. Logan."

The old woman smiled brightly and nodded her pleasure at the doctor's statement. "Thank you, Doctor. I shall appreciate a bit of a rest, as you can guess."

Chavasse "shushed" her away upstairs. Then he hooked a foot round the leg of a chair, pulled it up to the bedside and seated himself on it. He bent forward and watched the sick man's face intently. He was waiting for Jordan to emerge from his slumber and come to a state of wakefulness. Chavasse looked at his wrist-watch. He had intended to ask Mrs. Logan how long Jordan had been asleep. But he had forgotten to do so, and he didn't desire to trouble the staunch old Scotswoman during the period of her resting. Chavasse sat at the bedside, perfectly still, for the matter of close on half an hour. Then, to his satisfaction, he saw the first signs of the sick man's awakening.

Jordan flung an arm across the coverlet, sighed heavily two or three times, and then slowly opened his eyes. Some seconds elapsed before he recognised the man sitting at his bedside. When he did he began to speak. But owing to his repeated fits of coughing, he spoke with the utmost difficulty.

"Good morning, Doctor," he gasped. "Don't feel too good." Another burst of coughing shook him terribly.

"Good morning," returned Chavasse. "Don't talk if you're coughing. It will only make you worse."

Jordan shook his head. His impatience was easy to see. "I'm not so bad . . . perhaps . . . only sometimes . . . feel worse than others. Tell me, Doctor . . ." He thrust a shrunken, wasted hand from below the bed-clothes and caught Chavasse by the wrist. "Am I . . . going to get . . . better?"

Chavasse regarded him searchingly. "I don't think you are, Jordan. While there's life, there's hope, of course . . . but I think you must begin to realise . . ."

The doctor stopped rather lamely. Jordan's hand as he heard the doctor's pronouncement fell limply on to the bed. Neither man spoke. Jordan's head sagged a little, his eyes closed and his chin fell. Then by an intense effort which brought into play the entire resources left to him, he seemed to pull himself together and his eyes opened.

"The paper, Doctor," he croaked, "over there. Let me sign it. I must leave my affairs in order."

His lean, scraggy forefinger jabbed in the direction of an old-fashioned chest of drawers standing against a wall on the other side of the room. Chavasse turned his head in the direction indicated. Jordan saw that Chavasse's interest had been aroused. "Get it, Doctor! You won't be able to do many more things for me. In this world. And maybe there won't be any 'sawbones' knocking around in the next!"

He made a hollow, laughing noise at his own witticism. Chavasse stepped towards the chest of drawers. He saw when he came nearer to it that it had once before in its history formed part of a tallboy. There were three long drawers and in the top row two half-drawers.

"In the top drawer—left-hand side," came the harsh voice of Jordan's directing. Martin Chavasse pulled open the appropriate drawer. What he saw in the drawer rather dismayed him at first glance. For there confronted his eyes a miscellaneous collection of papers. They lay there in hopeless confusion, without even a sorry semblance of order. As far as Chavasse could see, at that moment, there were old letters, old envelopes, used and unused, postcards, old telegrams in their distinctive buff coverings, accounts, receipts, old theatre programmes, photographs of many varieties—amateur "snaps" and professional takings—labels, timetables and an assortment of old newspaper cuttings. Chavasse looked helplessly at the heap which his fingers were touching. Semi-instinctively, he half-turned his head back to the dying man in the bed.

"In the envelope" . . . came the gasping voice. . . . "It's marked on the outside . . . 'The last statement of Frederick Newcombe Bedingfield Jordan.' You can't miss it—or mistake it. A long, thin envelope . . . cream-coloured."

Chavasse said: "All right. Don't worry. . . . If it's here, I'll find it, if I have to sort through everything to get my hands on it. Just give me time—that's all."

Jordan made acquiescent noises from the bed. Martin Chavasse rummaged through the motley collection. The Spanish phrase, *olla podrida*, kept running through his mind as he stood there, searching through the contents of the drawer. Sandwiched between two old theatre programmes, Chavasse suddenly came on the envelope which Jordan wanted. Without turning, he called to the sick man.

"It's all right! It's here. The envelope that you're so concerned about."

To his surprise, remembering the acute anxiety which Jordan had just exhibited, there came no answering words. Chavasse turned and saw what had happened. What had happened so repeatedly during the last few days. Jordan had lapsed into unconsciousness again. Chavasse went to the fast-diminishing stock of brandy and moistened Jordan's lips with the spirit. But the treatment was ineffective. Chavasse shook his head dubiously and decided to sit down by the bedside and examine the contents of the long thin envelope.

He took out a sheet of ordinary foolscap paper covered with thin, spidery writing. It was headed: "The Last Will, Testament and Statement of Frederick Newcombe Bedingfield Jordan." With a glance at the unconscious man, Chavasse began to read what he presumed Jordan had written. When he had finished reading, he went to the door of the bedroom and called to Mrs. Logan. The old Scotswoman heard him and made her uncertain journey down the staircase. Chavasse gave her no time to think. He placed his demands before her in a flash.

"Mrs. Logan," he declared, and she observed that his voice was tinged with a note of excitement. "I must leave here at once. It's most important. Jordan's unconscious again, but I'll take my oath it's only temporary. His time hasn't come yet. I want you to stay with him until I return. Now listen to me carefully. Whatever you do, you mustn't let him out of your sight till I come back. And I shan't, I hope, be away too long. Understand me?"

Mi's. Logan looked a trifle nervous and bewildered. She fumbled with her hands on her apron as she nodded her acceptance of Chavasse's proposals.

"All right, Doctor Chavasse. I'll do as you say. I'll stay with him until you come back."

"Good," cried Chavasse. "Till I return, then. There's plenty of medicine left for him and there's brandy on the table."

"All right, Doctor," said Mrs. Logan.

IV

Chief-Inspector Andrew MacMorran made a tattoo on the bathroom door. The reason for MacMorran's relaying his morning message was that Anthony Bathurst was shaving inside the bathroom and that Andrew MacMorran had urgent news for him.

"Hallo," cried Anthony. "Open locks whoever knocks! What's the row about?"

"News—you mutt! Hot and strong! Just come crackling over the telephone. For me and for you. Open the door, Beau Brummell."

Anthony grinned and pulled the bathroom door to confront the Scotland Yard Inspector on the threshold. Anthony, let it be said, had one side of his face lathered and still therefore unshaven.

"What the hell?" said Anthony. "Can't a man remain comfortably cradled in his Kolynos? Without you appearing as a miniature Gabriel?"

"Mr. Bathurst," said MacMorran rolling his 'r's,' "you don't know what this news is. Otherwise you wouldn't be talking as you are. But the 'White Lion' murder case is over. Fini! We can play golf to-day and return to London to-morrow morning."

Anthony surveyed him kindly. "Come in, Andrew," he said sympathetically. "Come in and make yourself at home. Sit, I suggest, on the edge of the bath, and make a suitable noise by knocking the sponge on the back of the nail-brush. In the meantime, I will finish the very pleasant exercise of shaving."

Anthony pulled MacMorran into the bathroom and kicked the door to. MacMorran suffered the indignities with the utmost patience and good temper. Anthony resumed facial operations with his razor.

"You can talk your nonsense to your heart's content," remarked MacMorran, perched uncomfortably on the edge of the bath, "but the 'White Lion' murderer will be arrested this morning. If he hasn't been arrested already."

He spoke coolly and quietly. Anthony stopped—his razor poised in mid-air.

"What?" he cried incredulously.

"You heard," replied the Inspector.

"Go on telling me then, Andrew," rejoined Anthony, "and I'll promise to shave myself and stay silent. At the same time, I'm not promising to believe implicitly all the fairy tales you're going to put over."

"The murderer of Norman and the others has confessed."

Anthony took the blade from his cheek. "Oh—yeah," he remarked tersely.

"Your promises aren't worth much, apparently," retorted the Inspector.

"Sorry, Andrew," replied Mr. Bathurst. "It slipped. Tell me the worst."

The 'Yard' man started again to tell his story. "The murderer, as I said to you just now, has confessed. And—listen carefully—has put in a written confession! His name is"—and here MacMorran referred to a slip of paper—"Frederick Newcombe Bedingfield Jordan. He lives out near Sandals."

Anthony held up a finger. "You must let me out on this one. I'll apologise in advance. Where did you say, Andrew?"

"Near Sandals. That's near to where the Chief Constable, Sir Charles Stuart, lives."

"I can't bear to contradict you, Andrew. But keep on keeping on. I must confess to being interested at last."

"Jordan made a full and complete confession. It's in our hands. I should say that he's a lunatic. But, apart from that conjecture on my part, there's another abnormal complication."

MacMorran deliberately delayed his climax. Anthony waited for him, staring straight in front of him. But he said nothing. MacMorran yielded to the unspoken demand.

"He's a dying man. Doomed. Not the ghost of a chance, according to the vet. Growth on the lungs, or something of that kind. Absolutely incurable. Just a matter of time."

Anthony whistled under his breath. "Shades of Jefferson Hope! Still—proceed, Andrew."

"When this information was passed on to Venables, he communicated with me at once. I was amazed, of course, just as you were. But I listened to his story without interrupting him and agreed to the man's speedy arrest. I'd sooner he was under lock and key than anywhere else, even though it may spell hospital."

Anthony grinned. "Always the little gentleman—eh, Andrew? Well, it sounds peculiar to my way of thinking. I feel that I'd like to know a great deal more before I commit myself to the expression of a definite opinion."

"I expected that from you. And I've made all the necessary arrangements. After breakfast you and I are meeting Venables. We shall hear the whole story and Jordan's confession will be placed in front of us."

Anthony put his razor back into its case. He wiped the soap remnants from his face and his hands on a towel.

"Did you say 'after' breakfast, Andrew?"

"I did, Mr. Bathurst. I imagined that procedure would suit you."

"Andrew," said Anthony, "you have a positive flair for doing the right thing. It will suit me admirably."

V

Anthony Lotherington Bathurst and Chief-Inspector Andrew MacMorran were shown into the presence of three people. To be precise, Drs. Pegram and Chavasse and Inspector Venables. The venue was the official room of the last-named. Venables rose abruptly to greet his guests.

"Good-morning, Chief. Good-morning, Mr. Bathurst. You know the doctors here. Please sit down, make yourselves comfortable, and we'll get right down to business at once."

MacMorran and Anthony returned the greetings and took the chairs offered to them.

"First of all, gentlemen," opened the local Inspector, "I will call on Dr. Chavasse to tell you the story that he has already recounted to me. Dr. Chavasse."

Dr. Chavasse leant forward in his seat, his face alight with excitement. Quite simply, without any flourish of verbal trumpets, and with admirable restraint, Chavasse told the story, as he knew it, of his patient, Jordan. Anthony listened intently to every word. When Chavasse had finished, Anthony waited for MacMorran to speak. But Andrew shook his head and then nodded to Anthony to say what he had to say. Anthony took the opportunity immediately.

"This confession of Jordan's, Doctor—may we see it, please?"

Chavasse nodded and indicated Venables. "Here it is," said the latter. He produced a long, thin envelope, and took from it, a sheet of foolscap paper. He handed the latter to MacMorran, who spread it on the table in front of himself and Anthony Bathurst.

"That's the paper," remarked Chavasse, "which I took from the drawer in Jordan's bedroom."

Anthony saw that the paper was covered with handwriting of a thin, spidery character. He and MacMorran read it. "The Last Will, Testament and Statement of Frederick Newcombe Bedingfield Jordan. I, Frederick Newcombe Bedingfield Jordan of 9 Folly Buildings, Sandals, being in my right mind have much pleasure to state that I have nothing to leave behind when I depart this life except a few sticks of furniture of precious little value. These are to go to Mrs. Matilda Logan of the same address, a recognition of many kindnesses which she has shown to me during the past few months. In this particular respect, I'd like her to know that she occupies an almost unique position. If she sells the few things I leave to her I dare say they may realise a few shillings with which to drink my health when I'm in Hades or elsewhere, the odds being considerably in favour of the former-mentioned locality. Having disposed therefore of all my worldly goods, I will now pass on to the more important provisions of this statement. I hereby, voluntarily and of my own free will, confess to the murders of William Norman, Henry King, George Clarence and the boy, Richard Yorke. Not 'murders' really—-just elementary justice. At any rate, that's how I look at it. Years ago, I promised the only human being I ever loved in this world that I would administer justice in the way I have—and, thanks be to God, I have faithfully kept that promise. But I owe five lives to her blessed memory and up to now I have taken but four. But for the cursed and entirely opportune malady which has laid me so low of these recent days, the tally would have been five by now. As it is I hope to complete my task before I enter my own particular Valhalla. When there's a will there's a way! I know in my heart that God will grant me the necessary strength and give me the opportunity to complete my task. In that supreme hope and knowledge, therefore, I bid good-bye to this world! And I make this confession now', because I shall have no further opportunity. Signed Frederick N.B. Jordan. Witnesses to the signature of Frederick N.B. Jordan: Martin Thorne Chavasse and Matilda Logan."

Anthony waited again for MacMorran to finish reading Jordan's statement. The Inspector did so and then quietly handed the document back to Inspector Venables.

"Well," said the latter, with a glance in the direction of the two doctors, who were watching the others intently, "what do you think of it?"

"A remarkable document," commented MacMorran.

"What about you, Mr. Bathurst?"

"I can only echo what Inspector MacMorran has just said," replied Anthony.

"Well, there's one thing," contributed Chavasse, "there's no doubting its authenticity. I can vouch for that. Otherwise, I might very well feel as you gentlemen appear to be feeling."

"It is not dated," remarked Anthony.

Heads nodded at his statement. "We noticed that," added Chavasse. "But by implication it can have been written but a few days ago. It refers to the murder of the boy Yorke."

MacMorran acquiesced. "That's a fair assumption. There's no denying that."

"Where is Jordan now?" asked Anthony.

Venable answered the question: "At his lodgings at Sandals. Number Nine, Folly Buildings."

MacMorran turned to him with criticism in his eyes. "Is he aware that this confession is in the hands of the Police?"

Venables glanced towards Dr. Chavasse. The glance was an invitation to him to reply to MacMorran's question.

"In my opinion—yes—and no. As I've told you, he begged for me to find the paper so that he could sign it. When I found it, he had relapsed again into unconsciousness. I read it, came and consulted Dr. Pegram here as to the best course to pursue, then I returned to Jordan's place and, with Mrs. Logan, witnessed his signature. After a lot of deliberation and heart-searching over my position as medical adviser to my patient, I came to the conclusion that I must do my primary duty. I then left Jordan in the hands of Mrs. Logan and put the confession in the hands of Inspector Venables. I *think* I have done the right thing."

Venables nodded. "And I agree with you, Dr. Chavasse."

"Do you think it was safe to leave him," commented MacMorran.

"Safe?" echoed Chavasse almost contemptuously. "The man's almost unconscious nearly all the time now and, in addition to that, I saw that he had a shot of dope. You can rest assured I was taking no chances. When you fellows walk in this morning, he'll be like a log. If he isn't already dead."

MacMorran turned to Inspector Venables. "Have you made the necessary arrangements for the arrest?"

"Subject to your approval, yes! All of them."

"When?" demanded MacMorran curtly.

"As soon as you like."

"And then—"

"The prison hospital. There's no argument, I'm afraid, with regard to that. The procedure afterwards must depend—I take it you're in agreement with me?"

The Scotland Yard Inspector nodded sharply.

"Just a minute," intervened Anthony; "that is, gentlemen, if you don't mind. I want to ask a question of Dr. Chavasse. May I, Doctor?"

"Certainly," returned Chavasse. "What is it?"

"When did you last see this man, Jordan?"

Chavasse answered promptly: "Last night. Between ten and eleven o'clock."

"Were you alone with him, Doctor?"

"No, Bathurst. Mrs. Logan was with me all the time I was there and I left Mrs. Logan in charge of him. After we had witnessed his signature. You can rely on her. She's as safe as the Bank of England."

Anthony noticed Pegram flash a glance at Chavasse. He seized his chance immediately.

"What's your point, Dr. Pegram? I take it that there's something with which you aren't altogether satisfied." It struck Anthony that Pegram looked a trifle annoyed. When he replied Pegram spoke with some bitterness.

"You're quick, aren't you? But Chavasse knows what I mean and what I'm thinking of. Forget it!"

"No, no," said Anthony. "Let's have all the cards on the table, please. Don't hide anything from us. Otherwise—we may—"

Chavasse was, however, perfectly frank. "I know what's biting Pegram. And I'll tell you all about it. Again it comes back to this patient of mine—Jordan."

"Let's hear it then, Doctor," clinched MacMorran.

Chavasse told the story as he had told it to Pegram some days previously. Concerning his suspicions as to Jordan's actions, his remarkable rallying power and of the solution which Pegram had so quickly countenanced.

"Why didn't you mention this before?" said MacMorran.

"What do you mean?" countered Chavasse with definite asperity. "I have told Venables here and if he hasn't told you—it's his fault, so don't darned well blame me." Chavasse twitched his shoulders angrily.

"That is quite true," put in Venables. "I was coming to it later, but I regarded Jordan's confession as all-important."

MacMorran growled something under his breath.

"And I can vouch for all of it," supplemented Pegram. "Chavasse came and told me that he suspected Jordan might have been out during certain stages of his illness and that he was puzzled by it. I supplied the missing links. Together we pieced up the possibilities, little dreaming that they would so soon be corroborated."

"I was slow," said Chavasse frankly. "I admit that, but to me Jordan was a patient. A patient first, second, all the time and never anything more than a patient. I'm willing to cry 'Mea culpa'—but that's the explanation. Sorry if it seems too feeble for words."

"As a matter of fact," concluded Pegram, "I don't like any of it. It's all ugly and beastly. A man on the threshold of eternity making a pastime of bloody murder. Foul, I call it."

"Another thing which puzzles me about it," contributed Anthony, "is that Jordan gives no real reason for his murdering these people. Had they all been of a generation, one perhaps could have understood it a little better. But they're not—we have three men say of an age, and the other a boy."

"I agree with you over that," said Pegram. "I thought exactly the same thing myself."

"It is strange," mused Chavasse. "But the crimes were undoubtedly crimes of revenge. That's obvious to see, from the wording of Jordan's confession statement. Revenge, evidently for some wrong done to a woman in Jordan's life. The woman whom he promised to avenge."

"If that be so," commented Anthony, "then the woman, in all probability was Jordan's mother. That's my bet—and I regard it as a pretty safe one."

"Why?" demanded MacMorran. "I'd be interested to know that." Anthony shrugged his shoulders. "Merely from a study of the three dead men and the boy. One can visualise families running a vendetta of that kind. Had it been connected with a previous love affair, one wouldn't expect to find so *many* different families implicated. That's how I arrived where I did."

MacMorran nodded. "I see your point. I wondered—that was all."

"Will you come over to Sandals with me, Chief?" inquired Venables.

"I will. As soon as ever you like. And I think we ought to be getting along there at once and without any further delay. Are you fit?"

"That suits me," replied Venables. "And I also think that Dr. Chavasse should make the journey with us. After all, there's this to be considered—Jordan's his patient."

MacMorran turned to Chavasse. "What do you say yourself, Dr. Chavasse? Is the suggestion convenient to you?"

Chavasse answered him without hesitation. "Oh—yes. Quite. I shall be delighted to come over with you. In fact, more than that even. I want to come. And I should have been acutely disappointed if you hadn't asked me. You might just as well know that as not."

"Good," returned MacMorran. "That's settled then. We'll start half an hour from now. I'll meet you here."

Anthony walked with the Scotland Yard Inspector for a little distance along the Mallett High Street.

"Well—you know where I'm going, Mr. Bathurst. When I come back, I should like a few words with you immediately. Where shall I find you?" Anthony smiled. "What better place could I nominate, Andrew, than the saloon-bar of the 'White Lion'? Right in the very heart of things."

"Very well, Mr. Bathurst. I'll come there to you."

"Hope I shan't find Jordan there," grinned Anthony. "It would put me off my stroke."

MacMorran had turned away, but stopped short in his stride at Anthony's words. "Why, Mr. Bathurst, you don't think that likely, do you?"

"I can remember only one thing, Andrew. And that's this. That Jordan's tally is four—and not five."

VI

Anthony Bathurst walked away from his professional colleague and made his way to the nearest telephone call-box. When there, he rang the house of Sir Charles Stuart at Sandals. Having established contact, he asked to speak to the Chief Constable. Lady Stuart came to the telephone.

"Who is that?" she asked. Anthony thought that her voice was a little strained and anxious.

"It's Bathurst speaking," he said quietly. "May I have a word with Sir Charles, Lady Stuart? It's important—otherwise I wouldn't have worried you so early in the morning."

"Why—yes," she answered. "He's in the library. I'll get him to come to the 'phone to speak to you at once. How are things, Mr. Bathurst? Is a mere member of the weaker sex permitted to trespass into the territory of secret things?"

She heard Anthony's laugh at the other end of the line. "I think I may say, Lady Stuart, that we can report progress."

"Really, Mr. Bathurst?"

"Yes. Most certainly."

"And what is Mr. Anthony Bathurst's definition of progress? It seems to a humble person like myself that so much may depend on that."

"Well"—and here Anthony came to a quick decision—"we are in sight of an arrest. I might almost say that we are on the very eve of an arrest."

"When?"

"Within an hour, I should say. Sir Charles will know directly it becomes an accomplished fact. Scotland Yard's in charge of operations, you know."

"I've no quarrel with that. Er—who is it?"

"No—no! You mustn't ask me that. But you'll know all about it before bedtime to-night. Most probably before dinner."

"All right. I must accept what you say." Her voice was now definitely unsteady. "I'll ask Sir Charles to come to speak to you. Hang on, Mr. Bathurst, please."

Anthony waited for the Chief Constable to come to the telephone. Sir Charles's voice boomed down the line. "Morning, Bathurst. Everything's all right, you see, so far."

"I am relieved to hear that, Sir Charles. I get reports, of course, every morning and evening. Now, sir, I want you to listen to me. I'm going to ask you to grant me an extra special favour. And believe me, I'm not making the request idly. I want you to remain in the house all day to-day."

There came murmurs of protest from the Chief Constable of Glebeshire. But Anthony's voice assumed a note of insistence.

"I am certain, sir, that to-day will bring us to the crisis. Most probably to-night. Now, sir, may I have your promise? And wherever you go in any of your rooms, see that Lady Stuart accompanies you. In all emphasis, Sir Charles, my advice is vital."

"All right, Bathurst—I'll do as you desire. But it's a pestilent nuisance. I find it most—er—irksome."

"I don't doubt that, sir, but it's better than—well, you know very well what we're afraid of."

"I don't like the way you put it, man, but I understand what you mean. All right, Bathurst. I'm your man. Rely on me."

"Good. I'm delighted that you're seeing reason. I was afraid that I should have a harder job with you than it's proved to be."

"Thanks for the unnecessary compliment," came the grim rejoinder. Anthony grinned at his end and went on with the conversation. "Now, there's one more thing, Sir Charles. I'm coming over to your place early this evening. I feel that it's imperative that I should do. And I intend to bring one or two specialities with me. Is that all right."

"Of course. Come when you like. Let me know when we may expect you. Lady Stuart, I'm sure, will be delighted to have you over here."

"Thank you very much. After dinner, say. Don't worry about making any arrangements. It's going to be a purely business visit."

"All right. Have it whichever way you like."

"There's something else, too, Sir Charles. You must ask me to stay the night."

"'That's all right, too. Take it as read, Bathurst."

"Also, Chief-Inspector MacMorran. But he doesn't know yet where he's going to sleep to-night. I'm gate-crashing on his behalf. That all right too, sir?"

"I suppose so. Yes. You wouldn't ask it if you didn't regard it as necessary. But why doesn't the Inspector know about it? If it's so damned urgent—as you suggest it is?"

This time Anthony grimaced to himself. "He doesn't know *yet*, Sir Charles. But it's merely a question of time. He'll know within a few minutes of my next seeing him. Which will take place moderately soon."

He heard Sir Charles Stuart laugh at the other end of the line, but the laugh held little real merriment.

"All right, Bathurst. Do as you please in every way. I'll expect you soon after dinner, then. I'll tell Lady Stuart."

"Thank you again, sir. *Au 'voir* then—and please watch your step."

"Fee-fi-fo-fum," growled the Chief Constable. "I shall begin to think you got your Blue as a witch-doctor."

Anthony walked from the kiosk with thoughtful steps. He then made for the 'White Lion' and the saloon bar thereof—the rendezvous he had appointed for Andrew MacMorran.

The only man he knew who was in the bar when he arrived was Marnoch, the retired Inspector of Police. Marnoch's face brightened when he saw Anthony enter and he at once came up to his side.

"Good morning, Mr. Bathurst! And I'm not flattering you when I say that there's no one I'd rather have clapped eyes on."

"Nice of you," returned Anthony gaily. "Name your own fantastic brand of poison and I'll join you in the toast."

"I'll have a pint of 'B and B,' if you don't mind. At this time of the day, I seldom drink anything else." He sidled closer to Anthony. "Things moving?" he said in an undertone.

"Some things in all probability," returned Anthony. "A completely static world is surely appalling to contemplate?"

Marnoch smiled a slow semi-resentful smile. "Shucks—you know very well what I mean. I've been a 'busy' myself, don't forget—once upon a time."

Anthony gave him smile for smile. "Sounds, Mr. Marnoch, almost like a fairy tale."

Marnoch shook his head. "If you think that, Mr. Bathurst, you've got me all wrong. Fairy tales and the Metropolitan Police don't mix— by any manner of means. No"—and here Marnoch shook his head with a strong measure of solemnity—"I was perfectly serious when I said to you what I did, 'Things moving?'"

Anthony smiled cordially. "I'm wondering what it was, Mr. Marnoch, that made you say it. Perhaps you're merely drawing a bow at a venture?"

Again Marnoch shook his head. "No, sir. I'm too old a hand at the game to draw either false conclusions or even bows at ventures. And I usually go about with both these blue eyes of mine wide open."

"Good," said Anthony. "In that respect, then, you're a man after my own heart."

Marnoch nodded slowly and then drained his tankard with an air of finality. "No. I've met you before, Mr. Bathurst, and I've visited you at your private quarters—so we're by no means strangers. Up to a point, we should understand each other pretty well. No. I meant every word of what I said, 'Things moving?'"

"Exactly," returned Anthony. "Both of 'em."

Marnoch turned and eyed him suspiciously. "You don't get me! I've *seen* things—let me tell you! I'm not talking without having had a 'dekko' at the book of form." He came a trifle nearer to Anthony. "I wasn't over far from the station this morning. *And* at the right time! Put it down to accident. Or to the long arm of coincidence. Or even perhaps to my own acumen and initiative. I saw something that caused me to open my eyes. Not that they were shut before that! I saw that smart guy Venables, accompanied by your friend from the 'Yard,' MacMorran, plus that doctor fellow by name of Chavasse, sally forth! They were on a job. The signs were all there—much too obvious for me to miss. Too much experience of that sort of thing. I know the ropes, my friend, from A to Z." Marnoch paused. "You'll have one with me, Mr. Bathurst, I feel certain?"

"Thank you," said Anthony easily. "I'll have a bitter, if you don't mind."

Marnoch gave the appropriate order and threw a coin on to the counter. When the drinks were served, he pushed Anthony's tankard towards him with an almost imperial gesture.

"Your beer, Mr. Bathurst. Now where was I?"

"You had reached Z, Mr. Marnoch, if my memory serve me correctly. With regard to your professional knowledge and experience."

"Ah—yes. I recall it now. Well—there isn't a lot more for me to say. I spotted the three of 'em come out and I tumbled like a shot to what was doing. And what's more"—he lifted his tankard to his lips—"I've added up the figures and I'm darned sure I've made 'em come to the right answer."

He made more play with his tankard. Anthony offered no reply. Marnoch grinned cynically.

"You're giving nothing away—eh? Well—I don't think that I'll be blaming you for that. I'd probably feel the same as you do about things, if I stood in your shoes. Ah, well—there's no harm done. I've talked and you've listened. But if I was to have a shot in the dark, as you might say—I'd probably say, Sandals."

As he spoke, Marnoch looked straight ahead of him and pursed his lips in a whistle. Mr. Bathurst still remaining silent, Marnoch continued.

"You see," he said slowly and with weighty emphasis, "I'm not forgetting that car that passed me with the crying child inside it."

Anthony was about to reply to this remark when he felt a nudge at his elbow. Turning quickly, he saw Denton standing just behind him.

"I beg your pardon, Mr. Bathurst, but could I have a private word with you."

Anthony, glad to excuse himself to Marnoch, and, thinking hard over many things, stepped back and said, "Certainly."

Denton drew him to one side and said quietly: "Inspector MacMorran wants you at once in my private room."

Anthony walked away from the bar with Denton. "Come this way, Mr. Bathurst, please. The Inspector's been here about a quarter of an hour, but, seeing that you were not alone, he waited. But he wants to see you at once."

MacMorran was in the private room when Anthony entered. Anthony saw from the expression on the Inspector's face that everything had not been plain sailing. He waited for MacMorran to speak.

"He's sold us a pup," remarked MacMorran laconically.

"Who has?" demanded Anthony.

"Jordan."

"How?"

"Why—when the three of us got there, the swine had gone."

Anthony looked critical of the statement.

"It's no good your looking like that," returned the Inspector. "I've interrogated the old girl, Mrs. Logan. She fell asleep—so she says—in the night. Jordan took full advantage of it. When she woke up, he'd vanished."

Anthony made no reply to this statement. MacMorran went on. "Chavasse, of course, is tearing mad. Pegram's not much better now he knows about it, and Venables—well, I can't find words to describe Venables."

Anthony came to grips at once. "Did you put the woman through it?"

"I did."

"Thoroughly?"

"With a small-tooth comb. *And* I'm satisfied. So don't start me off on that side of it again. It's just a piece of rank bad luck—that's all. Poor old Chavasse will never forgive himself."

Anthony rubbed the ridge of his jaw with his finger. "H'm. There are one or two considerations, Andrew, which inevitably present themselves, that will require the best brains and attention that you and I can give them."

"There's one comfortable feature about it," said MacMorran, "and only one. The chap can't get very far. He's in too bad shape. When we do pick him up, I'm convinced that we shall find a corpse on our hands."

"Perhaps we shall. But—and I must stress this, Andrew—when we do lay our hands on that corpse, it may be too late."

Anthony shrugged his shoulders as he made the statement. MacMorran seemed slow to comprehend.

"How do you mean?" he asked.

"Why—that the tally of four may well have become five. Pretty obvious, isn't it?"

MacMorran stared at him. Then he slowly nodded. "Yes. It would be that! God, Mr. Bathurst—and what can we do? Beyond trying to find this man Jordan? And he may be in any one of ten thousand places. We can't watch 'em all. It makes me sweat with apprehension."

"We can do better than watch ten thousand places, Andrew."

"Again—how do you mean?"

"Why, watch *one* place! Watch the place where Jordan's bound for. At any rate, we'll call him Jordan for the sake of clarity."

"Why, isn't Jordan his real name?"

Anthony shook his head and smiled enigmatically: "Don't think so. But it will do as well as any other."

"How can we watch the place he's bound for—if we don't know it? Seems to be a pretty hopeless proposition, as far as I can see."

"That's where I come in, Andrew. And after me, where we come in." MacMorran screwed up his eyes. "Tell me. I can bear to hear a lot that I haven't heard before."

"You're going to have lunch with me, Andrew. Within the space of a very few minutes. I hope it will be a reasonably good lunch. After that we shall discuss certain aspects of the 'White Lion' murders with Inspector Venables. Amongst the matters we shall discuss will be our plans for to-night."

MacMorran wrinkled his brows. "To-night?"

"A-ha—to-night!"

"Why to-night?"

"Because, Andrew, I'm very much afraid that to-night's the night."

"For what?"

"For the last murder of the series. Which I hope to turn into a merely 'attempted murder.' With your valuable help, of course, Andrew."

"And where does all this take place, Mr. Bathurst?"

Anthony's eyes twinkled. "At the place where your friend Jordan's bound for. I thought you would have already guessed that."

MacMorran refused to be stalled off. "Cut the cackle, Mr. Bathurst, and let's get to the 'osses. As Marnoch once told us. We've no time to lose, as I see things. Where's the venue for this final encounter?"

Anthony shed his note of raillery. "In my opinion, Andrew, for what it's worth—and I'd lay a thousand to one on it—at Sir Charles Stuart's house at Sandals."

There was no mistaking the gravity of Anthony's words. Amazement showed in the Scotland Yard Inspector's eyes.

"The Chief Constable? What on earth can there be—"

Anthony stopped him with upraised hand. "I don't know why, Andrew—although I've a shrewd suspicion. Which I've been harbouring for some little time. But don't worry—lunch now, and then Venables! Come on!"

Anthony linked his arm in MacMorran's and walked with him to the luncheon-saloon.

VII

Anthony refused to discuss the problem with MacMorran until the courses of the luncheon were nearly finished.

"As this is something like a special occasion, Andrew," he said, "I propose that you join me in a liqueur."

MacMorran made a grimace. "I don't know that I'm exactly over-joyed at the prospect."

"Very likely," retorted Anthony; "but I am, you see—and the bloke that pays the piper calls the tune. At least, that's what happens in all properly conducted establishments. I suggest that we make it a Kümmel."

"I've no doubt you'll have it your own way," surrendered MacMorran. "You always do."

Anthony grinned at the waitress—a girl whom he hadn't seen before that particular afternoon—and ordered the two liqueurs. "There you are, Andrew," he said as he handed the Kümmel to his professional colleague. "Drink that. Personally, I find it grateful and comforting."

"It's not so bad," admitted MacMorran, "but I'd sooner have the money."

"That, my dear Andrew, is simply an expression of your North British temperament. You shouldn't parade it! You should always endeavour to hold it in subjection. Anyhow, the time has come to talk of many things. You know the rest, Andrew! So I won't bore you with it. But this afternoon, you and I will have the pleasure of interviewing Inspector Venables. I'm afraid—and I'm pretty sure that my fears are soundly foundationed—that we shall find serious difficulty in convincing him of certain extremely grave matters."

He stopped and pointed to MacMorran's glass, "Drink up, Andrew. To please me. I want your brain at its brightest and best for the next quarter of an hour."

"What a man you are, to be sure, for givin' orders." MacMorran disposed of his Kümmel.

"Now listen to me, Andrew! Unless I'm very much mistaken in my ideas, a murderous attack will be made during the hours of the night on no less a person than Sir Charles Stuart, the Chief Constable of the County. This attack will take place in Sir Charles's house."

"Why?" MacMorran cut in sharply. Anthony smiled.

"Because I have more or less forced that condition on our friend the assailant."

"Jordan?"

"Call him that if you like—as we agreed before."

"How have you done this?"

"Sir Charles has been generally warned and to-day he has been specifically warned. He himself by me myself. The warning has not been left to a third party. But I can give you my word, Andrew, that Sir Charles Stuart will not leave his house either to-day or this evening."

The Inspector wrinkled his forehead. "How about treachery inside the house? Have you covered on that?"

Anthony rubbed his top lip thoughtfully. "I think I've dealt with that possibility, Andrew. At any rate we shall both be there, and Sir Charles is no weakling. To say nothing of the excellent Venables. But we'll discuss the more intimate details later on. I'm confident that there'll be time."

"All right. I've trusted you before and I'll trust you again. But tell me, Mr. Bathurst—what's behind it all? What's the motive? Is it to do with Norman's farm? That belonged to the Rapson family? I've had that in my mind for some time now."

Anthony shook his head "I don't think so, Andrew. If it has, I'm entirely wrong in my calculations. It's altogether more deep-seated than that."

"All right, then! My second line of possibility concerns the Clarence part of the problem. The stamp collection. I've given a tremendous amount of consideration to that. What's your view of it?"

Anthony shook his head again. "And I'm not barking up that tree either, Andrew."

"You're not?"

"No. Very definitely—no."

MacMorran shrugged his shoulders. "Well then—I confess to my being 'bunkered.' I can't come again. You can put me with Barney's bull."

Anthony drew imaginary patterns on the table-cloth with the handle of his spoon. "There's one man in this show, Andrew, who's been right. And I've got to hand it to him. Right from the beginning. At the outset I was inclined to be in disagreement with him. But the more recent events that have come our way have brought me round to his way of thinking. Almost against my will."

"Venables, do you mean?"

"No. Not Venables. You've got to make allowances for him. Venables isn't bad as a country copper goes, but he lacks imagination and also the experience to handle a case of this kind successfully. He has remained a flat-foot. That, of course, is not altogether his fault."

"Sir Charles Stuart himself?"

"No, Andrew, Chavasse! Dr. Chavasse! His theory of the homicidal maniac is, I'm afraid, going to prove to be the right one. When he first put it up to me, I argued with him about it—but I *think* when it comes to the show-down, he's going to score off me over it. *Except* that this maniac we have to deal with is actuated by a motive that Chavasse, if we go by his expressed opinion, hasn't yet enunciated."

"And you have tumbled to it, you mean?"

"Yes. I think I have, Andrew. Although Chavasse had an initial advantage over me. You mustn't forget that. Not only has he been on the spot all the time, but he knows almost all the members of the cast and the locality in which they've been working."

"Makes a difference," commented Inspector MacMorran. "I'm ready to concede that."

"Thank you, Andrew," said Anthony cheerfully. "Your sense of fair play overwhelms me."

"Look here." MacMorran sat forward suddenly as he spoke. "One thing that surprises me. And which I find difficult to understand. Jordan is a man with a physical infirmity. As far as I know, there's been no question of his mental condition. Why is that?"

"Well—I don't know that you can criticise anybody for that. You must remember that Chavasse was called to treat him for his bodily affliction. Chavasse has never been required to examine him as to his mental capabilities. In all probability, the point has never arisen. As far as I can see—it wouldn't arise. Or, rather, it wouldn't have arisen—yet awhile."

"Yes. I suppose that does make a difference. I hadn't looked at it quite in that light."

Anthony pushed back his chair from the table. "Catch the eye—one of 'em will do—of our waitress, call her over here, and I'll pay the bill. I'm in one of my more generous moods. Then, Andrew, when that's been done, we'll away for the afternoon session with our friend Inspector Venables."

VIII

MacMorran rang up Venables from the telephone at the 'White Lion.' Venables, it didn't take him long to discover, was still tearing his hair.

"Not a sign of this fellow, Jordan, anywhere! Nice kettle of fish, I must say! I'll never take a chance again, Chief! Not half a chance. He might just as well have been spirited off the face of the earth. Nobody's seen him. Nobody's heard of him! He may be a hundred miles away by now. It will be the end of—"

MacMorran checked him abruptly. "Don't worry, Inspector. We're going to find him for you. And that before many hours are past."

"Oh—and who's 'we,' may I ask?"

"Mr. Bathurst and, I—and you're in it, too. Feeling better when you hear that?"

MacMorran heard Venables emit something which sounded suspiciously like a growl. "Sounds all right. But where does all this touching reunion take place? I'd be interested to hear that."

"And you will hear! As a matter of fact, that's what I'm 'phoning you about. Mr. Bathurst and I will be over to see you within the next half-hour. I'm 'phoning you from the 'White Lion.' We're coming over to make the final arrangements. He's asked me to discuss things with you before we make the last moves."

"Sounds all boloney to me, but if you want to come, I suppose you must come."

"Three o'clock suit you?"

There was a second's hesitation at the other end of the line. "Make it a quarter-past, will you, Chief? I've an appointment with the Deputy Town Clerk at three o'clock."

"O.K." replied the 'Yard' Inspector. "Three fifteen, then." MacMorran hung up and strolled back to Anthony, who was still talking to the waitress. Anthony turned when he heard MacMorran approaching. "Did you manage to get him?"

"Yes. He was there."

"Did you tell him?"

"No details. I withheld them, purposely. Just that we were coming over to see him."

"What time did he fix for us?"

"A quarter-past three. I suggested three—but he explained that he couldn't make it. Got an appointment or something."

Anthony frowned. "What a man! He must want to make an appointment at that time! If ours weren't so vital, it wouldn't matter so much. Whom's his with? Did he say?"

MacMorran nodded. "He did. But I don't think he would have done, if I hadn't asked him. He's meeting Hardwick, the Deputy Town Clerk of Mallett."

Anthony pulled at his top lip. "Hardwick—eh? Now, that's curious. I wonder why he's—Still, never mind. Surmising won't get us anywhere." He changed his tone. "All right, Andrew—a quarter-past three at the Police-station, and so be it. We'll make the journey together—which means that we shall be in good hands."

IX

Anthony Bathurst and Chief Inspector Andrew MacMorran arrived at the Police-station at Mallett when the hands of the clock showed exactly a quarter-past three. Venables was there in his room waiting for them and he was alone. Hardwick had evidently had his interview with him in good time and taken his departure. As Anthony took a seat, he put a question to the local Inspector.

"Any news of Jordan, Inspector?"

Venables shook his head dolefully. "Not a whisper, Mr. Bathurst. As I told the Chief here about an hour ago. Seems to me he's got clean away. And it's going to take a hell of a lot of explaining. That's what worries me."

"Cheer up," said Anthony. "It may never come to that."

"I'm afraid I don't share your optimism, Mr. Bathurst. Still—that's that! Now what's all this that the Chief was telling me on the telephone just now? With regard to to-night?"

"That's the style," rejoined Anthony. "That's what we've come here to talk about. Now please listen carefully, Inspector Venables—because I want you to understand everything thoroughly. It's only fair to you that you should. You want to arrest Jordan. Well, I think I shall be able to put you in touch with him before the day is out. I have every reason to believe that an attack will be made on the person of Sir Charles Stuart, in his own house, to-night. The intent, once again, will be nothing less than murder. Because I have every hope that we shall be able to circumvent that attack—forewarned is forearmed, you know, Inspector—Jordan will be delivered into your hands. How does that sound to you?"

Anthony watched the effect of his statement on Venables's face.

"You seem pretty certain of this," he ventured at length.

"Yes, Inspector." Anthony was emphatically positive. "All my deductions point in the same direction."

"Why do you think that this attempt on the Chief Constable's life will take place in his own house?"

Anthony smiled. "Because he won't leave his house. I've made that arrangement with him and I'm satisfied that he'll keep to it."

"And what do we do about it?"

"We shall be there—the three of us, and if we can't protect him between us, well, Inspector, who can?"

"Supposing the attack takes place earlier than to-night? How about it, then?"

"It won't. It won't be dark enough."

"It's a risk." urged Venables, and appealed to MacMorran for support. "Don't you think so, Chief? Don't you agree with me?"

"As Mr. Bathurst has put things to me, I don't," replied MacMorran sturdily.

"All right then," conceded Venables; "if that's how you feel about it, I guess you must count me in. But now that I've agreed to that I must ask you to give me the full details of our operation for this evening." MacMorran nodded to Anthony Bathurst to comply with Venables's request. Anthony signified assent and at once got down to actualities.

"I propose that we three leave here about half-past five. We will proceed straight to Sandals, Sir Charles Stuart's place. I've 'phoned him about it and he expects us. So that part of it's all in order. I shall be armed—so will Chief Inspector MacMorran. I advise you, Inspector Venables, to take the same precaution. We shall be faced by a murderer who will stick at nothing and who, if he gets the chance, and he considers it necessary, will shoot to kill. Any one of us who happens to stand in his path."

MacMorran intervened here. "He hasn't used a revolver yet. He uses fantastic methods. I feel that I should point that out."

Anthony shook his head slowly. "And he will still use fantastic methods to dispose of what he considers his legitimate victim. Make no mistake about that, Andrew. We shall belong, however, to a very different category. We shall be merely people in his way. Barring his escape and endeavouring to arrest him. He'll shoot at us—never fear—that is, of course, if we give him the chance. In our turn, we must attempt to be quick and too elusive for him. *Ça va sans dire.*"

The others nodded their heads. MacMorran then fingered his chin. "When do you really expect the attack on Sir Charles to take place, Mr. Bathurst?"

"Somewhere round midnight. The moon is late. He'll choose the darkest possible time. At least, that's my opinion."

"And *where* exactly do you anticipate that the attack will be made?"

"Well—that's asking me a rather tall question. But I fancy it will happen in Sir Charles's bedroom. The time would seem to suggest that. If things go well with us, Venables, your murderer will walk into our arms. And it will be your job to get the bracelets on him, Venables, in double quick time. Otherwise he'll let daylight through one of us. Got the idea?"

"Perfectly," replied Venables with curt emphasis.

"You're sure Sir Charles will co-operate to the full?" asked Mac-Morran.

"Yes," said Anthony. "He'll do that all right."

There was a silence which eventually Anthony himself broke. "Oh—and there's one more thing I must impress on you." His tone was grave. MacMorran and Venables realised this fact immediately.

"What's that?" asked the Scotland Yard Inspector.

"Not a whisper of our plans must be communicated to anybody. They must remain known to us three only."

Venables nodded. "I understand, Mr. Bathurst."

Anthony went on. "Those conditions of mine are absolutely and entirely inflexible. They are not to be varied in any way or to suit anybody. No matter in what shape or form the request or the invitation may be put. We three alone hold the keys. Is that clear, Inspector Venables?"

Venables nodded again. "I understand and I accept those conditions, Mr. Bathurst."

"Good," returned Anthony; "and considering that the Chief here hadn't heard them until we discussed them in this room there hasn't been the slightest chance of any leakage. With which condition I find myself content. Any other would have disturbed me profoundly."

Anthony took out his pipe and began to fill it. The two Police Inspectors watched him. Neither of them spoke. Anthony pressed down the tobacco into the bowl of the pipe and put a match to it. The flame lit up his face.

"I know exactly how you feel, gentlemen," he said. "I feel the same. That the final curtain is very near. Or, rather, to express myself more precisely, that the rag is going up on the last act and that I can hear 'Beginners—please.'"

He smoked steadily. MacMorran spoke his mind. "There's one thing I don't like."

Anthony smiled good-humouredly. "Only one, Andrew? What a superb optimist you always are."

"And that's this! In my opinion, this man Jordan is a homicidal maniac of the worst type. It's difficult to make plans to deal with chaps of that kidney. They're erratic. One can't foresee how they will act in certain circumstances. It's so easy to think you've countered them in every direction and then find that you've miscalculated."

Anthony shook his head. "I agree with you entirely, Andrew. But you're not to worry over Jordan. By this time to-morrow, you will be sure that it won't be we who have miscalculated."

" I hope you're right, Mr. Bathurst."

"And hope, my dear Andrew," said Anthony, "will on this occasion, at least, be emptied in delight."

CHAPTER VII

I

IN ACCORDANCE with his promise to the Chief Constable of Glebeshire, Anthony Bathurst, with his two professional companions, arrived at Sandals after Sir Charles and Lady Elinor had finished dinner. They were shown into the library and, after an interval of a few minutes, Sir Charles himself came in to welcome them. He looked tired and worn, but shook hands warmly with each of the three visitors.

"Evening, Bathurst! Evening, Chief. Evening, Venables. Make yourselves comfortable before we are called upon to face this ordeal which this fellow Bathurst is so glib about."

MacMorran knew at once that the levity was forced. Anthony, however, laughed, and in this instance the laughter was genuine.

"If you ask me, Sir Charles, both the Inspectors here are thoroughly relieved to see you still hale and hearty. On the way here, they reminded me of a couple of undertaker's mutes."

MacMorran moved his hands in silent protest and Sir Charles smiled nervously. Anthony turned to the two Inspectors.

"While I'm having a few words with Sir Charles, I'd like you to go over the house. Please pay particular attention to all doors and windows—especially those to do with bedrooms."

Anthony looked straight at the Chief Constable as he put forward the suggestion. Sir Charles saw what Anthony intended him to see.

"Yes. Good idea, Bathurst," he said. "And I'll tell you what. I'll get Lady Stuart to show them over." He went to the door and called "Elinor. Come here, my dear, will you, please?"

The four men waited for the appearance of Lady Stuart. The wait was of but short duration. Lady Stuart came into the room. Anthony watched her intently. The same look of strain which was noticeable on the face of the Chief Constable was discernible on her face.

"Good evening, people," she said pleasantly with a smile at each. "You called me, Charles?"

"I did, my dear. I want you to take these two gentlemen over the house while I have a word or two with Bathurst. Chief-Inspector

MacMorran. You know Venables well enough! Tell them all they want to know, my dear, and answer any questions they ask of you."

"Certainly," returned Lady Stuart. "I shall be only too delighted." She turned to MacMorran and Venables. "Come with me, will you? I'll take you all the way round while these two people talk to each other. And I'll guarantee that they'll still be talking when we come back to them."

MacMorran and Venables followed her out of the room. As soon as the door closed behind them, Anthony spoke earnestly to Sir Charles Stuart. At several points of his speech, Sir Charles made interruptions. Anthony heard each one of these reasonably and with infinite patience. One by one, he was able to dispose satisfactorily of all Sir Charles's remonstrances. When he had completed what he had to say, he asked a direct question of the Chief Constable:

"Well, sir, do you find yourself in complete agreement with me?"

"That's all right, Bathurst. Don't worry. I'll frankly admit that I don't like any of it—but I've placed myself in your hands and I'll do as you tell me. You'll inform the others, of course?"

Anthony hesitated. "I don't know, sir. I haven't quite made up my mind yet. It's quite on the cards that they *might* function better if they *didn't* know all the details." He glanced at Sir Charles. "See my point, sir?"

"Perhaps I do. I'll leave it to you, then."

"Thank you, Sir Charles. Leave it to my judgment when we get close to the correct time. I shall be in a position to weigh things up more accurately later on."

Sir Charles passed a hand across his forehead. "All right, Bathurst. I'll agree to leave things to you." He stopped suddenly and listened. "I fancy I hear the others coming back. From now onwards, you understand, I'm placing myself unreservedly in your hands. Yes, here come the others."

Lady Stuart arrived back with the two Inspectors. "I've obeyed your instructions," she said brightly. "These two gentlemen have seen all over the house. I've explained everything that needed explaining and I think that they're thoroughly satisfied."

"There's one thing," said MacMorran with a look in Anthony's direction, "that I'd like to know. To feel sure about it. And that's this. In which room are you sleeping to-night, Sir Charles?"

Sir Charles made no reply to the question. He looked rather as though he expected Anthony to answer it. Anthony realised what was expected of him.

"In your own room, sir. If I may be allowed to answer Inspector MacMorran's question."

"Do you think that policy a wise one?" inquired Venables.

Anthony saw again that the answer was anticipated from him. "Not 'wise,' perhaps, using your adjective, Inspector Venables. But necessary. The condition is almost forced upon us."

"How so?" Venables wrinkled his brows.

"For this good reason. We *must* catch our murderer red-handed. If you prefer it—*in flagrante delicto*. If we don't—the burden of proof, I fancy, will prove too much for us. I offer Sir Charles, therefore, in the words of Bacon, as a hostage to fortune."

Sir Charles boomed in here. "Don't mind about me! Reminds me of the days when I went tiger-shooting in India with the Jam Sahib of Nawanagar. He was entertaining one of the touring English cricket sides. Put up a tiger-shoot for their delectation. Tethered a poor little blighter of a kid in a sort of trap-pit arrangement to encourage His Majesty 'Stripes' to call in and pass the time of day. The kid would be there for hours bleating away like the devil before the fun began. Damned good sport for a lot of people, no doubt, but a pretty thin time for the kid. Well—you—er—see my analogy—put me down as the kid in this 'ere cast."

Sir Charles growled and shook himself as a dog does when leaving the water.

"What I propose," said Anthony, "in a nut-shell is this. There are two methods of entry to Sir Charles's room—the door and the window. The latter can virtually be ruled out of our calculations. There is no foothold near it on the outside of the house, and it would puzzle an acrobatic tabby to make an ascent that way. Still—no risks should be taken, and I can assure you that no risks will be taken! Inspector Venables will have charge of the watch on the outside of the house. Nobody will be able to put in an appearance even, without Inspector

Venables being aware of it. There remains the bedroom door. The corridor itself and the bedroom will be guarded by Inspector MacMorran and me. Which in my humble judgment should afford ample protection. To allay any anxiety, however, on the part of Sir Charles here, I may say that there will be one other precaution. It won't affect our working arrangements in any way, so that it needn't be discussed here at the moment."

Anthony paused and looked round. "Well, gentlemen, have I made myself clear to all of you?"

Sir Charles took upon himself the responsibility of reply. "I think so, Bathurst. I'm clear, at any rate, and I expect our two friends here are also. You are, aren't you?" He addressed his question to Inspector MacMorran.

"Ay," came the response.

"I understand," contributed Venables.

There came a silence. Sir Charles looked at his watch. ' Look here—I've a suggestion to make. I'm certainly not going to bed yet and it won't be dark for a long time, Lady Stuart wants to listen to a play on the radio. What do you fellows say to an adjournment to the billiard-room? We can play billiards, or, if you'd prefer it, snooker. What do you say? Are you on?"

"Suits me, sir," Venables said quickly and Anthony and MacMorran nodded in assent.

The four men, therefore, trooped up to the billiard-room. The two Inspectors elected to start and play snooker. Before they began and while the Chief Constable was placing the balls on the table, Venables came across to Anthony Bathurst.

"Mr. Bathurst," he said, "I've been thinking. Has Jordan any idea, to your mind, that we shall be waiting for him when he turns up tonight?"

Anthony shook his head. "As far as I can see, Inspector, he hasn't an inkling of it. In fact, nothing should be further from his thoughts. Why do you ask?"

Venables rubbed-the tip of his nose with his forefinger. "Well, it might make a big difference if he did know. But as you say that he doesn't, it leaves me much easier in my mind."

He chalked his cue and walked back to the table and Andrew MacMorran. Anthony linked his arm in the Chief Constable's and walked him a few yards down the floor of the billiard-room.

"Come over here, Sir Charles, and sit down for a moment or two. Till it's our turn for a game. I want another private word with you."

Sir Charles suffered himself to be taken to a wall-seat. Anthony offered him a cigarette. They lit up.

"Sir Charles," said Anthony, "I don't want you to go to bed at all to-night. But I don't mind Venables thinking you've gone. That won't interfere with my plans at all. Do you mind?"

"Not a bit. Lady Stuart can sleep in one of the spare bedrooms. What do I do in substitution for my ration of shut-eye?"

Anthony grinned. "Sit up with MacMorran and me. Then you'll be as safe as houses."

"That's all right, Bathurst. I'm not worrying."

"I don't suppose you are, sir, if the truth's known. But there's this to it. If we do as I've just suggested, it will relieve MacMorran of a considerable amount of anxiety. Because he will have you under his eye all the time. Whereas, if you were ever out of his sight, he would be suffering untold agonies. And where you are exactly, won't really concern Inspector Venables. As long as he does the job allotted to him, smoothly and efficiently, that's all that matters. See what I mean, Sir Charles?"

"Yes, Bathurst. And I agree with you. And if we go over to the billiard-table, we can start knocking the balls about directly after MacMorran and Venables have finished. Come along with me now, there's a good fellow."

II

The evening wore on. But the atmosphere round the billiard-table remained bright and cheery, no matter which couple of the four men was playing. Following on a desperately close game of snooker between MacMorran and the Chief Constable, which went to the condition of 'all on the black,' and which ended in the Inspector being defeated (hailed vociferously by Sir Charles Stuart), Anthony looked at his watch. "By Jove, sir! It's turned half-past eleven. I think it's time we—" He paused significantly.

"Time we what," inquired Venables?

"Took up action stations," responded Anthony. "We oughtn't to leave it much later. What do you say, Andrew?"

"I agree with you entirely," urged MacMorran.

"That's settled, then," cried Sir Charles genially. "Venables! You'll find sandwiches and a whisky and soda all ready for you in the dining-room. Go and help yourself, man."

"Very good, Sir Charles and thank you. And when I'm finished with that, I'll take up my position."

"A little bite and a little drop of something for us are also indicated. Come along, you fellows."

Anthony and MacMorran followed Sir Charles Stuart. The Chief Constable took them to a table standing close to his bedroom door. On it had been laid a plentiful supply of sandwiches, a bottle of liqueur whisky, a siphon of soda water and an appropriate number of glasses.

"Here we are," said Sir Charles. He rubbed his hands. "And very nice, too—if I'm any judge. We'll collect a few chairs and then we'll fall to on this little lot. What do you say?"

Chairs were brought and the three men began to do justice to Sir Charles's prepared tray. Suddenly there came the sound of a clock chiming the hour and immediately afterwards the big clock in the main hall began to chime the hour of midnight. Anthony Bathurst put his glass on the tray.

"I think, Sir Charles," he said quietly, "that it would be as well if we prepared for action."

"I place myself unreservedly in your hands, Bathurst," replied the Chief Constable.

III

Sir Charles Stuart remained on the landing with MacMorran. From where they sat in their chairs, their eyes commanded the ascent of the main staircase from the hall below. That is to say, they could see any person who came into the hall, but could not be seen by that person until, ascending, he came to the top stair.

"What about lights, Inspector?" asked the Chief Constable.

"Can you control the electric lights in the hall and up the staircase from here?"

"We can," answered Sir Charles. "There's the switch over there." He indicated where he meant. "Within a hand's stretch of where you're sitting, Inspector."

MacMorran turned, saw the switch and nodded his understanding. "They can also be switched on, I take it, down below there?"

"They can. Both down there and up here."

"Good. In that case, then, we'll have than off." MacMorran leant across and pushed up the switch.

"Now we're in the dark," said Sir Charles.

"Not for long, sir. That room there, through which Mr. Bathurst just passed, leads to your bedroom, or so I understood from her Ladyship when she conducted us round a little while ago."

"That is so, Inspector. Why do you ask?"

"Well, I was on the point of saying this, sir. If we switch the light on in that room, it will give us enough light to see by as we sit here and it's scarcely enough, seeing where it is, for anybody to notice from the hall or from the foot of the staircase."

The room to which MacMorran had made reference lay to their immediate right at a distance of about ten yards and was the farthest away from the top of the staircase. Sir Charles looked in the direction of the room.

"All right, Inspector. Try the light now. Then I can judge the effect."

MacMorran rose, walked across to the room and switched on the inner light. Sir Charles expressed instant approval.

"That's satisfactory, Inspector. That will give us enough light for what we want to do."

MacMorran returned to his chair. "If I knew what that was going to be, sir, I might be in a better position to answer you. As it is—" He shrugged his shoulders.

Sir Charles finished the sentence for him. "As it is, you're hoping for the best—eh?"

"That's it, sir." MacMorran took out his tobacco-pouch and began to fill his pipe. As he did so, Anthony came from the further room and joined them.

"Your bedroom's all ready, Sir Charles. All ready for visitors. I've even put a mat down with 'Welcome' on it."

"Red carpet—eh, Bathurst?" chuckled Sir Charles.

"Almost, sir," smiled Anthony. "By the way—what's your fun and games with the light, Andrew?" he inquired of the Inspector.

MacMorran explained the arrangement he had just made with Sir Charles Stuart. "I hope you're in full agreement, Mr. Bathurst," he added.

"Oh—altogether," Anthony replied. "As a matter of fact, I intended to propose something of that kind myself."

MacMorran puffed steadily at his pipe. Anthony and Sir Charles lit cigarettes. The clock in the hall below chimed twice for half-past twelve.

IV

Anthony Lotherington Bathurst has since said to more than one of his closer friends that the vigil he spent in the house of Sir Charles Stuart was the most trying that he has ever known. One o'clock came and went and then half-past one. The hands of the various clocks and watches crept relentlessly and inevitably towards the second hour of the day. Just before two, MacMorran made an impatient sound with his tongue against his teeth.

"Our friend's not coming, gentlemen. For once, Mr. Bathurst, I'm afraid that your plans have miscarried."

The Chief Constable spoke quietly immediately after him.

"I'm inclined to agree with the Inspector, Bathurst." But there was neither censure nor petulance in his voice.

Anthony shook his head: "I don't think so, sir. I may be wrong, of course, but I expect him within the next half-hour. I'm going by the incidence of the moon and the general conditions of light and darkness. But if you want to stretch your legs, Inspector, go down and pass the time of day with Venables. Be as quiet as you can. But don't be away more than ten minutes."

MacMorran accepted the offer gladly. They heard him descend the staircase and make his way through the hall.

"He'll find Venables," whispered Anthony, "at the end of the row of latticed windows."

"They're the kitchen windows," answered Sir Charles.

MacMorran found Venables almost exactly as Anthony had fore-told. As he walked towards him the farther wall of the garage was only just visible. The trees in the distance stood out like a row of gaunt sentinels, dutifully devotional to the cause of the house round which they stood, and that house's occupants. MacMorran slithered silently towards the vigilant Venables.

"How goes it, Venables?" he whispered.

Venables nodded assurance. "All quiet. Has been ever since I came out here. Quiet as the inside of a church. If you ask my opinion, Mr. Bathurst has backed a loser."

"Maybe," replied the cautious MacMorran, "but the night's not through yet. Another hour and maybe I'll be disposed to agree with you."

"I shall have had more than enough of this before another hour has passed."

"Don't you worry yourself. It'll pass quicker than you think, Venables. Well—I'll be getting back to my post. Cheer-o."

MacMorran turned and started on his way back. Venables squared his shoulders and turned on his patrol. He heard the soft swish of MacMorran's footsteps as they receded into the distance and within a few seconds he had left the line of latticed windows. Venables pulled his coat more closely round him and thrust his hands into his pockets. At that moment, through the hedge that skirted the bottom of the garden, there stepped the man whom he and the people upstairs were awaiting. But Venables failed to see him and was therefore totally unaware of his presence. The man took a couple of steps and emerged into the half-light half-darkness of the night. He advanced towards the house . . . and Venables . . . and Sir Charles Stuart.

V

The man who had broken through the hedge saw Venables as soon as he had taken half a dozen steps towards the house. He halted in his advance. He was certain in his own mind that, although he had seen Venables, he himself had not been seen. He therefore retraced his steps and went back in the direction by which he had came.

In a few steps, he had disappeared from view. But for a few moments only. When he showed himself again, he was carrying something in his hand. Keeping on the blind side of the waiting Inspector, he began to walk forward again. When within twenty yards or so of

Venables, he dropped flat and started to crawl towards the house. Venables remained entirely oblivious of the figure which was slowly approaching. The dark figure on the grass crept nearer. Although his progress was slow, it was certain . . . and for the unsuspecting Police Inspector, ominously certain. The crawling man came to within a few yards of Venables and then stopped. An owl hooted away in the distance of the countryside. Venables heard it and, under the influence of some whim, walked a few paces away from the menacing figure lying prone, with chin in the grass. The sound of Venables's footsteps gave his adversary the opportunity for which he had been waiting. Noiselessly, he rose to his feet and then to his full height. Equally noiselessly, he came to within striking distance of the Inspector. With an incredibly quick movement of his right arm, he struck hard at the back of Venables's head. The Inspector went down like a felled ox. His assailant bent over him and listened. He stayed listening for the space of a few seconds. Then he nodded in an expression of satisfaction. Looking round, he turned and ran quickly towards the strip of garden nearest to the dark line of the garage. From there he emerged carrying a ladder. He placed the ladder against the wall and began to climb. He took each rung silently and swiftly. Until he reached the window he had marked as his objective.

VI

Andrew MacMorran, after his short conversation with the luckless Inspector Venables, returned to the landing where Anthony and Sir Charles Stuart were still sitting in the subdued light offered by the electric bulb within the room adjoining the Chief Constable's bedroom. They greeted the Inspector quietly as he came up the staircase and sat down again with them.

"Everything O.K.?" inquired Anthony Bathurst.

MacMorran nodded acquiescence. "Yes. Except that Venables is beginning to run a grouse. If we draw blank, I rather fancy he'll tear you off a strip."

Anthony chuckled. "He will, will he? Well, well! Accidents will happen you know, Andrew."

"Ay. The man that never made a mistake, never made anything."

Sir Charles moved uneasily in his chair. "What's the time now, Bathurst? This night reminds me of the death-bed of Charles the Second. It's an unconscionable time in going. Must be—"

He stopped abruptly. Anthony had gripped him by the arm.

"What's the matter," demanded the Chief Constable a trifle irritably.

"I thought I heard a noise."

MacMorran stood up and listened with them. "I can't hear anything," he said after a short interval.

"No. Perhaps not," returned Anthony. "Must have been my fancy."

He had risen when MacMorran rose and the two men sat down together again. Anthony held his breath. He wasn't yet satisfied that his previous idea had been a mistaken one. MacMorran bent over to whisper something to him, but Anthony shook his head and put a finger to his lips. The three men sat there as though carved in stone.

Suddenly MacMorran noticed the tense expression on Anthony's face. Anthony nodded to him almost imperceptibly.

"He's here," he whispered. "He's got by Venables. Wait, don't rush things—it may spoil all to be too precipitate. You, Sir Charles, stay here, please! Don't move an inch away from that wall. I don't like it."

Anthony rose and the Inspector rose with him. "When we move we'll move together. Get your revolver, Andrew, and I'll have mine handy. He's in the bedroom now."

He motioned with his head towards the inner room and MacMorran nodded again to show that he thoroughly understood what Anthony wanted. Then, without the slightest warning, action was demanded of them. There came the sound of a smashing blow within the inner room and then the noise of two successive softer thuds. Anthony and MacMorran dashed into the bedroom that was Sir Charles Stuart's. A figure stood by the bed with a weapon something similar to a butcher's cleaver in his hand. Before either Anthony or MacMorran could cross the threshold, he struck another blow at the thing in the bed.

Anthony flung himself forward. MacMorran came on his heels. The figure turned. Across the top part of his face was stretched a strip of black felt. He hurled the axe at Anthony and then plunged headlong for the window.

VII

The axe struck Anthony on the right shoulder and the force of the blow sent him reeling backwards and on to the Inspector just behind him. The respite, thus gained, helped the assailant materially. For it gave him the fraction of a start which of necessity must be his, to enable him to make the getaway. His feet were on the ladder and he was halfway-down it, before either Anthony or MacMorran recovered from his setback. Before they could grasp the ladder, the flying figure jumped the rest of the journey and kicked the ladder away from the window-sill against which it had been resting. It lurched away and fell with a slanting slither on to a line of apple trees on the edge of the orchard.

"Down the other way. Andrew," shouted Anthony. "Run like hell. There's just a chance we may head him off."

MacMorran turned and dashed towards the staircase. Anthony followed him and Sir Charles Stuart, looking thoroughly scared and amazed, brought up the rear. They were outside the house in a matter of flying seconds. MacMorran spotted the escaping figure near the hedge. "There he is," he shouted. "By the hedge. After him."

The three men ran towards the gap in the hedge. But the start which they had been forced to give away proved too big a handicap for the pursuers. When they reached the road, there was no sign of any living person. MacMorran looked blankly at his two companions.

"Given us the slip! And in this light we haven't the ghost of a chance of catching him."

He turned and spoke directly to Anthony. "Did you notice anything when he was down there by the hedge?"

"No, Andrew. Nothing particular. What's the reference?"

"Well—it seemed to me that he threw his arms up in a rather peculiar manner just before he vanished. Still—if you say you didn't notice it—" he broke off. "Where's Sir Charles?"

"He stayed behind, just outside the house, to give a hand to Venables."

"Where was Venables? I didn't spot him."

"He's out, poor devil. Slugged good and proper. I should say, from the look I caught of him—he was taken from behind, probably. That would account for things."

"What a mess," moaned MacMorran. And we're no nearer than we were when we started."

"I wouldn't say that," returned Anthony. "Who knows what the morning may bring forth? Still—let's find out about Venables."

Sir Charles had aroused two of the servants and had ordered them to assist him in carrying Venables inside the house. MacMorran went over and looked at him.

"Concussion," he said curtly. "Something like a sandbag, I should say." He ran his fingers along the bones at the back of the Inspector's head. "Nothing broken, I fancy. He'll be all right a little later on."

Sir Charles came up to him. "What happened in my bedroom?" he asked. "I heard the noises, of course, and when you ran out I joined in and ran behind you."

MacMorran looked towards Anthony for the explanation for which Sir Charles was asking. Anthony smiled.

"Come upstairs with me now and I'll show you," he said. "We can leave one of the men with Venables."

The three men made their way upstairs again. "Before we go in," said Sir Charles, "I suggest we improve the shining hour and have a 'spot' each. I'm a firm believer in self-fortification. What do you say to the suggestion, gentlemen?"

"Carried nem. con.," replied MacMorran. Sir Charles poured out the drinks.

As. Anthony replaced his glass on the table he said, "What I'm going to show you may be a trifle dramatic, but it proved effective and I think, served its purpose."

The light was still burning in the ante-room. Anthony went first. As he crossed the threshold of Sir Charles Stuart's room, he switched on the second light. The Chief Constable and MacMorran came close behind him. Anthony pointed to the bolster and pillows at the head of the bed. His two companions looked at once to the spot at which he was pointing. They saw what looked very much like the head of Sir Charles lying shapelessly on the right-hand pillow.

"That is the object," said Anthony, "which was designed to attract our visitor's attention. It did not altogether fail in its design, as you can see."

MacMorran and the Chief Constable went close to it to inspect it more carefully.

"A simple contrivance," explained Anthony Bathurst, "a wig, one of Gustave's very best, coloured to Sir Charles's natural hair, an old-fashioned round collar-box placed inside it, pyjamas arranged loosely and carelessly round the bottom of the pillow, and in the subdued light, it served its purpose of attracting the assault intended for the living person of Sir Charles. That axe lying at the foot of the bed there made a sorry mess of the ancient collar-box. When I arranged this—shall I say decoy—I figured that the murderer would swing the axe in such a manner as to—"

MacMorran cut in abruptly. "Hold hard there, Mr. Bathurst! Just a minute! You didn't know that the weapon used would be an axe."

Anthony's eyes twinkled. "I'm sorry, Andrew. And let me apologise in advance for shooting a line. But I anticipated that the weapon would be an axe—or at least something so much like an axe as to make no difference."

MacMorran showed signs of impatience. "Well—I'm sorry, but I don't see how you deduced that. He'd never used an axe before. If you cast your mind back over the other crimes, you won't find an axe figuring in any of them. So how you can come to say—"

This time it was Anthony who was guilty of the interruption. "There's no Friday in any week until it comes, Andrew. And no June or July in the year's calendar before their respective arrivals. So that you can't always establish an argument by basing it on precedent. I expected the use of an axe. I can't prove that. You must take my word for it. But an axe turned up. Sorry, Andrew, and all that, but I'll promise to give you an adequate explanation in due course and I fed pretty sure that the explanation will satisfy you. In the meantime, Andrew, 'patience and shuffle the cards.'"

Sir Charles listened intently to the conversation between Anthony and the Inspector before breaking in on it. "I think we ought to be seeing how Venables is. And after that it became a question of future plans. I still happen to be Chief Constable of the County carrying certain responsibilities—and, frankly, I'm worried. What have you to say to that, Bathurst?"

Anthony deliberated a moment or so before replying. When he did reply, he spoke quietly and gravely. "We'll hold a council of war in the morning, Sir Charles."

VIII

When Anthony came down to breakfast in the morning, to which he helped himself, he learned from Lady Stuart that Venables, on medical advice, had been removed to the local Cottage Hospital. He noticed that his hostess looked tired and worn.

"My husband has told me something of what happened last night," she said, "or, rather, as I should have said 'this morning.' It's all very bewildering to me. I can't understand why any of it should have happened. But Inspector Venables should be all right in a day or two, so the Doctor said. He's had a nasty blow somewhere near the base of the skull, but the doctor doesn't think that the damage is too serious." She smiled rather deliciously, but it was a tired smile all the same.

"I'm glad to hear that," replied Anthony. "I've been a bit worried about poor old Venables. Has Chief Inspector MacMorran been down to breakfast yet?"

"Yes, Mr. Bathurst. The Inspector was a distinctly early bird. The only missing member so far is my husband. But I think that; bearing in mind all the circumstances and seeing what he's been through, we must forgive him the delinquency, don't you?"

"I suppose we must," conceded Anthony. "And we must school ourselves to remember too that Sir Charles isn't as young as he was."

"No," she replied a little guardedly. "That is so, of course. Although you must admit, Mr. Bathurst, that he's a truly remarkable man for his age."

"I do," said Anthony. "Whatever it may be."

Lady Stuart flashed another shrewd glance in his direction. But Anthony's face remained completely impassive under her scrutiny. She was on the point of considering the advisability of launching a further remark when MacMorran entered. His face was flushed and his whole bearing showed that he was thoroughly excited.

"It's all right, Mr. Bathurst—pardon me, your ladyship—but we've got him."

"Got whom, Andrew?"

"Jordan. The murderer. He didn't get very far last night, after all. I doubted whether he would, by the way I saw him go through that hedge. You remember I remarked on it to you?"

Anthony was listening gravely. "Where is he, then, Andrew?"

"His body's about a hundred yards away from the hedge. Just lying there. On the Mallett side. He rallied to a point, probably, and then no further. The effort he had made proved too much for him and he just dropped down there to die. In the shadows."

"How do you know it's Jordan, Andrew?"

"I don't. But I'd like to be as sure of a thousand quid."

"Ever seen him before?"

"I have. By Sir Charles's bed last night doing his axe stuff. He was easy to identify with that in mind."

Anthony thought hard. "I see. I think perhaps I'd better come and have a look at him."

"I thought you'd probably like to do that. Before I have him moved." Lady Stuart shuddered realistically. "How awful! Dead bodies everywhere now. Strewn all over Mallett and the adjoining districts! How long is it going to last, I wonder! It will bring me with grey hairs in sorrow to my grave."

Anthony strove to reassure her. "In answer to your question, Lady Stuart, not long now. I can give you my word of honour that the end of the road is in sight. All right, Andrew. I'll come along with you right now."

He followed MacMorran out of the room and down the garden, towards the hedge boundary of Sir Charles Stuart's property. MacMorran conducted him to the place where the man had broken through just prior to the attack on Inspector Venables.

"This," said MacMorran a little pompously, "is the spot where I thought he threw up his hands in a rather peculiar way. Now I'll take you to the body. Turn to the right and we haven't much more than a hundred yards to go."

Anthony kept pace with the Inspector for the distance mentioned. MacMorran pointed.

"There you are, Mr. Bathurst. There's our man. Just as I found him about a quarter of an hour ago."

Anthony went straight along and looked at the prostrate figure. He saw the body of a man dressed in grey flannel trousers, grey pull-over and blue jacket. The shoes he wore were brown. His face was strangely white, even in death, and a tumbled shock of black hair fell on to his forehead. Anthony judged him to be somewhere between forty and fifty years of age. Across his eyes and covering a small portion of his nose was a piece of black felt. His hands were bare. He lay on his back with his legs wide apart and his arms sprawled helplessly away from his body. His neck and throat were gaunt, dry and stringy and Anthony could see at a glance that the man had been a victim of a virulent disease.

"Last night," commented MacMorran, "was his last fling. And ten to one we shall find he's a homicidal maniac. Escaped from a mental hospital, in my opinion. Dr. Chavasse's theory was right."

Anthony made no answer. "You feel certain, I suppose, Andrew, that this man is Dr. Chavasse's patient? You have no doubts in the matter?"

"I shall be surprised, Mr. Bathurst, if it isn't." He pointed to an object lying on the ground a few feet away. "See that? A small sand-bag. That's what he walloped poor old Venables with."

Anthony bit at his underlip. "Finger-prints, Andrew! That's what I'm thinking of. The small axe in Sir Charles Stuart's bedroom and the ladder and the window-sill, possibly, and the window-frame itself. Get a man on them as soon as you can. Do you mind, Andrew? I'm rather more curious about things than usual."

"I've thought of all that. I've already sent up to Mallett for a photographer and for a finger-print man. I hope they've got the apparatus. Shall we move this chap to the house, Mr. Bathurst."

"I think so, Andrew. And then our next step must be to get Dr. Chavasse to identity him."

Anthony bent down to look at the dead man's brown shoes. MacMorran noticed the intent look on his face.

"What's the matter, Mr. Bathurst?"

Anthony grinned. "Good old Andrew. You'll never alter, will you? What size would you say that shoe is?"

MacMorran inspected the brown shoe. "Either a seven or an eight. On second thoughts, the latter. Why?"

Anthony's eyes twinkled. "Nothing. He's smallish feet, though, for a man of his height. Don't you think so, Andrew?"

MacMorran shot a suspicious glance in Anthony's direction. He had an uneasy feeling that he was the subject of a little and misplaced irony.

"I don't know," he replied defensively. "Some tall men have small feet and small hands. I've known quite a few in my time who would qualify for that description."

Anthony nodded. "Very likely. I wouldn't attempt to contradict you."

He walked towards Sir Charles Stuart's house. MacMorran followed him. When the Inspector caught up with Anthony, he noticed the latter examining the broken part of the hedge where MacMorran had said he saw Jordan break through, after the attack on the house of the early morning. Anthony turned to the Inspector when he came up.

"Unhappily, Andrew, there has been but little rain during the last fortnight. There are no footprints which show either across the grass or near the house. But Andrew—and I stress the 'but'—what about that little fellow there?"

MacMorran's eyes followed the direction of Anthony's pointing linger.

"The earth there," said Anthony, "just under the hedge is a trifle on the soft side. It's been shielded and protected from our old friend, 'Sol the sun.' And on that blessed plot, Andrew, I fancy I detect something more than a suspicion of a footmark. What's your own opinion?"

MacMorran bent down and shook his head. "No evidence much. And none at all to say that it was made by the man you're attempting to pin it to."

"Shouldn't expect hordes to tramp along there, Andrew. An occasional individual, but certainly not battalions."

There was a gleam in the grey eyes which MacMorran had seen many times before. Anthony straddled the ditch and inspected the mark more closely. Then he jumped back to his former position. MacMorran began to feel impatient.

"I must be getting back to the house. I've got several things to do. Firstly, there's that finger-print business, then I've got to get Jordan to the mortuary and, thirdly, I must 'phone the two doctors. Both

Chavasse and Pegram. The former for the identification of Jordan and the latter in his official capacity."

"I agree. And all of them, the sooner the better."

The two men walked back to the house of the Chief Constable.

CHAPTER VIII

I

WHEN the fingerprint expert arrived with the insufflating apparatus, Sir Charles Stuart, who had breakfasted late, joined the others. MacMorran more or less supervised the operations. The small axe, the ladder, the window-sill and the frame and the catch were all tested for the tell-tale fingerprint. Eventually the Inspector made the announcement that the various efforts had been barren.

"Our friend wore gloves. Mr. Bathurst. I was afraid that would turn out to be the case. And there they are."

MacMorran tossed a pair of old worn woollen gloves on to the table. Anthony raised his eyebrows.

"Where were they, Andrew?"

"In Jordan's coat pocket. I expected to find them there."

"Anything else in the pockets, Andrew?"

"Nothing at all, Mr. Bathurst."

"H'm. Bad Luck. Still it was worth trying. I should have done the same myself."

Anthony relapsed into silence and MacMorran bustled out to superintend the arrangements for the transfer of the dead man's body to the mortuary at Mallett. Sir Charles Stuart sat down at a table in the writing-room to write what he had termed an important letter. Anthony thoughts things over and decided to take no further positive action until he had heard what Martin Chavasse had to say in relation to the body of the dead man. It was Anthony's hope that Chavasse and Pegram would arrive before the ambulance came. He wanted to avoid everything in the nature of unnecessary delay. In less than half an hour his wish was gratified. Pegram drove up in a car with Dr. Chavasse at his side. MacMorran brought them in to Anthony and the Chief Constable.

"Job for you, Chavasse," said Sir Charles. "Job after your own heart. According to Chief Inspector MacMorran here, we've had a visit from your murderous patient."

Chavasse's eyes bulged with curiosity. "Is that so? Really?"

"So MacMorran says. But you're the man that can settle it. Probably the only one. But come along with us now and we'll soon be able to clear the matter up."

"I shall be only too pleased, Sir Charles. But I can tell you that you've set me blazing with curiosity. What the hell's the fellow doing here in your house?"

Anthony intervened. "Before we go, Chavasse, you might be good enough to put me right on one little matter. Do you mind?"

"Not at all. What is it?"

"How long is it since Jordan vanished?"

"The day before yesterday."

"I see. Thank you, Doctor. I'm fit now, if all of you are."

Pegram, who had been listening intently to the conversation but who, strangely, had said nothing, slipped along at the rear of the party. MacMorran conducted them to the tool-shed. There on a hurdle lay the dead man from the hedge.

"Now, Chavasse," said Sir Charles Stuart. "Is that your patient?"

Martin Chavasse walked across to the hurdle. Anthony saw him begin to shake his head. Then a look of doubt crept slowly into his eyes. He seemed very unsure of himself.

"Doubtful?" inquired Anthony.

Chavasse smiled at the question. "Well—I am and I'm not."

"Explain please, Dr. Chavasse," cut in the Chief Constable curtly.

"It does sound a bit daft, doesn't it?" supplemented Chavasse. "Not knowing my own mind as it were. But there you are! I don't want to say anything that may mislead you or even come back on me afterwards. Still, let me have a good look at the chap."

Chavasse went closer to the body. For some seconds, he stood there silently.

"What's your trouble, Doctor?" asked Anthony again.

Chavasse pushed his fingers through his hair. "Two things are troubling me. His eyebrows and his hands. They don't look familiar to me. You must remember that Jordan was my patient for weeks." He bent over the body with a puzzled look in his eyes.

"What are the differences, Doctor?" Anthony asked again.

"His hands seem much rougher and his eyebrows nothing like so well-marked and defined as they were. Still—when all's said and done—"

Chavasse paused and hesitated. Then his puzzled frown gave way to a look of intense relief. "Good Lord, what a consummate ass I am! I can settle this question of identity in a matter of a few seconds."

"How?" demanded MacMorran.

Chavasse grinned. "Jordan had a small pigmented wart on his chest. I've noticed it dozens of times when I've been attending to him. We can soon check up on it on this fellow. Why the heck didn't I think of it before?"

Chavasse thrust his fingers into the dead man's shirt and undid his vest. As he did so he bent over the body and his face changed.

"Yes, gentlemen," he said quietly. "This is my patient, Frederick Jordan. Come over here and look for yourselves."

II

The others satisfied themselves that what Chavasse said was true Anthony thought that Pegram looked a little annoyed.

"A wart of that kind and in that particular part of the body is by no means uncommon, Martin. I think you are bound to agree with me as far as that goes."

Chavasse shook his head. "You can't deceive me over this particular one, Pegram. As I said, I've seen it too many times before not to recognise it."

He looked up and noticed that Anthony was beckoning to him. Chavasse went over to Anthony.

"How long has he been dead, Doctor? I'd like to know that as accurately as possible."

"You must address that question to Dr. Pegram, Mr. Bathurst. He's here entirely professionally. I'm not, I'm afraid."

Anthony repeated the question to the Divisional Surgeon. Pegram went over and examined the body on the hurdle. He made certain tests before returning to Anthony. "It's difficult to say," he said, "but at a rough estimate anything between say nine and twenty-four hours. But don't bank on my accuracy."

"Which would be the nearer in your opinion?" persisted Anthony.

"I really couldn't say. I simply cannot tie myself down on a time like that."

"In that case, then," said Anthony again, "have I your permission to apply for a second opinion to Dr. Chavasse?"

Pegram shrugged his shoulders. "I've no objection," he said stiffly. Anthony smiled. "Thank you, Dr. Pegram. Now, Dr. Chavasse, can you help me?"

Chavasse looked towards Pegram.

"I don't mind, Martin, if that's what's troubling you," said the latter. "Don't be concerned about me."

Chavasse walked over to the hurdle again. He remained there for some few moments. Slowly he returned to his seat. "If it's any value to you, Bathurst," he remarked, "in my opinion that man's been dead less than twelve hours. And I say that with some degree of confidence. He was my patient, you see, and I'm fully aware of what he died of." There ensued a silence. Chavasse riveted his attention on the Chief Constable. Anthony broke the silence.

"Ever seen the dead man before, Sir Charles?"

"Never, Bathurst. To the best of my knowledge, that is. But, of course, I've had hundreds of people through my hands in my time. And it's impossible to recollect one per cent, of them. But as far as I am able to tell, the man's a complete stranger to me."

"Is the name familiar to you?"

"Not in any real sense of association."

"You can think of no reason why he should have made this attack on you?"

"None whatever, Bathurst. I am just as bewildered as you are."

"You are convinced that he doesn't belong to the past at all? Nothing to do with any—I am sure you will forgive me, Sir Charles, for introducing the point—*affaire du coeur* that may quite legitimately have come your way? Or even with any previous incident belonging to your official career?"

"Nothing whatever. I have been guilty of singularly few indiscretions. Either privately or officially."

The silence came again. MacMorran consulted with Dr. Pegram. Anthony overheard the Divisional Surgeon say: "All right, Inspector; that will be quite convenient as far as I am concerned."

He realised that they were discussing the removal of the body. He became aware that the Chief Constable was watching him studiously. "Well, Bathurst," said Sir Charles, "what's the next step going to be?"

"The next step, Sir Charles?"

"Yes. Where are we heading for? Where do we go to from here?"

Anthony rubbed his lip. "Well, sir," he said. "MacMorran's got plenty of work on hand. There's that sand-bag, for instance, requiring some little attention. But as to the next step—the really vital step—"

Sir Charles cut in forcibly. "The next step, Bathurst—whether vital or not! What is it?"

"Well, sir, since you compel me to a proclamation—the next step that counts is the arrest of the murderer."

"Obviously," returned a nettled Chief Constable, "but how do we get there? Ferry across the Styx?"

MacMorran saw the gleam in the grey eyes again.

"My trouble," said Anthony, "is proof. I know the difficulties only too well."

Dr. Pegram nodded his agreement with Anthony's statement. "I can see and understand all that."

"But, on the other hand," continued Anthony, "all the rest of the complicated story is only too clear to me."

MacMorran looked up at him. Anthony went on, "Any doubts I may have entertained were dispelled by the evidence which Dr. Chavasse so kindly gave us a few moments ago. By the way, Doctor, I'm indebted to you."

Chavasse waved away the compliment. "Only too delighted, Bathurst."

Pegram seemed on the point of saying something, but checked the impulse. Sir Charles Stuart, however, had no such qualms.

"Well, this may sound all right to some of you, but it's a damned sight too 'airy-fairy' for my liking. I must repeat what I said earlier on. Where do we go from here, Bathurst? And I mean every word of that question."

Anthony looked at MacMorran. MacMorran returned the look. Anthony rose. "I think that the situation will be best suited," he said quietly, "if I have a chat with a very well-known Mallett personality. You see, I want a letter written. I am not sure yet whether that letter *will* be written. If it is—I have great hopes that benefit will ensue. To almost all of us. Although, of course, Sir Charles, there is no gainsaying that fact 'that the evil that men do lives after them—the good is oft interred with their bones.'"

The Chief Constable stared at him. "And what about me? In the meantime? What about those dramatic and elaborate preparations for my personal safety? Am I to continue them?"

Anthony stood in the doorway, a far away look in his eyes. "I think, Sir Charles, that now, the circumstances being what they are, you may regard yourself as being reasonably safe. Indeed, I feel sure that is so." He turned to the others. "I wonder if Dr. Pegram would give Chief Inspector MacMorran and me a lift into Mallett—say in about a quarter of an hour's time?"

"Certainly, Bathurst," replied the Divisional Surgeon. "Only too pleased."

"That's very decent of you," returned Anthony Bathurst.

III

Throughout the entire journey back from Sandals, Anthony was grave and thoughtful. He scarcely spoke at all. Once or twice Chavasse made terrific efforts to enliven the party and to set the ball of conversation rolling, but Anthony only smiled in return and Martin Chavasse eventually surrendered the struggle. As they neared Mallett, Anthony spoke.

"I think it was James Agate who said, "I want Valhalla to be a home and not a palace. Where there must be familiar grog and laughter and good fellowship. A heaven in which horses shall run and the laying of odds allowed a sinless occupation. I want Sayers and Heenan fighting it out again, to roar at Dan Leno, to watch old Grace again (or Bradman, Trumper, Hobbs, Ranji, Lionel Palairet, or, again, whom you will), and the atmosphere of bar-parlours, pint pots of jasper, playing fields with well-matched teams, keen-eyed umpires, hysterical supporters and tapering goalposts—crysoprase if it must be, but common deal will do—and the feeling that once in every week, will come Saturday afternoon.' I may have misquoted—no doubt I have, gentlemen—but the kernel's there."

The car drew up before the Police-station at Mallett. "And what's the point of all that, Bathurst?" asked Pegram.

"Why, that's my Valhalla, too," said Anthony, "but it wouldn't be everybody's. I've been wondering how our murderer regards his Valhalla. That was all."

He turned and looked the Doctor straight in the face. Then he alighted with MacMorran. "Many thanks, Dr. Pegram, for the courtesy of the car-ride."

IV

Anthony walked with MacMorran to the "Laughing Angel." By this time the Inspector had fallen into Anthony's vein. He had few words. Anthony has often stated since the happenings at Mallett that his own handling of the 'White Lion' murders was undistinguished and for a long time proceeded without inspiration.

"It was almost entirely my fault," he has been heard to say, "and very largely due to my rag-bag of a mind. Sometimes this is a condition which helps me—at others it retards the smooth working of my mental machinery. Snatches of old half-remembered times, odd lines of poetry, nebulous musings or old fragments of stories flash in, and then out, of my mind, without my being able to place them. It is, perhaps, the penalty of a strangely operating memory which holds as blurred impressions, at least, most of the things which have come to me down the avenue of my five senses and their attachments."

On the way to the 'Laughing Angel,' he surprised MacMorran with two statements.

"I want two more stages covered, Andrew, and then I fancy we may reasonably regard ourselves as in the straight and with the winning-post in sight. But even then, Andrew, I am not without one or two of life's little worries. There still remains that awkward problem of driving home the *proof*. I doubt whether any jury of twelve good men and true would convict on the evidence that you and I are going to put in front of them. Especially if Campbell Patrick is briefed for the defence."

MacMorran grunted. "What are the two stages to be covered now, Mr. Bathurst?"

"When we were at Sir Charles Stuart's, I mentioned that I wanted a certain letter written. Well now, Andrew, I want to know that that letter has *been* written, has been committed to the channel of the Post, and has been received by the person to whom it was addressed. That's the first of the stages. The second one is that I must call on a certain doctor who practises in Mallett."

"Which doctor's that?" inquired MacMorran.

"Dr. Cuthbertson," replied Anthony, "the medical adviser of the poisoned King . . . that poor devil who was suffering from a malignant growth in the region of the pylorus. And I propose, Andrew, to have that interview with Dr. Cuthbertson as soon after lunch as possible."

MacMorran rubbed the tip of his nose, but made no reply.

V

Anthony telephoned to Dr. Cuthbertson as soon as he got back to the 'Laughing Angel.' The doctor was a little frigid on the telephone, but agreed that he would see Anthony before surgery at three o'clock that afternoon.

When Anthony was shown into his consulting-room he found himself confronted by a big, broad-shouldered man, with a large, leathery-looking face, shiny, flat-brushed hair and pleasant, laughing eyes.

"About fifty," thought Anthony when he first saw the doctor, "amiably-distinguished, and very much on his guard."

"How do you do?" said Dr. Cuthbertson, rising from his desk and holding out a friendly hand.

Anthony shook hands with him and as he did so the telephone rang.

"Pardon me for a minute." The doctor excused himself and reached for the telephone. Anthony heard him speaking into it.

"No, Raven, old man, I'm sorry but I can't make it. Unless you're very short and can wait till I arrive. If that will suit you, you'll have to field a 'sub' if you lose the toss, and put me in about Number Nine if we win it and bat first. All right . . . if that will do for you. I don't mind. But I can't help it. I must be at the Hammeridge hospital until midday at least. All right, then—that's O.K."

Dr. Cuthbertson replaced the receiver and looked at Anthony again. "Sorry to keep you waiting, Mr. Bathurst. But I still try to play cricket at odd times. Years ago, you know, I played for Glebeshire."

"Really? Congratulations! As a matter of fact, I remember you, now you mention the fact. You were contemporary with Bickford-Brown and Tregonna. Am I right?"

"Quite right. Glebeshire weren't a bad second-class side twenty years ago. But that's beside the point. What can I do for you?"

Anthony eyed the blunt, heavy face.

"Cigarette?" said Cuthbertson. He passed over a solid-looking silver case. Anthony helped himself to a cigarette. "Now come to the point, Mr. Bathurst, if you please."

"Nothing will give me greater pleasure, Doctor. In conjunction with a professional colleague, I am investigating the 'White Lion' murders." Cuthbertson thrust his leathery face across the desk. Then he flicked his fingers impatiently, picked up a pencil, put it back in its groove again and pushed back his chair. "In plain English, what do you want to know?"

"Not a lot, Doctor. But of enormous importance to me. King, the man poisoned at lunch in the 'White Lion,' was a patient of yours?"

"Quite true."

"The P.M. undertaken by the Divisional-Surgeon revealed the fact that when he died he was suffering from a malignant growth in the proximity of the pylorus."

"Quite right." Cuthbertson spoke slowly . . . almost resentfully. He took his cigarette from his mouth and blew a cloud of smoke to the height of the ceiling.

"The man's dead," continued Anthony, "so that nothing you may say can harm him—how long would he have lived, assuming that he hadn't been poisoned?"

"Well," said Doctor Cuthbertson a little warily, "questions of that type are always difficult to answer. And, when all is said and done, I can give you only an opinion. *My* opinion! But I wouldn't have given King much more than six months to live. And, taking it even finer than that, I would have said under that rather than over." Cuthbertson blew a second smoke-cloud to the ceiling.

"Thank you, Doctor. That fact will certainly be of assistance to me."

"Glad to hear that. Hate wasting time in any direction."

Anthony smiled. "My next question, Doctor, is more of a personal nature."

Cuthbertson eyed him shrewdly. "I may decide not to answer it."

"You may—but somehow I don't think you will. Do you hold any appointments of an official nature?"

Cuthbertson stared at Anthony as though he had made an announcement of the most devastating nature. There was an interval of almost oppressive silence. Cuthbertson eventually broke it.

"Besides being an ordinary G.P., I hold one appointment that may be described in the manner that you just mentioned. My predecessor held it and I hold it after him. I am M.O.H. to the Glebeshire and Dartshire Hospital Board. For which I am paid the princely annual salary of £250 per annum, less superannuation contributions. But I'll admit this! I don't suppose if I'm strictly honest with myself, that I earn even the two-fifty quid."

Anthony nodded. "Thank you, Doctor. Is there a hospital, under the aegis of the Board, in this district, or comparatively near here?"

"There is, Mr. Bathurst. And that's probably the chief reason why my predecessor in this practice was appointed to the position. Dr. Honeywell. He was the first to fill the post. The hospital itself is just outside the village of Hammeridge. I expect you've been there. Unfortunately for me, from the point of view of the monetary consideration, a great deal of the work that falls on my shoulders is of a clerical nature. And I prefer being a doctor to being a mere administrator. I'm better at it." He swivelled round and pointed to a shelf at the back of him. "Let me explain more fully. Those files you can see there, Mr. Bathurst, are all records to do with the hospital at Hammeridge. And I curse every one of 'em."

Anthony offered his cigarette-case to the doctor. "One of mine, doctor," he murmured.

"Thank you."

Anthony knew that he was very near to the end of his case. He lit a match and held it to Cuthbertson's cigarette. "Would you oblige me, doctor, with a slip of paper?"

Cuthbertson looked surprised at the request. "Certainly; use this."

He took a slip of paper from his desk, glanced at it and then pushed it across to Anthony. Anthony unscrewed the top of his fountain pen and wrote a few words on the paper. He read carefully what he had written and handed the slip back to Doctor Cuthbertson. The latter pulled his chair forward so that he might the better read it. When he had finished reading it, he raised his eyes and looked up into Anthony's face.

"This is very remarkable," he said, "but the answer is 'Yes' to each of your two questions. I lost my mother in the spring of this year. But I can't for the life of me see how you—"

Anthony smiled at his bewilderment. "You forget, Doctor, that I've had access to many matters and to much detailed information. Stuff which you yourself haven't seen, for instance."

Cuthbertson nodded at the explanation. "Yes. I suppose that is so."

Anthony rose. "Well, that being so, Doctor, I have the information which I came here hoping to obtain. Many thanks for your help. Nobody else in Mallett was in a position to furnish me with what I wanted. You were in a unique position as far as that was concerned. So it had to be you."

Cuthbertson followed Anthony's example and got up from his chair. "Only too pleased to help in those circumstances, Bathurst. Although I'm still wondering about things. Despite that explanation you gave me."

He held out his hand and Anthony shook hands with him. "Don't bother to come out," he said. "I can see myself to the front door."

Cuthbertson nodded genially and said, "All right, Bathurst. Do as you please. That suits me."

Outside Doctor Cuthbertson's establishment, Anthony made his way to the nearest telephone kiosk. Luckily for his convenience, it was empty. He entered, therefore, and dialled a number.

"Is that you?" he said eventually. "This is Anthony Bathurst this end. I just rang up to find out if you'd written that letter? . . . You have? Good . . . and posted it! Even better. . . . When? Soon after I asked you? Good again! Should come to hand, then, by to-morrow morning at the latest. Yes . . . that will do excellently. . . . I can't answer that. . . . You're asking me to forecast with regard to somebody else. . . . What? . . . Psychology? . . . Yes. I know all about that. But that runs true to form on paper. No. . . . Not only on paper, I agree . . . but better on paper than anywhere else . . . you must admit that. . . . Well, then, if you insist on a prophecy . . . I shall expect it to mean the end of everything. . . . I don't know that it would do that; . . . it might, I agree. But we must wait until the actual time comes. . . . Good-bye."

Anthony hung up and left the box. When he returned to the 'Laughing Angel' and found Andrew MacMorran there, he told him all that he had done during the afternoon. MacMorran listened to his story without comment until Anthony had finished. When that occurred, MacMorran shook a sapient head.

"I would never have credited it," he said, "but if you say so—"

VI

Anthony came down from his bedroom to the smoke-room lounge of the 'Laughing Angel.' MacMorran was there to meet him on the threshold. He noticed that Anthony's face was a little flushed.

"What's the matter, Mr. Bathurst?" he inquired. "I've been looking for you, but I couldn't find you."

"Been packing my suit-case, Andrew, and you'd better do the same. As I told you yesterday, we shall be leaving here in the morning. The 10.22, I am told, is an excellent train. Stops Plymouth and Salisbury. That suit you?"

"As well as any other. Now, how many chairs will you be requiring in here?"

He indicated the room behind him. Anthony made a rapid calculation. "Nine, Andrew. Nine! That's strange, by the way. Does it strike a chord of reminiscence?"

MacMorran nodded "Ay. It does that! You're referring to those murders at the Royal Sceptre Hotel at Remington and Mrs. Clinton's nine guests. That's a coincidence."

"We shall want nine chairs. Seven visitors and our two selves. That reminds me of something else, Andrew. How's poor old Venables progressing? Have you heard anything to-day?"

"Going on as well as may be expected. There's no fracture of the skull, it appears. The doctors are satisfied on that now."

"Good." Anthony fished in his pocket. "Here's the plan as to how I want them to sit. Sir Charles Stuart here." Anthony put a finger on the paper. "And Hardwick there. Cox and Waghorn along that side by us."

MacMorran studied the plan carefully. "What about Marnoch?" he asked.

Anthony seemed absent-minded as the Inspector asked the question. "Who?" he said.

"Marnoch. Where do you want Marnoch?"

"Oh—between the two doctors. That will do."

"And the time?"

"Nine o'clock this evening. I've made arrangements with the landlord that we have the lounge to ourselves from that time. After nine, he's promised that we shan't be disturbed."

MacMorran accepted this last piece of information in silence. He ran his eye round the room in an endeavour to understand the full implications of Anthony Bathurst's proposed seating plan. He cleared his throat before speaking.

"I'm not too confident," he muttered with a shake of the head. "I'm sorry to say that, because I know that confidence is nearly always more than half the battle. And I'd like to know how you feel yourself about things."

Anthony's response was slow. "Well, Andrew—I hope and think that things will pan out all right. The letter, I fancy, will turn the scale. It should do. if it doesn't—" He broke off and shrugged his shoulders.

"What will you do—if it doesn't?"

Anthony pondered over the question. "I don't know, Andrew. And that's a fact. I *may* have to pull a fast one. But on the whole I'm optimistic enough to think that we shall bring it off. And there's always this to remember. My indictment may sound more terrifying and proof-packed than it actually is in stark reality. Our friend may not have the necessary time to work all that out. No, Andrew, on the whole and taking everything into consideration, I think we shall do the trick."

MacMorran put the paper with the seating plan into his pocket. "I only hope you're right, Mr. Bathurst. For the sake of all of us."

VII

By ten minutes past nine the seven guests had arrived. Anthony had a few words with the landlord of the 'Laughing Angel' and was assured that he and his companions might count on absolute privacy until the need to use the room no longer remained. MacMorran took careful stock of the seven guests as they arrived and went to the places which had been allotted to them. Anthony employed himself similarly. He strove to find a suitable adjective for each individual description. Pegram, he thought, looked ill-tempered. Chavasse looked eagerly curious. Marnoch, between them, looked jaunty. Cox looked scared, Waghorn wary and Hardwick debonair.

MacMorran walked behind the Chief Constable so that he might close the door that opened out into the corridor. The Inspector came back to the circle.

"If you would be good enough to take your seats. gentlemen? Mr. Bathurst here has a few words to say to you. He feels that every one of you has a right to be present, bearing in mind that in some shape or form you have all been connected with this chain of murders at the 'White Lion,' which (and this is news to many of you') culminated a few days ago in a savage attack on no less a person than the Chief Constable of the County, Sir Charles Stuart. Cigarettes are on the table, and if you let me know what drinks you would like, I'll order them now. That will get it over and done with. Now, gentlemen, if you'll let me know, please. Thank you."

The orders were taken, the drinks were brought, the barman disappeared again and MacMorran closed the door for the second time. He looked across the room and spoke to Anthony.

"I'm ready now, Mr. Bathurst, if you are."

Anthony nodded and rose. "As Inspector MacMorran has already stated, gentlemen, he and I thought it only right that we should give you all this opportunity of coming here this evening. Each one of you has been in contact in some way with this extraordinary series of murders which has shocked this beautiful little town of Mallett: and the adjoining countryside. I shall be able this evening to present to you the truth of what has happened and I will preface my remarks with an astounding statement. That statement is this."

Anthony paused and lit a cigarette. The whole action was coolly deliberate. He shook the flame of the match he had used into extinction and tossed the stick into an ash-tray.

"The murderer is in this room! And—which is more to the point—he knows that I know he's the murderer. Despite the fact that the Police hold a signed confession to the crimes."

There was a chilled silence. It was broken eventually but only just broken by the scrape of a chair-leg on the carpet. Somebody in the circle had moved awkwardly and uneasily.

"I propose, however," continued Anthony, "to unfold my story and to make him acquainted with my facts. The murderer will then see plainly and mercilessly that I hold all the cards in my hand. In other words, I am going to expose the workings of his mind so relentlessly and inexorably that he will be under no doubts and will harbour no illusions as to the fate which waits for him just round the corner. He alone will recognise the exposed brain I am going to present to you. In the first place, there was but one murder that really mattered to him. That was numbered 'five' on his bloody list. I use the adjective, gentlemen, in its appropriate—not in its colloquial sense. It was the murder of Sir Charles Stuart. The murder which, thanks to the prompt counterstroke of Inspector MacMorran here, became translated into mere attempted murder."

MacMorran shook his head and seemed on the point of saying something. But Anthony held up his hand and the Scotland Yard Inspector desisted. Anthony went on:

"I have begun, as you will notice, at the end of the chain. I have done that of malice aforethought. When I was first called to the case, with Inspector MacMorran, I wasn't able to do that. I could deal with only that which I had placed in front of me. The first murder was of William Norman, a farmer. He was killed by the extraordinary method of having hot cinder pellets put down his back after having left the saloon-bar of the 'White Lion.' I mention that method of killing specially because I want you to regard it as of the highest importance."

"The second murder was of Henry King, a baker. He was killed through partaking of poisoned fish whilst lunching at the 'White Lion.' Again please observe very carefully the mode of extinction."

Anthony bent forward and pressed out the burning stub of his cigarette in the ash-tray. He straightened himself to standing again. "The third murder was of a scallywag named George Clarence, who was concerned, mind you, in the theft of a valuable stamp collection. Clarence was killed by drowning. He was drowned in a wine-butt in the courtyard of 'White Lion' premises. For the third time, gentlemen, I commend to your earnest notice the method of the murdering. Once again—highly illuminating. Number four link in the murder-chain was a young boy by the name of Richard Yorke. He was found dead on a settee inside the premises of the 'White Lion,' having met his death by suffocation. Again—please note, gentlemen, the way and manner of the killing. Which brings me to my starting point. The attempted murder of Sir Charles Stuart. The Chief Constable was attacked in his own house by a masked man wielding an axe. Not quite so bizarre a method on this occasion, gentlemen, but an axe for the good reason that the situation, as delineated by the murderer, demanded an axe."

Anthony paused again here and watched the faces of his hearers carefully, to assess the effect of his words. Nobody spoke, but on the features of each could be discerned a look of strained intensity. Anthony began again.

"Having reached that point, gentlemen, I will retrace my steps again and we will examine the names of the four people who have met their sudden and violent deaths. William Norman! May I recall to your memories, William of Normandy? The Conqueror? The Bastard? The King who defeated the Saxon Harold at the Battle of Senlac? 1066 and all that? I wonder how many of you, in addition to our murderer, will remember how William the Norman died! The cause of his death was hot cinders! His horse trod on them! Interesting—don't you think?" Three people in the room coughed. Neither MacMorran nor Anthony could be sure of their identity. Anthony helped himself to another cigarette.

"The next man to die was Henry King. Can you recall a Royal Henry on the English Throne who died of a surfeit of lampreys? I suggest that poisoned turbot makes a reasonable substitute! Lampreys are not found on every fishmonger's slab. The interest grows!"

There came sharp exclamations from several of the people present. Anthony ignored them. "Death number three was that of a man hearing the name of George Clarence. Here our historical sequence takes somewhat of a deviation from what I may term the main royal track. I will explain. George, Duke of Clarence, was the brother of Richard Crook-back. The third Richard. Tradition has it that he was drowned, by order of the King, his brother, in a butt of Malmsey. Malmsey is the wine of Malvasia. You will recollect, gentlemen, once again, the circumstances of the murders under review. And how our George Clarence was found to have met his death."

By now the entire circle was gazing almost spell-bound at Anthony as he unfolded the dramatic particulars. Once again be carried on with his recital:

"When the name of Clarence appeared on the list, I got my first really satisfactory clue. It came to me on the railway platform at Mallett. I had Norman—King—Clarence! The boy, Richard Yorke. followed. May I call to your attention the story of the Princes in the Tower? Edward and Richard, Princes of the House of York, were murdered there by the same Richard Crookback mentioned just now, in the year 1433. It is believed that they were smothered. The Yorke of this story died in very much the same way."

Anthony thrust an accusing forefinger at the people sitting round him. "Gentlemen, it was an easy cry from Norman. King. Clarence and Yorke to Sir Charles Stuart. The man against whom this fiendish plot was directed and because of whom the four previous deaths were merely fortuitous happenings, by reason of their names and their names only."

Almost everybody turned and looked towards the Chief Constable. Sir Charles bore the scrutinies with admirable composure.

"I will not go into the reason behind this murderer's intent, either here or at this time. The genesis lies in the years behind. But I will call your attention to yet one more chain of—coincidences? Well— hardly that. Call them rather definite selections. Norman had serious cardiac trouble. King was already doomed as the victim of a malignant growth, Clarence was in the last stages of tuberculosis and the boy Yorke a 'status lymphaticus' case. To say nothing of the condition of a certain man named Frederick Jordan. Note carefully, please, the intricate working of a master mind. The operation of a new type of euthanasia!"

Anthony looked at his watch. He frowned at what he saw. But the frown had scarcely died from his face when there came a light tap to the smoke-room door. MacMorran crossed to the door and a boy in uniform handed in a telegram and a letter. Anthony took them a moment later from the Inspector.

"Here's a telegram," he said, "for Dr. Chavasse and a letter addressed to Ex-Inspector Marnoch, and I'll pass them along."

He noticed that Marnoch opened his envelope with unsteady fingers. Chavasse looked at Anthony and slightly shifted the position of his chair as Anthony nodded to him.

VIII

Anthony commenced to speak again. "I am positive that by now, the murderer in our midst must be convinced that I know all. And if he thinks that I lack proof to bring his crimes home to him, I can assure him as solemnly as I can, that in that idea he is clinging to a broken reed. He has convicted himself out of his own mouth. Thus for the spoken word. He has also convicted himself by what he has penned on paper. Thus for the written word."

Anthony paused. To resume again after but a few second's interval: "He also knows by now that the goal he visualised as a result of his crimes is eternally unattainable as far as he is concerned. . . . That all he has perpetrated has been wanton folly and wicked futility. . . . That he is held in absolute loathing and supreme contempt by the person who dominates his thoughts. . . . That if he were the only man left in the world. . . ."

A shout rang through the room . . . a shout of fierce anger and baffled rage. . . . Its interruption effect was as much as a pistol shot's would have had. Anthony saw Marnoch spring to his feet and MacMorran move swiftly away from where he had been standing. Marnoch's face was white and strained and the veins in his forehead stood out unnaturally. Anthony threw aside all pretext at further speech and all finesse and dashed towards MacMorran. But as he did so, the doubt flashed through his mind as to whether he would be in time to avert disaster.

IX

His worst fears were realised. Quickly as he had acted, and quickly as both MacMorran and Marnoch had moved, they were powerless to prevent Martin Chavasse throwing up a challenging arm and then conveying something to his lips.

"Euthanasia—eh?" he snarled. "Well, if that's the case, here's a physician who can heal himself."

He swayed for a moment or so and then crashed to the floor. The rest of the company, bewildered and amazed at the astounding turn which things had taken, crowded round. But the sinner was beyond help. The poison had done its work and MacMorran took charge of the room and the necessary arrangements. The other men who had been present gradually withdrew to their respective homes.

X

Anthony Bathurst sat with Sir Charles Stuart and Chief-Inspector MacMorran in a quiet corner of the Chief Constable's house. Anthony had previously promised that he would endeavour to clarify any of the points of the problem which were not clearly understood.

"The main motive force behind it all," he said, "was a love affair which Chavasse had had with a charming girl some fifteen or so years ago. I have been enabled to have a chat with the lady in the case and she tells me that she gave him up for you, Sir Charles, and has never regretted her decision. I believe her and I think you can too, Sir Charles."

Stuart flushed and mattered under his breath. The words sounded like: "I knew nothing about it."

Anthony went on. "But Chavasse never gave up hope. He went abroad for a time, but returned and found out where you were living. He followed you into this district, determined to end your life and marry your widow. His vanity was such that he took the lady for granted. But herein lay his problem. He had to kill you without evoking the slightest suspicion. So he determined on his series of murders—all perpetrated by a semi-homicidal maniac who always chose a family of royal historical association. Sooner or later, the names were *bound* to be noticed and the 'Stuart' end of the tangle would then be taken as a matter of course and automatically chalked up to the score of the killer. I fancy that Norman gave him the sinister idea in the first place. Thank you, Sir Charles, I don't mind if I do."

Anthony acknowledged the Scotch and soda that the Chief Constable poured out for him. He drank and then continued:

"He'd seen Norman in the market-place, noted his appearance, and his medical knowledge told him that the man had serious heart trouble. Here was victim number one. We'll deal with the manner of the deaths later. Victims numbered two, three and four fell from the tree almost into his lap. I'll tell you how. Chavasse used to act as *locum* to Dr. Cuthbertson whenever the latter went away. King was a patient of Cuthbertson's—Chavasse had access to the papers and the relevant medical records—and Clarence and Yorke had been patients during the last few years at Hammeridge Hospital."

Anthony paused here, waiting for the inevitable question he knew would emanate from Andrew MacMorran:

"What's the point of that, may I ask. Mr. Bathurst?"

Anthony smiled at his questioner. "Why—this. Dr. Cuthbertson was M.O.H. to the Glebeshire and Dartshire Joint Board, which has jurisdiction over the Hammeridge Hospital. Chavasse picked them up from Cuthbertson's hospital files. Their names filled the bill and so did their states of health. Of course, he had many names from which to choose and which would have suited his book just as well. For example, Prince, Tudor, Harrold, Percy, Warwick, Edwards, Lancaster, Saxon, George, Orange, Howard, Bullen, Seymour, Parr . . . you can think of dozens, no doubt, if you apply your minds to the job."

Sir Charles smiled. "I never realised how perilous my name was to other people. But tell me how he committed the four crimes."

"I'll tell you how I think he brought them off. He induced Norman to pick him up in his car. Wet night. Pedestrian wanted a lift badly. Chavasse had the pellets in a container. It wouldn't be large and he was able to hide it, probably, under his overcoat or mackintosh. When Norman bent forward to peer through the driving-screen, as he was almost bound to, owing to the weather, Chavasse, sitting behind him, emptied the pellets down his neck inside his collar. The shock killed him, I should say, instantaneously."

Sir Charles shivered. "Cold-blooded swine."

"He would argue that Norman felt scarcely anything. King was easy, because of his audacity. Chavasse's—I mean. Garbed as the electrician, he doctored King's lunch as it stood on the ledge of the serving-hatch. Clarence he picked up in Hammeridge. Probably in the 'Gardener's Arms.' It was the name 'Clarence,' by the way, that first put me on the right track. Coming as it did after Norman and King. I don't think that Chavasse was 'Smith.' He may have been, but I don't think so. I fancy he hung about listening to the deal between Clarence and that gentleman. When the chance came, he struck up an acquaintance with Clarence, offered him a better price for the stamp collection than Smith had, filled him silly with booze, shoved him in the car which he always used when he went to Hammeridge, got to the 'White Lion' in the small hours and shoved Clarence in the water-butt. The port wine was introduced of course, as the best substitute for the historic Malmsey. The courtyard is accessible from one side at all hours of the day and night. When he reached home, knowing of Waghorn's stamp-collecting activities, he posted the collection to the bank manager and thereby immediately brought him into the area of suspicion."

"What about the boy, Yorke?" demanded MacMorran.

'Yorke falls into the 'conjecture' class. What I think happened was this. The killer inveigled the boy into the car. Caught him when he was on his own out shopping for his mother. Promised him a ride, I expect. At a convenient moment he smothered him with a cushion of some kind. One he had with him in the car. Then he disposed of the body much in the same way as he had Clarence's. Through the 'White Lion' courtyard. There you are, gentlemen. There are your four murders, nicely docketed."

MacMorran leant forward. "Now for one matter that I can't fathom, Mr. Bathurst. The matter of the man, Frederick Jordan. That's got me beat to a frazzle."

Anthony's grey eyes twinkled at the Inspector. "Ah—Jordan! That was a touch of touches, wasn't it? Almost that of a master hand. But not quite, thank God! Jordan was a genuine patient that came to Chavasse all in the day's work. He hadn't had him long before an idea began to germinate in his fertile and unbalanced brain. At least, that's how it appeals to me. Jordan alternated regularly between fits of consciousness and unconsciousness. In some of the former, he evinced an overwhelming and consistent desire to make his will. As he put it to his doctor, 'to sign a paper.' This desire on Jordan's part gave Chavasse the idea of getting Jordan to put his signature to a confession to the 'White Lion' murders under the impression that he was merely signing the paper which he considered to be his will."

"Ingenious," muttered Sir Charles. "Highly ingenious."

Anthony smiled. "I agree. Chavasse then proceeded to build up the story. Planted in Pegram's mind—I have Pegram's authority to say so—that Jordan had bouts of recovery during which he left his bed and went out. By subtle implication, he made the dates of these 'truantries' coincide with the murders with the pretence all the time that he himself hadn't considered such a possibility. All very clever, but not quite clever enough."

"I'm still a little in the dark," declared MacMorran. "What about the time when Jordan disappeared? How was that managed?"

"I think in this way, Andrew. After the confession incident, he realised that to prosecute his full plan properly, he must still hold Jordan's body. Dope in the medicine and also in the drink of the old girl who looked after Jordan gave him the chance to get Jordan away in his car. To his own house. Where he kept Jordan until the man died. Directly that occurred, it gave him the signal for the attack on Sir Charles. He would finish off Sir Charles, leave Jordan's body to be discovered outside the house and everything would fit in with the terms of Jordan's confession. You know how the plan went wrong. When he pretended he was unable to identify Jordan and gave that opinion as to how long Jordan had been dead, I knew without the shadow of a doubt that I had the right man. Also, the footmark we found near the hedge had been made by a much larger shoe than that which the dead man was wearing. The difficulty was to drive the guilt home. After a lot of thinking, I decided to enlist the help of Lady Stuart. He has given her a bad time for months now. It struck me that if she turned him down absolutely and irrevocably and let him see that all his malice had been futile, it might turn him to mordant bitterness and cause him to throw up the sponge. Lady Stuart responded admirably. She wrote to him and also sent a tele-gram in similar strain which I timed to arrive at the psychological moment. The receipt of this goaded him to blind fury—and *voilà*! You know the rest."

"What was the message Marnoch received at the same time?"

"That was another little arrangement of mine," smiled Anthony. "A request to move to Chavasse the moment the latter moved. But Marnoch was too late, as it happened. All the same, on more mature thought, what did happen eventually may have been all for the best. What do you think, Sir Charles?"

"I agree with you, Bathurst, *in toto*. I'll go even beyond you and assert that the 'best is yet to be.' I'll tell Lady Stuart the same thing."

The Chief Constable puffed out his cheeks.

"Sir Charles," said Anthony, "you're a man after my own heart."

FINIS

Printed in Great Britain
by Amazon